TRY EASY

JILL BRASHEAR

MOMENTUM PRESS

ISBN 978-0-57843-793-4

❀ Created with Vellum

UNTITLED

This book is dedicated to the Islands of Hawaii, for inspiring me, and to my family for encouraging me to reach for my dreams.

PROLOGUE

SUNSET BEACH, NORTH SHORE HAWAII
    A Saturday in March 1966

THREE MEN CARRIED THEIR SURFBOARDS INTO THE GLASSY BLUE water of Hawaii's North Shore. The sun was high overhead, and not a single white cloud dotted the blue ceiling of sky. Sunset Beach didn't have the biggest or the longest waves on Hawaii's 208 miles of shoreline, but it did have consistency. Sunset Beach wasn't fickle. It didn't rage during a storm like Waimea Bay or flip riders into somersaults like the backwash of Makaha's Bowl, but it did offer steady, year-round waves.

For those who sought them, Sunset Beach always offered a wave to surf.

The three men were best friends and closer than brothers. They were from different backgrounds, but one thing had brought them together: their love for the ocean. They were the descendants of a sailor, a warrior, and a merchant. They had all been born in Hawaii, but only one of them considered himself to be Hawaiian.

The men were three of the best surfers in Hawaii, and therefore, the world.

Each of them had big plans for their future and dreams of a life just beginning.

One of them was planning to propose to the girl he had loved since high school.

One had just signed a contract with a surfboard company and was poised to compete in every major surfing contest across the world for the next two years.

The third man was Hawaii's beloved son. At twenty-three years old, he was already a legend in big-wave surfing. He dreamed of bringing Hawaii the world recognition it deserved, and he was willing to risk everything to make a name for himself on the waves.

The three men strode into the turquoise waters of Sunset Beach with their boards under their arms and their minds on their dreams. Only two of them came out alive.

WALLS OF WATER

WAIMEA BAY, OAHU
   A Sunday in January 1968

THE WHOLE CAR SHOOK AS KEONI MAXED IT OUT AT TOP SPEED, racing across the island to the North Shore.

"Come on," Keoni urged the car. "We're almost there."

He rounded the cliffs of Waimea and gasped as the shoreline unfolded before his eyes. He had seen big waves before, but nothing like this. This was crazy. Violent. Unsafe. *Perfect.*

Walls of water two stories high sprayed into the air, shrouding the entire North Shore in a lavender-hued mist.

Keoni slowed down, wanting to remember every moment of the day. There might not be another one like it for years. Then he punched the gas again and headed straight for Waimea Bay.

The other surf spots along the eight-mile stretch of sand on the North Shore would be no better than boiling cauldrons of water. They would eat a surfer alive. Only Waimea Bay could handle a storm like this one.

Keoni screeched to a stop in the church parking lot that overlooked the bay and jumped out of the car. He stood in the same spot where his ancestors had once stood, studying the conditions of the surf. He noted where the waves broke, how many were in each set, and how fast they were coming. People assumed Keoni had a magical gift for predicting where the best waves would break, and for always being in the right spot at the right time. But it wasn't a gift, it was a skill that had been passed down for generations. Keoni's father had taught him how to listen to the voice of the ocean, and his mother had explained how to feel the mood in the wind.

Surfing was in his blood.

Keoni could still remember the days when the locals had said that only gods could ride the wild waves of Waimea Bay. They all said the waves were too big, too angry. They believed the bay was haunted from above by the *heiau* in the cliffs and from below by the bones of a dead surfer.

Keoni had been a child when the locals had been proven wrong.

It had been a sunny day in the winter of 1957. Keoni was in sixth grade, and his dad had let him stay home from school to watch the *haole* surfers from California try to commit suicide on the giant waves.

Cars had lined the Kamehameha Highway. Everyone sat on their hoods, watching the show. Keoni, his four siblings, and his parents had climbed onto the roof of their Studebaker and eaten a picnic of fried chicken and macaroni salad while the surfers wiped out. It had been better entertainment than a World Series baseball game.

The surfers had been pummeled by the waves and had nearly died, but they had also caught some of the biggest waves Keoni had ever seen.

"I will catch even bigger waves someday," twelve-year-old Keoni Makai told his father. "I will make our name famous all over the world."

Once Keoni got a taste of the power of the waves at Waimea, he was hooked. Two years later, he quit school to surf full-time. He didn't belong in a stuffy classroom all day, learning the literature and history of white people from the mainland. He belonged on the water. The ocean became his classroom.

Watching the waves strike the sand with the force of a power plant, Keoni thought today might be the day.

There were a handful of surfers in the water, not really doing much more than clinging to their boards. Keoni knew all of them.

Rabbit Jones, an old-timer who had been one of the first surfers of the North Shore, looked to be the only one doing any riding.

Keoni saw the flash of Rabbit's board fly down the face of a giant wave. Rabbit was well over six feet tall with a wiry frame, but he looked as tiny as an ant in the giant swells of water.

Rabbit made the bottom turn and then got pummeled by the closeout.

Keoni could hear the groan of the spectators on the beach as he jogged across the sand with his board under his arm. They were all disappointed to see Rabbit go down.

Keoni scanned the water anxiously for a sign of his friend and sighed with relief as he saw his dark shaggy head pop up. Rabbit turned toward shore, flashed the shaka sign, and paddled back for more.

"Somebody's gonna die today," said a woman in the crowd.

There was a group of housewives with small children clustered together, watching the entertainment just as Keoni had done on that day long ago.

Keoni reached out and tousled the hair of a small boy of about ten years old.

"Ey, kid," he said. "You wanna be out there someday?"

The boy tore his eyes away from the waves long enough to nod at Keoni. "Yes, sir."

"What's your name?" Keoni asked.

"Benjamin Kealoha," the boy said.

"I'm Keoni Makai," Keoni said. They shook hands with an air of professionalism, as if they were two businessmen getting ready to close a deal. "One day I'm gonna see your name on a trophy," Keoni said.

"Yes, sir," Benjamin said, lifting his chin proudly.

Flashing the boy the shaka sign, Keoni stepped toward shore. The waves were slamming the sand. It would be suicide to charge into them while the set was closing out. Keoni counted in his head, remembering the pattern he'd observed from the parking lot.

When all five waves of the set had closed out, Keoni dove into the water, and popped up on the other side. He started the long, grueling paddle out to the lineup. Every few feet he gained; he was pushed back toward shore by the angry waves. The ocean was determined to keep him from reaching the lineup, but Keoni was even more determined to get there. He crawled over the massive waves, feeling the thunderous power of the ocean beneath him.

Keoni should have been more frightened, but all he felt was a detached sense of calm and the belief that the day to make a name for himself had finally come. These were the biggest waves in the world, and Keoni was going to ride them.

When he finally reached the lineup, he glanced around at the other surfers bobbing on top of their boards. He saw fear in their eyes. Most of them were wondering how to get back to shore alive. There was only one way back to the beach, and it was back the way they had come, through the violent crash of the waves. Even getting this far was either an act of stupidity or extreme bravery.

"Ey, maybe we should go surf Queen's," Bones said, hunching over his board while a wave rolled under him, threatening to spill him into the sea.

Keoni smiled at his cousin. Queen's Beach was for tourists, but it had once been their stomping ground. They'd gotten their first rides at Queen's Beach, where long, gentle waves caressed the sparkling sands of Waikiki. It was hard to believe those sweet waves inhabited the same ocean as the angry behemoths thrashing the sand of Waimea Bay Beach.

Keoni watched a blue bump in the distance, sensing promise in its obscure shape. It lumbered toward them, and when it hit the reef, it exploded. The other surfers scrambled to paddle over the top, but Keoni turned toward shore, stroking calmly to catch the swell.

This was his wave. It would be good to him. Keoni could tell. He listened closely and heard the voice of the ocean speaking to him.

This wave was going to be a force of nature.

Keoni paddled as hard as he could, racing to get ahead of the wave. The key was strong paddling. It was essential to stay in front of the wave for as long as possible. Although that was an extremely difficult feat when the waves were roaring toward him faster than he could drive his VW Bug.

The wave that had been a lump in the sea a moment earlier became a mountain, and it was bent on crushing Keoni to dust. The inevitable moment came, and the wave caught him.

Keoni stopped paddling and let the wave lift him into the air. He jumped to his feet, landing with feline grace on top of the thin, wet board. He kept his weight centered in his hips, crouching low over the board as the wave threatened to toss him off its lip.

It was already too late for him to change his mind. If he did anything other than drop in, he would wipe out. He stood on top of the cliff, peering over into the watery abyss. Knowing that one moment of hesitation could mean his death, Keoni pushed the limits of time, waiting as long as possible on top of the wave before making the drop.

It was moments like this, the split seconds between life and death, that Keoni lived for. It was the rush of leaning over and staring potential death in the face that made his heartbeat and his blood pump. There was nothing like standing on top of a giant wave, feeling the weight of your own mortality. It was physical and spiritual at the same time. This was Keoni's church and his playground. It was his passion, his lifeblood.

He inched forward, pushing the narrow nose of his board over the top of the wave. He leaned into the wind, letting the roar of the ocean fill his ears and the rays of the sun shine down on him as if for the last time. He tasted the bitterness of fear mixed with the salt of the ocean and smelled his own nervous sweat.

The moment for hesitation was gone. Keoni dropped into the wave. His board slid along the moving mountain at top speed. Throwing out his arms and bending his knees in a wide warrior stance, Keoni leaned into his toes and plunged down the face of the wave.

One. Two. Three.

Keoni counted silently, savoring each second that he plummeted into the blue abyss. *Four. Five. Six.* Keoni smiled triumphantly. *Seven!* He settled his weight in his heels and began to turn the long, heavy board to the right. His smile spread over his whole body as he relished the milestone of getting to the number seven.

Seven seconds. Seven incredible seconds of sliding, of conquering. The ride had felt like forever, and yet it had gone by so fast.

He'd done it. He'd ridden the biggest wave in the world.

Keoni turned back toward the lineup with a triumphant smile and paddled out for more.

THE BEST AND THE WORST DAYS

BY THE TIME THE SUN SET ON WAIMEA BAY, THE SAND WAS littered with broken surfboards. Keoni sat with his back to the bonfire, watching the sun slip behind the horizon line. He wished for more daylight. He could have kept surfing for hours.

Nursing his cold beer, Keoni shifted on the sand, trying to find a comfortable position.

Keoni was legendary for his skills at avoiding wipeouts, but even he couldn't avoid them every time. After a long day of surfing the biggest waves in the world, Keoni was bruised and battered. He had a black eye, a gash on his forehead, and his mouth was bleeding. The tenderness in his ribs told him something was broken. It hurt to sit or stand, and even breathe.

Keoni couldn't have been happier.

All that he wanted was a simple life: heavy waves, a cold beer to wash down the taste of sand in his mouth, friends to share a bonfire with, and eventually a close-knit family of his own.

It didn't seem a lot to ask.

He pressed the can of beer to his forehead, letting the cold metal soothe the split skin.

The best days always held a tinge of sadness. They were the days when Keoni missed Eddie the most.

Nearly two years earlier, on a beautiful sunny day in March, Eddie Alvarez, a twenty-five-year-old, third-generation Portuguese immigrant, best friend, son, and brother had died on the waves.

They had been at Sunset Beach, only a few point breaks up Waimea Bay. Eddie had wanted to go to Patterson's, but Declan and Keoni wanted to go to the North Shore. Eddie was outnumbered. They'd gone to Sunset Beach.

If they had stayed at Patterson's would things have been different? Would Eddie still be alive?

Keoni had been raised on Christianity, but he found himself drawn to the old religion of Hawaii. He believed in the Christian God, but also the ancient gods of his ancestors. All of them could be unbearably cruel. Keoni believed in the ultimate power of the earth and the ocean, and that some of that power sang in his veins.

He believed that he could have saved Eddie.

Keoni had rescued countless others from the waves. There was no lifeguard service on the North Shore, and the surfers had to look out for each other. Whether in the lineup or standing on the beach, Keoni always kept an eye out for someone in danger. Dramatic rescues happened so often that Keoni had been featured in the *Honolulu Advertiser* in an article about the dangers of the ocean.

Keoni's history of heroic rescues was one of the reasons Eddie's death caused him so much pain. He'd been on the very same wave as Eddie, and he hadn't been able to save him. Keoni hadn't even seen Eddie go under. Keoni had tried for ten minutes to revive Eddie with CPR, but it hadn't worked. The ocean had already stolen Eddie's life by the time Keoni had dragged him to shore.

If only Keoni would have gotten to him sooner. If only he'd been paying better attention. If only they had gone to Patterson's instead of Sunset. *If only.*

Keoni shook his head, trying to stop his internal dialogue.

There were too many "if only's" for Keoni to count. Eddie was dead, and Keoni could only blame himself.

"You're crazy. You know that?" Bones asked.

Keoni looked away from the ocean, up at his cousin, whose tall frame blocked the setting sun. "Yeah. I know." He'd been told that a hundred times. It hadn't stopped him yet.

Bones dropped to the sand next to Keoni and handed him a plate of fish. Their mothers were sisters, and descendants of the most celebrated war chief of Hawaii. They were cousins, but also friends. They had grown up on the water together, from their first waves at Queen's Beach when they couldn't afford surfboards and had to make their own out of sheets of plywood, to winning surf contests at Makaha.

While Keoni dominated on the big waves, Bones was more suited to body-surfing and diving. Between the two of them, there was nothing in the water they couldn't do.

"I got something I wanna run by you," Bones said.

Keoni braced himself for Bones's latest scheme. Bones was an entrepreneur who had a knack for coming up with crazy ideas that were sometimes profitable, and sometimes disastrous. It had been Bones who'd talked Keoni into giving surfing lessons to the wealthy tourists at Waikiki when they'd been teenagers. They'd made a killing. Keoni would have quit his job at the marina if he didn't hate giving the lessons so much.

"What is it?" Keoni asked, already knowing he wasn't going to like it.

Bones lowered his voice and glanced around to make sure no one could hear him. "You remember that time we found that black coral in Maui?"

"Yeah."

Keoni took a bite of the fish. The skin was salted and crispy. The white chunks of flesh melted on his tongue, but Keoni hardly tasted it. His stomach was in knots just remembering the dangerous dive in Maui last year. They had found an underwater field of rare coral, but it had been purely by accident. The depth gauge on their boat had been broken, or they would have never been diving that deep.

"I found it again," Bones said.

Keoni put the fish down, his appetite gone. "What were you doin' out there so deep?" he asked.

"Lookin' for the coral," Bones said, as if it was obvious.

"Alone?"

"Nah. Kenny was driving the boat."

"You dumbass. That was, what, 250 feet deep?"

"More like 300."

"Shit, Bones." Keoni felt like he might throw up. He got to his feet and paced back and forth on the sand. His ribs screamed with pain whenever he moved, but he was so angry he didn't even feel it. "What the hell is wrong with you? You got a death wish, or what?"

Bones unfolded his long legs and got to his feet, glaring down at Keoni. Bones was one of the few people Keoni knew who could do that. Most people were shorter than Keoni, but everyone was shorter than Bones. Ever since Bones had grown taller than Keoni when they were teenagers, he'd used his height to his advantage.

Bones's thick eyebrows were drawn together over his stormy gray eyes, and a muscle bulged in his neck.

"You're the asshole who just spent all day trying to commit suicide! Had us all fucking scared to death." He shoved Keoni's shoulder. "And I got a death wish, yeah?"

Keoni winced as the shove sent a fresh wave of pain through his injured ribs. He drew himself up to his full height, still three inches shorter than Bones, and raised his chin.

"I know what I'm doing," he said.

The cousins glared at each other for a long moment, neither one of them wanting to be the first to give in. They had inherited more than height and build from their warrior ancestors. They had also inherited passion and a stubborn streak. Bones and Keoni argued loudly and often, but they hadn't come to blows since they were fourteen.

Bones gave in first and looked away. Keoni let out the breath he'd been holding and relaxed his fists. He knew Bones was right: he took too many chances on the waves. Ever since Eddie had died, Keoni had been pushing harder and harder to make a name for himself. His risks had so far paid off—he was famous all over the islands for his big-wave riding—but he knew that one day his luck would run out.

"I got a boat lined up," Bones said after a long silence. "I could use another diver."

"And you want me?"

"I need somebody I can trust."

Keoni finished his beer, tasting blood from his cut lip as he swallowed. There was no one he trusted more than Bones, not even his own brothers. Keoni guessed Bones felt the same about him.

"Those trees are worth about a grand each," Bones said, lowering his voice.

It was a lot of money for only a few hours of work, but the danger involved raised the stakes.

"You're the best diver I know," Bones said, sweetening the pot. "Not just anybody can dive 300 feet."

That much was true, Keoni thought. But it wasn't skill he needed. It was luck. Anything over 200 feet was plain stupid.

"When?" Keoni asked.

"Two weeks."

"Alright."

"Alright?"

"Yeah, that's what I said."

Bones grabbed two more beers out of the cooler and tossed one to Keoni. They popped the tops, tapped their cans together, and drank to their agreement.

"Now all we need is a driver," Bones said. "Somebody who will stay on the boat while we dive and get us out of there quick-like if anything happens. Not that anything is gonna happen," he said. "Just in case, yeah?"

Keoni raised an eyebrow but didn't comment. He knew all too well what could happen. The deeper the dive, the greater the danger.

Henry came over to join them, catching the tail end of the subject.

"What do you need a driver for?" he asked.

Bones looked at Keoni, his eyes glittering in the darkness. Keoni shrugged. Driving the boat was an easy job. Anyone could do it, even Henry, a *haole* from California. *Haole* was a word that Hawaiians used to describe white people from the mainland who were ignorant of their culture. In Hawaiian *Ha* meant *breath* or *life*, and *ole* meant *without*. So, *haole* literally meant *without breath*. It was what the first Hawaiians had called the first Europeans, and the insult had stuck.

Keoni gave Henry a hard look and decided he would do fine for a driver. Henry wasn't so bad. He was even decent at surfing. Keoni nodded at Bones and tipped back his beer.

Bones nodded back. "Heh, you wanna make fifty bucks?" he asked Henry.

"Depends on what I gotta do."

"Just drive the boat while me and Keoni go on a dive."

"That's all? For fifty bucks? Are you crazy?"

"Nope," Bones said. "You in or what?"

"Yeah, I guess," Henry said, stroking the stubble on his chin. "But I need a favor."

"What?"

"I'm supposed to pick up my cousin and her friend from the airport on Tuesday," Henry said. "But I can't get off work."

"No one else can bust their ass for money?" Bones asked, and they all laughed.

Henry worked as a stuntman for a TV show that was filmed on the east side of Oahu. Some days Henry had to run through glass windows, other days he crashed motorcycles. His friends all teased him, but he took it good naturedly because he made more money than any of them.

"Come on," Henry said. "I don't want them to show up and not have a ride."

"Your cousin look anything like you?" Bones asked.

"No, why?"

Bones grinned. "What time does the plane land?"

"Three o'clock."

"We'll be there," Bones said.

"We?" asked Keoni. "I never said I could go."

"What else you got going on?" Bones asked, laughing.

Keoni was notorious for doing nothing but surfing or working. His friends and family were constantly trying to drag him out to a party or fix him up with a girl, saying he needed to live more.

Keoni tried to think of an excuse to get out of the chore, but he drew a blank. Reluctantly, he agreed to go.

MONDAYS AT JEFFERSON'S

SEATTLE, WASHINGTON
A Monday in January 1968

MARY LOU HUNTER HOPPED OVER A POTHOLE ON THE STREET AND landed in a puddle. Dirty water splashed over her legs, soaking her stockings.

Holding tight to her umbrella, she hurried across the street to her car, an early '50s model Pontiac Star Chief that had seen better days. Lou had a fondness for the Star Chief that she called Bertha. Even though Bertha had more scratches than paint and refused to start on cold or rainy days of which today was both, Lou loved the car she'd bought with her own money.

Lou could hardly blame Bertha for not wanting to start. She shared the car's disdain for Seattle's weather.

"Please start," Lou whispered before turning the key in the ignition. "I'm going to be late."

The engine rumbled and then sputtered out. Lou leaned her head on the steering wheel and closed her eyes tightly, willing Bertha to start. She didn't want to be late on her last date with Paul before she left for vacation. Paul hated it when she was late, and dinner would not go smoothly.

Lou tried turning the key again, and this time after a bit of grumbling, Bertha roared to life. Lou smiled and patted the steering wheel, then pulled away from the curb. Before she met Paul at their usual Monday night spot, Lou had one stop to make. She'd called the camera store and told them she was coming by, and since she was such a good customer, the owner was staying open late for her. Lou swung into a parking spot in front of Pacific Camera and ran through the rain to the storefront.

Standing under the protection of the awning, Lou knocked on the glass door. She stood shivering in the cold until the owner opened the door.

"Come in, dear girl. Come in out of the cold." Oliver Tollison opened the door for Lou and welcomed her inside.

Pacific Camera was Lou's favorite store in Seattle. It consisted of a tiny storefront with cameras and equipment for sale and a darkroom for processing pictures in the back. It was family owned and operated. Mr. Tollison and his son did all the developing, and Mrs. Tollison usually ran the front counter.

Lou walked into the store, looking first at the wall of photographs that served as an inspiration to customers. There was nothing new, so she continued to the counter and bent down to inspect the lenses behind the glass.

"I need that 300mm lens," she said, tapping the counter over the one she wanted. "And four rolls of film."

Mr. Tollison's bushy mustache lifted as he smiled. "Saved up enough, did you, now?"

Lou nodded. Ever since she and her roommate, Penny, had decided to take a vacation to Hawaii, Lou had known she wanted a telescopic lens. Between the plane tickets and the lens, she'd pretty much cleaned out her bank account, but she knew it was worth it. This trip was a once-in-a-lifetime opportunity, and the lens was an investment.

Mr. Tollison reached behind the counter and pulled out the lens Lou wanted. "Black and white or color?" he asked.

"I'm going to Hawaii," Lou said, smiling.

"Black and white, then?" Mr. Tollison said with a straight face.

Lou shook her head. "Color."

"You need black and white."

Mr. Tollison was a purist who believed that good photographers shot in black and white only. Lou had listened to countless lectures about the virtues of shadows and contrasts between light and dark. Color film was too new, too gimmicky for Oliver Tollison's tastes.

"Fine," Lou said, not wanting to hurt his feelings since he had stayed open late for her. "I'll take three color and one black and white."

Mr. Tollison rang up her purchases, and Lou handed over her hard-earned money.

"When you bring the film back here for processing, I'll give you a good discount," he said, walking her slowly to the door. "I can't wait to see what you do." He gave her a wink. "Especially with that black and white."

"Thank you," Lou said and hurried out the door into the rain.

Bertha was still warm from her recent drive and started on the first try. Lou rushed to Jefferson's, where she and Paul had been meeting regularly on Monday nights for almost a year.

When Lou arrived, Paul was already sitting at a table with a view of the waterfront. Behind him was the lake and Mt. Rainier in the distance.

Lou smiled, realizing Paul had intentionally left her the best seat with the panoramic view. She took a moment to appreciate her good fortune. She was going on a fabulous trip to an exotic island tomorrow, but tonight, she had the best-looking man in the restaurant waiting for her arrival.

Paul noticed Lou and stood up to greet her. Half of the men in the restaurant were following Lou with their eyes, but she didn't notice. She never noticed.

Paul looked her over from head to toe. "You look beautiful," he said. "You're always worth the wait."

"I had trouble with my car," Lou lied smoothly.

Paul's eyebrows drew together. "I can't wait until you get something decent to drive."

"I don't mind the Star Chief."

"You need something new. I don't want you driving our kids around in that thing."

Paul was always looking to the future. He and Lou had their entire lives planned out together, including how many children they wanted to have and what neighborhood they wanted to live in.

The waitress came up to the table with a fresh Manhattan for Paul. She put it down with a smile.

"The lady will have a vodka martini, straight up, with a twist," Paul said. When the waitress had gone, he leaned across the table and touched Lou's hand. "I'm going to miss you next Monday."

"I'll be home before you know it."

Paul nodded and reached for a cigarette. "I was planning to take you to Hawaii for our honeymoon." He pinched the cigarette between his lips and squinted at Lou as he lit the tip. "You're spoiling it for me."

"Don't be silly. Hawaii isn't going anywhere. We can go again."

"I'm the one who needs a vacation." Paul blew out a steady stream of smoke. "I've been working day and night."

The waitress brought Lou's martini, and Paul ordered their usual appetizers. They were quiet for a minute while Lou sipped her martini and Paul smoked.

"Don't spend your entire time hiding behind that camera."

Lou choked on a sip of her drink. "What?"

Paul blew a stream of smoke into the air and tempered his

words with a smile. "Just lift your head up every once in a while and take a look around, will you?"

"I will. I promise."

Paul pinned Lou with his brilliant blue gaze. "And don't have so much fun that you forget about me."

"Impossible." She reached across the table and took his hand, thinking it was time they changed the subject. "Tell me about your day."

Paul squeezed her fingers, then released her hand and sat back in his chair. "It was a very good day."

Paul launched into a retelling of his day. Lou listened, nodding when it was appropriate and making noises of agreement, but she was only half listening.

She studied Paul as he spoke, watching his elegant gestures and charming smile. Paul was what people called classically handsome. He had hair so black it had a blue tint and dazzling eyes the color of an inky sky. His best feature was that cheeky smile that got him whatever he wanted. He was taller than average, physically fit, and athletic. Somehow he managed to beat everyone at tennis and golf, even though he smoked too much and never practiced.

"You should have seen the look on his face." Paul laughed, slapping the table with his palm and leaning forward. "And then he had the nerve to say, 'Are you just going to stand there all day?'"

Lou laughed along, even though she hadn't really been paying attention. Paul looked younger when he laughed, and it reminded her of when they'd first met in high school.

They ordered another round of drinks with dinner, and they spoke of their summer plans. They hoped to sail around the Puget Sound if Paul could get the time off. He loved sailing, and Lou loved relaxing on the water. They hoped to have a boat of their own someday.

They finished dinner, declined dessert, and walked to their cars. The sky was cloudy, and the stars were hidden. The moon was only a sliver of light, and the night had turned colder.

Lou huddled inside her jacket, dreaming of the sunny skies that awaited her in Oahu.

"It looks like snow," she said.

"I doubt it," said Paul. "It isn't that cold."

"Hmm," Lou said, studying his chiseled profile. She wasn't going to miss the weather, but she would miss Paul.

When he leaned down to kiss her, she wrapped her arms around his neck and held him close. It had been weeks since she'd gone to his place. Lou never made the first move, but she considered it now because she was leaving in the morning. Paul was old-fashioned. He liked to be the one to initiate sex, which was usually fine with Lou. Except tonight, she was feeling bold.

"Do you want me to come over?" She pressed against him.

Paul stiffened and pulled back so that they were barely touching. "Not tonight. I have an early morning." He dropped a quick kiss on her upturned cheek. "It will give you something to look forward to," he said.

He waited until she'd fished her keys out of her bag before stepping away.

"See you in two weeks." She paused at her door, giving him a chance to change his mind and invite her over to his place.

"Don't forget about me." He winked.

"I won't."

Lou turned the key, and Bertha roared to life without hesitation. Paul waved one last time and then walked away.

AIRPORT IN PARADISE

Honolulu Airport
   A Tuesday in January 1968

"Hurry up," Penny said, poking Lou in the shoulder. "The rest of us want to see Hawaii, too."

"I'm going." Lou could only move so quickly in her high-heeled espadrille sandals, and she didn't want her first steps on Hawaiian soil to be flat on her ass. "Stop breathing down my neck, would you?"

"I told you not to wear those shoes." Penny poked her again. "You're too clumsy for heels."

Penny's voice was teasing, but it was true. Lou was hopelessly clumsy, partly because her camera was usually glued to her face, leaving her no room to look where she was going. When she made it to the tarmac without incident, she twirled in a circle, tilting her face to the sun. "I love it here already."

"Me, too." Penny linked her elbow with Lou's. "Let's stay forever."

"You think Paul and Joe would mind?"

"Who are Paul and Joe?" Penny pulled Lou closer, laughing. "Maybe I'll marry a Hawaiian man instead. Maybe I'll live in a grass shack instead of a brick house in Seward Park."

"Surf all day and go to luau parties every night?" Lou asked, joining in the fantasy.

"I can learn the hula."

"And I can take pictures and sell them to rich tourists."

They strolled arm-in-arm across the sunlit tarmac. If Lou noticed the people staring at them, she just assumed they were looking at Penny. Her roommate was gorgeous. A former ballerina, Penny's long legs and glossy red hair caused heads to turn wherever they went.

Lou never considered people might be looking at *her*. She thought of herself as the girl next door—like Gidget, while Penny was every man's dream woman.

"I need my camera." Lou stopped to dig in her purse.

"Oh, for goodness' sake, Lou. You'll look like such a tourist."

"We are tourists."

"I know, but it doesn't mean we have to look like them. And there's nothing to take photographs of here. It's the airport."

Lou ignored Penny and brought her camera to her face. She snapped a few pictures of the palm trees and then scanned the tarmac for another shot. She slowly panned her camera across the tourists walking into the airport, and then over the people waiting to pick up their loved ones. They stood in a line behind a rope, carrying flowers and colorful Hawaiian leis. Lou took a picture of a little boy riding on his father's shoulders and then swept her camera over the other faces in the crowd. She froze her lens on a tall, dark-haired man standing behind the rope.

Unlike most of the travelers, he was dressed casually in a worn T-shirt and shorts. He was tall and tanned with broad shoulders and a headful of wavy dark hair. A Native Hawaiian, he had been blessed with perfect bone structure, bronzed skin, and chiseled features.

He was one of the most striking men she'd ever seen, but his good looks weren't the reason she zoomed in on his face. Despite the proud tilt to his head, he looked fresh from a fight. His lip was split and crusted with blood, and a large gash on his forehead marred the perfection of his face. Dark sunglasses hid his eyes, but a purple bruise peeked out from under the metal frames.

Just as Lou pressed the button to take a picture, he lowered his sunglasses and stared straight at her. *She'd been caught.* Her cheeks burned, and she dropped her camera.

Penny was a few paces ahead, and Lou hurried to join her.

"Whoa. Get a load of those guys. They don't make them like that in Seattle." Penny nodded toward the man Lou had just photographed. "He's the biggest man I've ever seen. I wonder if he's that big all over?"

"Penny!" Lou laughed and swatted her friend on the shoulder. "You're terrible."

Lou risked another glance at the tall Hawaiian man. "He's not that tall," she said, unable to tear her eyes from the man. Despite the bruises marking his skin, he had a noble appearance, like a prince dressed down for the day. There was something almost majestic about his lean, muscular build. He reminded her of a sculpture. A work of art.

"He's enormous," Penny said. "Look at his shoulders. They look like mountains."

"What?" Lou asked. "They don't look like mountains." His shoulders were broader than average, but otherwise perfectly normal.

Penny followed Lou's gaze, and she snorted. "Not him," she said. "The other one."

Lou dragged her gaze away from the man in the sunglasses to the man next to him, and her eyes widened. His shoulders *did* look like mountains. His neck was thick with muscles, and his arms were bigger than her waist. He looked like he could snap her in two without breaking a sweat. Except for his modern clothing, he could have been ripped from the pages of a book on Hawaiian warriors.

"Lou!" Penny cried. "I think they're here for us."

Lou's throat went dry. "What?"

"Oh, geez," Penny said as they got closer to the rope. She grabbed Lou's hand and squeezed it hard enough to make Lou cry out in pain. "That's me!"

Lou saw that the big man was holding a handwritten sign with Penny's name on it.

"Henry said he would send a friend if he couldn't get off work." Penny was practically jumping up and down. "They are here for us!"

"Be cool," Lou said under her breath, holding Penny's arm.

"Me? You're one to talk with that camera stuck to your face."

"Are you sure they are Henry's friends? That guy has bruises all over his face. He looks like he's just been in a fight."

The two men made a striking pair, but there was something dangerous about them.

"Bruises? Oh, you're right. I hadn't even gotten to his face yet. I got hung up on the rest of him. And the big one is mine."

"Penny!"

"I'm just having a little fun, Lou. Don't be such a square. Joe will never know if I flirt a little." She grabbed Lou's arm and jerked her forward. "Neither will Paul." They halted in front of the men, and Penny beamed up at the big one. "I'm Penny Longchamp."

He smiled, and something magical happened to his face. He went from looking dangerous to sweet. He had a wide, genuine smile that made Lou relax instantly. His eyes were warm and welcoming, an unusual shade of gray, flecked with sparks of silver.

"Henry sent us," he said. The words rolled off his tongue in an exotic lilt. "He told us to pick up the two prettiest girls who got off the plane." His eyes roamed over Penny from head to toe. "And that's you."

Penny opened her mouth, but nothing came out. Lou realized her friend was speechless. Penny was never speechless. Lou came to her rescue.

"It's so beautiful here!"

The taller man laughed and said, "This is the airport. Wait till you see the beaches, yeah?" He offered Penny the lei he was carrying, and she bent to accept it. "I'm Bones," he said. "And this ugly guy right here is my cousin Keoni."

Lou glanced away from Bones to look at Keoni. His face was battered, but he didn't seem menacing to Lou. Up close, he seemed even more like a sculpture. Despite his casual clothing, there was something refined in his stance. He seemed confident, but not arrogant.

"Welcome to Hawaii," Keoni said, offering Lou the colorful lei.

His accent called to mind the sultry beaches of the islands. *Ha-vhy-ee.*

Lou lowered her chin, and Keoni placed the lei around her neck. It was a surprisingly intimate gesture for something so common. Keoni's fingers brushed her skin, and Lou's heart quickened.

She looked up and met her own reflection in the lenses of his dark sunglasses. Her gaze dropped to his mouth, which was swollen and split in the middle. The ghost of a smile played around his lips. His injured mouth should be ugly, but it lent him an air of vulnerability.

"What's your name?" Keoni asked.

"Mary Lou. My friends call me Lou."

"Mary Lou," he said. "Pretty."

Lou raised an eyebrow at him. No one had ever told her that her name was pretty. She'd always thought it was old-fashioned. She'd never liked it. But coming from Keoni's lips, her name sounded lovely.

"Thank you."

"Let's get your bags." Keoni led the way to the airport.

Lou hung back, letting Penny and Bones walk ahead of them. Penny was very tall. It was why her dance career had ultimately failed. She was too tall for all of her partners. But she wasn't too tall for Bones. Even in her high heel sandals, Penny barely came to his shoulder.

"Is his name really Bones?" Lou asked Keoni.

"Nah," Keoni said, taking off his sunglasses and hooking them in the neck of his shirt.

Lou waited for Keoni to elaborate, but he never did. Without the sunglasses covering his face, she could see the full extent of the bruise covering his eye. It looked horrible. She'd never been hit in the eye, but she imagined a mark like that must be painful. The bruise covered his eye from brow to cheek in varying shades of purple and yellow.

"First trip to Hawaii?" Keoni asked.

"How can you tell?"

"Just a guess." He smiled and pointed to the camera around her neck.

"Oh." Lou's cheeks heated. "I'm always taking pictures. I do this at home, too."

"Yeah?"

"It's kind of a hobby of mine."

Keoni placed a hand on Lou's elbow, steering her around a large pot of flowers that seemed to have appeared out of nowhere. "Watch out."

"Thanks," she said, laughing nervously. His hand on her arm awakened a curiosity in her. She wanted to know everything about him. What did he do for work? Did he have a family? How did he get that bruise?

"No worries." He smiled and dropped his hand, continuing through the crowd.

Lou followed along, trying not to gape at the surroundings. She'd never been in an airport like this before. It was so full of life and energy. There were young girls handing out flowered neck-laces, a gift shop stocked with souvenirs, and a band playing Hawaiian music from a stage.

As the high-pitched sounds of the ukulele filled the air, Lou stopped and turned toward the stage, automatically raising her camera.

"You want to listen?" Keoni asked.

"Yeah, sure." *But she'd rather watch.* Lou focused the lens on the singer. "Can we get a little closer?"

Keoni steered her toward the front of the crowd. Lou panned her camera over the members of the band. With their dark hair and eyes, they looked similar enough to be family. Lou zoomed in on the singer. She was petite and curvy, with waist-length curling dark hair. Even with the heavy makeup, Lou could tell she was young. Early twenties at most, she had a sultry voice that was seasoned beyond her years.

Lou snapped a few pictures of the woman as she wrapped up her song. The singer waved her hand and waved at someone in the crowd as she drew out the last note.

"Thank you," the singer said as the crowd applauded. She waved again, and Lou turned to see Keoni wave back.

"Do you know her?" Lou asked, glancing between them.

"Sure," Keoni said. "That's Ryla."

"Is she calling you up there?"

"Yeah, but..." He shrugged.

"Ladies and gentlemen, we have for your pleasure—the fabu-lous Keoni Makai." Ryla waved at Keoni again, smiling broadly.

"Not today, Ryla." Keoni raised his voice to be heard over the audience.

"Come on, Keoni," she said. "Don't be shy."

"I'm busy." He took Lou's hand and tugged her closer.

Lou felt a jolt of awareness as his big hand wrapped around hers.

"Ah," said Ryla. "Next time, then?"

He nodded and waved, pulling Lou back into the crowd.

"Did she want you to sing?" Lou asked.

"Something like that," he said.

"But you didn't want to?"

"Nah," Keoni said.

"I hope it wasn't because of me," Lou said. "I'm sorry for the inconvenience."

"Nah, it's not that." Keoni raised an eyebrow and gestured to his face.

"Oh." Lou looked at him, taking in the cut on his forehead, the bruise on his eye, and the split lip.

The bruises lent him an air of mystery, and she wondered again how he'd gotten them. A man pressed into Lou from behind, and thanks to her clumsiness, she nearly went down.

Keoni's hand tightened on hers. "You okay?"

"I'm fine." Except for now her heart was thundering in her chest like a storm about to break. She sucked in a breath. "It's very busy today."

"Always is."

Lou imagined how she would feel if Seattle was bombarded by hundreds of thousands of tourists every year. "You must hate all this."

"I'm used to it, but..." He shrugged. "That don't mean I gotta like it."

"How'd you get roped into coming to the airport to get us?" Lou asked.

He lifted his shoulders an inch. "I didn't have anything better to do."

Lou laughed. "That's too bad for you," she said. "I'm sure there are plenty of other things you'd rather be doing than playing chauffeur to a couple of tourists."

"Nah," he said.

Lou doubted it. "Are you from here?"

"I'm from Maui."

"Maui?" Lou said, trying to pronounce it with the same lilt as Keoni. "Sounds beautiful."

"It is. There are a lot less tourists." He froze as he realized what he'd said. "Sorry. I didn't mean…"

"It's okay." She smiled. "I get it."

His eyes came back to hers, and he smiled. Lou felt like it was the first genuine smile she'd gotten out of Keoni. The power of his smile rocked her to the core.

His dark gaze turned serious as he studied her. "Your hair is about a dozen different colors." Reaching up, he rescued a strand of her hair that was caught in the lei.

Awareness knotted in her belly. Every time Keoni touched her, she wanted it to last a little longer.

"It's pretty," Keoni said, wrapping his finger around the strand of hair.

"Thanks." Lou had never paid much attention to her hair. It was thick and wavy—a nuisance most of the time. She had to wear it back at work, but other than pinning it up in a knot, she didn't bother much with styling. It was Penny who spent hours in the mirror trying to get her straight hair to cooperate.

"There's your stuff," Keoni said, nodding at Bones who was carrying their luggage. "You ready, or do you want to take some more pictures?"

A bubble of joy burst in her chest at his question. No one ever asked her if she wanted more time to take pictures. Everyone always hurried her along, annoyed with her preoccupation of watching life from behind her camera lens.

Lou looked up at Keoni, wishing she had a whole roll of film and hours to capture the way the light hit his brown eyes. She dragged her gaze away from his, knowing there wasn't enough time and film in the world to do him justice. But she had an entire Hawaiian vacation ahead of her, might as well get started. "I'm ready," she said.

RED VELVET INVITATION

Bones's station wagon had two giant surfboards strapped to the top. Lou stopped short when she saw it and raised her camera for a picture. At this rate, she was going to run out of film in one day. She cautioned herself to go slowly. She wasn't made of money.

Penny came up beside Lou and nudged her with her elbow. "What do you think? Do I have a chance?" Penny nodded at Bones as he tossed their luggage in the trunk as if it weighed no more than a grocery sack.

Lou narrowed her eyes at Penny. "What about Joe?"

"Joe who?"

"*Penny.*"

"*Lou.*"

"Keoni?" a man's voice called from a distance.

Lou turned and looked at the man who was striding down the sidewalk toward them. He had a confident walk that chewed up the sidewalk, wheat-blond hair, and a gorgeous, white-toothed smile. He wore a navy blazer, white pants, and sockless Weejuns. Black-framed Wayfarer sunglasses covered his eyes.

Keoni walked stiffly across the sidewalk to greet him with a handshake.

"Look who's back," Bones said, coming up to join them.

There was an awkward moment of silence, and then the man took off his sunglasses and inspected Keoni's face.

"What the hell happened to you?" he asked.

"Waimea Bay," Keoni said.

"I thought maybe you got some girl pregnant again," he said, laughing.

"That wasn't me," Keoni said, not laughing.

"I know, but…" He shrugged. "You got your ass beat anyway."

"You just fly in, Declan?" Bones asked.

"Yeah, I came from Huntington Beach. The waves were this big," he said, raising his arm over his head.

Keoni smiled, and some of the stiffness left his shoulders. "Sure, brah, whatever you say."

Declan smiled back at Keoni. "I swear. They were monsters." Declan glanced over at Penny and Lou as if noticing them for the first time. "Aren't you going to introduce me to your friends?" he asked.

"Mary Lou and Penny. This is Declan Bishop."

Declan bent over Penny's hand and kissed it, then did the same with Lou's. He looked up at her as his mouth brushed over her knuckles, giving her a cocky smile. His blond hair fell over his forehead and he swept it aside in a practiced move.

"What are you two lovely women doing with these chumps?" Declan asked.

Lou straightened her shoulders and did her best to look down her nose at Declan. "They were kind enough to give us a ride."

"You gonna give them a tour of the islands, too?" Declan grinned mischievously. "Show dem da reel Ha-vhy-ee?"

"Sounds like a good idea," Penny said, gazing up at Bones. "I bet you know all the best spots."

Declan laughed. "You bet he does."

Bones glared at Declan. "What you doin' home?"

The color drained from Declan's face and he glanced at Keoni, concerned. "You didn't hear?"

"Hear what?"

Declan shifted from one foot to another, then reached into his jacket pocket and pulled out a red envelope. He handed it to Keoni, who held it reverently with both hands before opening it and reading the card inside.

"I'm surfing in the Duke," Declan said.

Keoni wet his lips and cleared his throat, then handed the invitation back to Declan. "Congratulations."

"Yeah, well," Declan muttered, looking down at the curb. "It shoulda been you," he said.

Bones defused some of the tension in the air with a hearty laugh. "You better be glad they didn't invite Keoni to surf the Duke, or you woulda had no chance."

Declan laughed along with Bones, nodding. He tucked the invitation back in his pocket. "You girls are coming to watch the Duke, right?"

"What's the Duke?" Lou asked.

"It's a surfing contest," Bones said. "The entire island comes out to watch. Everyone will be there. Right, Keoni?"

Keoni nodded. His jaw was clenched so tightly that Lou thought his teeth might be in danger of cracking.

"You'll come, won't you?" Declan asked.

After a moment, Keoni nodded again. "I'll be there." He reached out to take Declan's hand. "I hope you win."

Declan swallowed and nodded. "Thanks."

They shook hands, then hugged briefly.

"I gotta go," Declan said. "My car's here."

Lou looked down the sidewalk to see a white Rolls Royce parked at the curb. Declan waved and left. Keoni watched him get in the car.

Bones clapped a hand on Keoni's shoulder and said something

in a low voice that Lou couldn't hear. Keoni shrugged his hand away with an unintelligible response.

Chuckling, Bones went to the passenger door and held it open for Penny. "You ready?" he asked.

Penny nodded and climbed in, leaving Lou no choice but to sit in the back with Keoni.

Lou got in the back, then slid over as Keoni got in beside her. He leaned his head back on the seat with a heavy sigh and pinched the bridge of his nose between his thumb and index finger. Lou could feel the tension rolling of his body in waves. She wished she knew him better, so she could comfort him, but she had no words of wisdom.

"Are you okay?" She kept her voice soft. If he wanted to ignore her, she would understand.

Keoni glanced at her from the corner of his eye. "It looks worse than it feels, yeah?"

She hadn't been asking about the bruises, but she wasn't sorry he'd brought it up. He'd said something about Waimea Bay, which rang a bell in Lou's memory. She'd seen a movie about surfing that had been filmed at Waimea Bay. The waves had been monstrous.

"Did you do that surfing?" she asked.

"Nope." He grimaced and pointed to the gash on his forehead. "I did this wiping out."

Lou laughed. Keoni's eyes narrowed on her, and she realized too late that he hadn't been trying to be funny.

"And your ribs?" she asked.

"What about 'em?"

Lou reached over and touched his side with a gentle hand. "They're broken."

"Nah."

"Are they as bad as your face?"

"Nothin's as bad as his face," Bones joked from the front seat.

"Shut up," Keoni said.

"In this movie I saw, the waves at Waimea looked fifty feet high. Are they really that big?" she asked.

Keoni pressed his tongue to the raw cut on his lip. "We don't measure the waves in feet," he said. "We measure them in fear."

Lou stared at Keoni in horror, and then realized from the quirk in his smile that he was teasing.

"That must have been pretty scary," she said.

"Yeah."

"But you went out there anyway?"

"I live for days like that."

This time Lou sensed he was serious. There was something far off in his gaze as if he was planning out his future.

"So, you girls want to start the tour right away, or what?" Bones asked from the front seat.

"Sure," Penny said. "But you'll probably have to feed Lou pretty soon. She turns into a beast if she doesn't eat every two hours."

"That's not true," Lou said.

Bones laughed. "I could eat too."

"Me, too," Keoni said.

Lou glanced at Keoni to see that some of the tension had gone from his body. He looked almost relaxed with his legs sprawled into the space between them. When Keoni smiled, the temperature in the car suddenly rose ten degrees. Lou grabbed the tourist pamphlet she'd taken from the airport and fanned her face. After a moment, she turned her attention to the pamphlet and spread it over her lap. She tried to ignore Keoni as she pretended to study the map.

But it was no use.

He was too big. Too close. His leg brushed against hers as Bones switched lanes. If Lou took a deep breath, she could smell the ocean in his hair.

"Waimea Bay is right here." Keoni leaned his arm over the back of the seat and pointed at the map with his other hand.

Now he was even closer. So close that she could see the individual hairs of the scruff of his beard and the fine lines radiating from the corners of his eyes. His long hair was nearly dry, and it flopped over his forehead, hiding the worst of the gash. If they'd been in Seattle, Keoni would be in desperate need of a haircut and a shave, but in Hawaii, he was perfect.

"Is that where they will have the Duke contest?"

"Nah." Keoni shook his head. "Waimea's too wild. They'll have it here," he said, trailing his finger north along the map to stop at Lou's knee. "Sunset Beach."

"You have to be invited?" Lou asked.

"Yeah."

Lou waited for him to go on, but he didn't. From what Declan and Bones had said, she thought Keoni must be pretty good at surfing. Then again, judging from his injuries, maybe not.

TROPICS DRIVE-IN

T<small>HEY STOPPED AT</small> T<small>ROPICS</small> D<small>RIVE-</small>I<small>N AND ORDERED BURGERS,</small> fries, and shakes.

Keoni ate automatically, even though he didn't feel hungry. Seeing Declan had taken him back two years to Eddie's death. The last time Keoni had seen Declan had been at Eddie's memorial. They hadn't parted on good terms.

Keoni had seen Declan's name on the list of invitees to the Duke last month, but he'd put it out of his mind, too angry that he hadn't been selected.

Maybe next year, Keoni hoped.

He'd been hoping that for three years, but he didn't let that discourage him. He knew he needed to be patient. Times were changing. They couldn't keep ignoring Hawaiians.

Even though the Duke Kahanamoku Invitational Surfing Championships was named after the most famous Hawaiian surfer in the world and held in Hawaii, it was an exclusive contest. No Native Hawaiian had ever been invited. Keoni planned to be the first.

It shoulda been you, Declan had said.

And he was right. There was no one better at surfing on the

North Shore than Keoni. But if he couldn't win, then Declan was the next best thing. Keoni had meant it when he'd told Declan he hoped he'd win.

Declan could do it, too. He was as talented as anybody, and he knew the waves better than most. The only problem was that the contest was at Sunset Beach—where Eddie had died.

Declan had to keep from pressuring out on the same waves that had stolen their best friend.

"You gonna eat those?" Lou asked.

"Hmm?"

"Do you want your fries?" She pointed to the uneaten fries on Keoni's tray.

"Nah." He passed her the fries.

She smiled and polished them off, then climbed out of the car, taking her camera with her.

"So, where should we go first?" Penny asked.

Keoni got out of the car, leaving Bones to answer the question. He watched Lou wander off to the edge of the parking lot with her camera in front of her face. She was so absorbed in looking through the lens that she nearly stumbled over a curb.

She righted herself quickly enough and then bent down and aimed her camera up at the Tropics Drive-In sign. When she got the shot she wanted, she stood up and dropped her camera to her chest, then headed back.

Keoni liked watching Lou take her pictures. She was so completely absorbed in what she was doing that she didn't notice what was going on around her. A hurricane could be coming and she wouldn't see it blow by.

It reminded Keoni of how he felt when he surfed. He got lost the same way Lou did.

It was easy to watch her. She was pretty. She was tall and curvaceous, and she had unusual eyes—more green than blue. Her hair was her best feature. She had it pinned on top of her head, but most of it had escaped to curl around her neck and shoulders. The sun picked up the blond and copper highlights among the strands of brown, turning it a dozen technicolor hues.

Lou saw Keoni and smiled at him. She did that a lot, he'd noticed. Something squeezed in his chest, and he amended his earlier assessment that Lou's hair was her best feature. It was definitely her smile.

When she smiled, a dimple winked in her cheek, and her whole face lit up. Even though it hurt his mouth, Keoni felt himself smiling back.

With the lei of flowers around her neck and the camera in front of her face, Lou looked like the very definition of a tourist fresh off the boat. Keoni hated tourists, but he couldn't help thinking Lou was cute.

No- *cute* wasn't the word. The only thing cute about her was her delicate nose. The rest of her, from her long legs to her wide smile, wasn't cute—it was sexy as hell.

"It's beautiful here," Lou said, coming to stand next to him.

"Hmm," he said, dragging his eyes away from Lou to the scenery. When he saw what she was looking at, Keoni laughed. They were on a busy road in Honolulu. "This is nothing."

"I can't wait to see something, then."

"What's it like in Seattle?" he asked.

"Rainy. We hardly ever see the sun."

"I couldn't live like that."

Lou glanced over Keoni's shoulder to the car where Bones and Penny were chatting with their heads together in the front seat. They looked to be hitting it off nicely. Bones was probably already planning on giving Penny the deluxe tour of Hawaii that ended at his apartment in his bed.

Bones didn't discriminate against tourists the way Keoni did. The legendary Beach Boys of Waikiki had gone out of style years ago, but Bones did his best to make sure tourists got an authentic experience. Especially the pretty ones like Lou and Penny.

"I think they are planning out the tour," Keoni said, noticing the way Lou watched Penny protectively.

"Yeah. Looks like it."

"Anywhere in particular you want to go?"

Lou smiled, making the dimple in her cheek wink again. "Everywhere."

Keoni laughed. "How long are you staying?"

"Twelve days."

He shook his head, his eyes lingering on her wide mouth. "That's not nearly enough," he said.

Lou's mouth dropped open, and her eyes flew to Keoni's. He realized he was flirting with her, and he stiffened and pulled away. He hadn't meant for it to come out that way, like a come-on.

That wasn't Keoni's style. He didn't flirt with tourists.

He turned away from her and headed back to the car.

"Heh," he said, leaning in the window of the driver's seat. "I just remembered Kimo is coming by today. I better get home."

"Kimo's coming home?" Bones asked.

"That's what I said."

"That's perfect!" Bones said. "We were just deciding where to go first, and your parents' place is perfect. Everyone will be there, and Auntie Palu probably has *malasadas* in the oven." He turned to Penny. "You ever had a *malasada*?" he asked.

"No."

"Let's go," Bones said.

"Can I holler at you a minute?" Keoni asked, opening the car door.

"Yeah." Bones climbed out and they walked off a few feet from the car. "What's wrong?"

"Nothing." Keoni took a deep breath and then looked at Lou. She was leaning into the car talking to Penny. She glanced up and caught his eye, then looked away quickly. "I said I would go to the airport, but I ain't gonna spend all day showing around some tourists."

"Why not?"

Keoni sighed. "I got better things to do."

"You got better things to do than hang around two girls who look like that?" Bones asked, raising his eyebrow at Keoni.

"I gotta work tonight."

"Not until midnight. It's 4:30."

Keoni cast around for another excuse, but he couldn't think of anything.

"Come on," Bones said, slapping Keoni on the back hard enough to make his ribs rattle. "Be cool."

"I am cool," he said. "Just take me home, will you? Then you can do whatever you want after that."

Bones shook his head at Keoni as if he was crazy. "What's the matter, you?"

"Nothing," Keoni insisted, walking back to the car.

He opened the door for Lou, and she slid along the seat, making room for him. Bones got in the front and started the car.

"Everything okay?" Lou asked.

"Yeah."

"We're going to Keoni's parents' house," Bones said. "It's not far."

Lou unfolded the pamphlet again. "Where is it?" she asked, seeming genuinely interested.

She spread the map on the seat between them and leaned over it, her hair spilling forward. Keoni breathed in the honey scent of her shampoo and felt the soft sweep of her hair on his forearm.

He turned toward her and pointed on the map, running his finger south along the mountain range that ran the entire length of the windward side of the island.

"Here," he said, stopping at a brown valley that was tucked into the steep green slopes of the mountains.

She leaned forward to study it. "Right between these mountains?" she asked. "Must be beautiful."

"It is."

Keoni's parents' house was his favorite place on the island besides Waimea Bay. Set deep in the valley of the Ko'olau Mountains, his parents' place had views of the mountains, the city, and the ocean.

Keoni folded up the map. He made sure to hand the brochure back to Lou faceup, because he was pretty certain his picture was on the back cover. He didn't want her seeing it and thinking he was some kind of big deal.

"My house might not be what you're expecting, yeah?" he said.

Lou put the brochure back in her bag and looked up at Keoni, waiting for him to go on. After a moment, her eyebrows drew together, and she asked, "What do you mean?"

"You'll find out," he said.

Soon after they exited the city, Bones turned onto a hilly road that ran parallel to the coast. The road was made up of small houses with postage-stamp-sized yards. As they wound higher into the hills, everything got bigger.

The yards stretched out, the houses grew, and the trees reached higher. The dark green foliage on the trees looked like something out of a fairy tale. Flowers grew on shrubs, in pots, and up the sides of fences. The car climbed higher into the mountains and then dipped down a steep descent.

At the bottom of the hill, Bones turned onto a gravel road that led to a valley between the green ridges of the mountain range. He took another turn, and they came upon a gate that was guarded by two large Chinese-style stone lions.

Keoni glanced over at Lou as they drove past the red-roofed pagoda that held a sign for a cemetery.

Her mouth dropped open, and she reached for her camera as if on auto pilot.

"You live in a graveyard?" she asked.

"No, but my parents do."

THE GRAVEYARD

KEONI HAD BEEN TEN YEARS OLD WHEN HIS FAMILY HAD MOVED TO the graveyard. Those stone lions with their all-seeing gray eyes had scared him and his brothers and sister half to death.

In their country home in the mountains of Maui, Keoni had run free and wild. In Honolulu, they lived in an apartment with two bedrooms for seven people. In Maui, his father couldn't find work, but there was plenty of work at the docks of Honolulu for a strong, hard-working man like Keoni's father. Loki Makai was used to working the ranches of Maui from sunup to sundown. He was tall and broad, and even though he was uneducated, he was smart. Loki worked at the docks for a few months before he found out about a job where his family could live rent-free on thousands of acres of land. The only catch was that they had to maintain the property, and it was a cemetery.

Keoni and his siblings had learned to love the cemetery. The land stretched out like their own private park, with the Ko'olau Mountains as the backdrop. Views of Waikiki and Kane'hoe Bay could be seen from the tops of the hills. Keoni could ride his bike a few miles and arrive at the cliff-side beaches of Black Point or Diamond Head.

But it wasn't all play for the Makai children, they had to work hard to keep up the grounds of the cemetery. The sprawling acreage didn't take care of itself, and the family had to put in a lot of hours of work. Keoni and his brothers and sister had spent countless hours doing mundane chores like weeding and mowing. And then there were the less ordinary jobs of digging up graves to excavate the bones and prepare them for the Bone House according to Chinese customs.

Once their work was done, they were free to do as they wished. They didn't have a television, but five thousand acres of land was plenty to keep them entertained.

The Makais didn't have a lot of money, but they never went without the necessities. There was always food to eat. Mango, papaya, and guava trees dotted the hills of the graveyard, and the ocean was a short drive away. There was an ancient fishpond, with curving walls made of stone at Black Point. Fish swam in through the sluice gates at high tide and became trapped. Keoni or his brothers and sister would be sent down to collect fish if food was short, and his mother canned enough fruit to feed everyone in their extended family.

Whether it was work or play, there was always something to do on the graveyard. The Makais were well known on the island for their hospitality. Keoni had grown up with a revolving door of guests and relatives. There was always an extra seat at the table. There was always food and drink to share. There was always aloha.

And the graveyard became the center of Keoni's world.

He glanced over at Lou, wondering what she thought of his universe.

She was looking out the window. The breeze caught her hair and tossed it into her face, and she shoved it away with an impatient hand. Feeling his stare, she turned to look at him, and Keoni saw that her eyes were ablaze with curiosity.

"You grew up here?"

He nodded, plucking a strand of her hair that had stuck in the short hairs of his beard.

"What was it like?"

Keoni's eyes softened. "It was everything."

He had nothing but fond memories of growing up in the grave-yard. It had been hard work for him as a kid, and it still was for his parents, but it had been full of joy. He felt guilty sometimes that he had left and moved to Hale'iwa.

It helped that Keoni's older brother, Tau, had built a small house on the property and lived there with his young family. There was a whole new generation of Makais to grow up on the cemetery.

"It's beautiful," Lou said.

Keoni felt a surge of pride. "Thanks."

"It didn't spook you out living here?" Penny asked.

"Nah," Keoni said.

"Keoni has all kinds of crazy stories about growing up here," Bones said.

Penny and Lou both turned to look at Keoni. Bones met Keoni's eye in the rearview mirror, and they shared a smile. One of the most entertaining stories was the one of Bones's nickname, but that wasn't Keoni's story to tell.

They drove along the narrow road that cut through the mani-cured lawns of graves until they reached the center of the valley, where several small houses were built in a clearing. Half a dozen cars were already there. Keoni recognized Kimo's truck among the others. He gritted his teeth and looked away.

Keoni would be glad to see Kimo one last time before he left, but he wasn't looking forward to another confrontation with his bull-headed brother. Suddenly feeling cooped up in the small back seat, Keoni couldn't wait to jump out and stretch his legs. Bones had barely rolled to a stop next to the other cars when he opened the door and climbed out.

"How big is this place?" Penny asked.

Keoni glanced over the top of the car to look at Penny. "Five thousand acres," he said.

Lou climbed out of the car and walked to the far end of the gravel drive, staring up the hills at the tombstones.

"She's gonna want to take some pictures." Penny rolled her eyes.

Sure enough, Lou already had her camera raised to her face. Keoni thought she would love the view from the top of the hill.

"I'll show you the view," he said impulsively.

He wanted to see Lou's face when she saw the cityscape surrounded by blue ocean and sky.

Penny laughed. "Not in these shoes," she said, pointing to her heels.

Keoni glanced from Penny's shoes back to Lou, who was in her own little world behind her camera.

"You go on inside," he said. "Tell Mom I'll be right along."

After Bones and Penny went inside, Keoni crossed the yard toward Lou. "Want to see the view of the city from the top?"

She lowered her camera, resting it on the strap around her neck. Her eyes sparkled like the turquoise ocean. "This place is unreal."

"Wait till you see it from up top. Would you like that?"

She didn't hesitate. "Yes."

They started off up the hill. The pace was much slower than Keoni usually took it because Lou kept stopping every few steps to take a picture.

Keoni leaned against a statue of an angel and watched her adjust dials and press buttons. She was so engrossed in what she was doing that she'd seemed to forget his presence. He took advantage of her distracted state to study her while she wasn't looking.

At first glance, Lou had intrigued Keoni. There was a spark about her, a curiosity that lit her from within, making everything about her shine. Her blue-green eyes sparkled. The reddish-blonde streaks running through her brown hair gleamed, and her skin glowed fresh as a peach.

At first glance, she was pretty, but the more he looked, the more she grew on him. Taken individually, her features were pleasant, but put together, they were striking. She was quick to smile and blush, and there was a softness to her that touched something calloused inside him.

A smile crept over his lips as he watched her. She was clearly passionate about her photography. There was something very sexy about watching a woman doing what she loved. The look of pleased concentration he saw on Lou's face must be similar to what he looked like while surfing or playing guitar.

She stumbled over a root, and Keoni's hand shot out to steady her before she could fall. So far the only fault he could find about her was that she had two left feet. And of course the fact that she was a tourist. Nothing could be worse than that.

"Careful," he said, holding her elbow until she got her feet under her properly. He reminded himself to heed the warning. He didn't want to get involved with a woman like her who came to Hawaii only to leave again.

"I'm not wearing the right shoes for a hike." She glanced down at her sandals as if they were to blame for her clumsiness.

"You women and your shoes." Keoni shook his head. "I'll never understand."

"I'm planning on going barefoot on the beach for the rest of the trip." She let her camera rest on its strap. "Does that make you feel better?"

Keoni pictured Lou on the beach, toes buried in the sand, and every muscle in his body tensed. He wouldn't mind seeing that.

She raised her camera and snapped a photo of him mid-smile.

"I might break your camera." He pointed to his bashed-up face.

"Highly unlikely." She grinned. "Tell me a story about growing up here. I bet it was… interesting."

Keoni didn't need to be asked twice to tell a story. He was a natural story-teller, and there was always one on the tip of his tongue. Most of his friends just rolled their eyes and tuned him out when he launched into a story, but Lou was a fresh audience. She lapped up his story about the ghost they were trying to trap, listening with wide eyes. He hammed it up a little, adding embellishments.

About halfway to the top of the hill, Lou interrupted him. "You're making this up."

"Nah. It's true."

Lou shook her head. "You're only trying to scare me."

"Why would I do that?"

She lifted her camera and aimed at him. He grinned and held up his hand in the shaka sign, fingers tucked against his palm, thumb and pinky spread wide.

Lou froze and then blinked slowly at him as she lowered her camera.

"What? Did I break it?" He pressed his tongue to the cut on his lip, hoping it wasn't really possible.

"No." Color stole up her cheeks. "I just realized something."

"Yeah?" Keoni wondered if it was the quickening of her heart whenever they touched.

Lou reached into the pocket of her dress and pulled out the travel pamphlet with the map. She flipped it over and pointed to the picture on the back.

"That's you," she said.

Keoni shrugged, looking away from the photo of him sitting on his surfboard flashing a grin and the shaka sign. That must have been how she put it together. There was no denying it was him.

"You're famous."

"Nah."

"Don't be embarrassed. It's a good picture."

Keoni started up the hill again. "Do you want to hear the rest of the story, or what?"

"Do you have a better one," she asked.

"You don't like my story?"

"I just don't buy that you and your brothers trapped a ghost. I know I'm naive, but even I'm not falling for that."

"Good thing I'm not trying to impress you." He reminded himself that he didn't mess around with tourists who were only in town for a few days, not even ones as pretty as Lou. Keoni smiled and held out his hand to Lou. "Close your eyes these last few steps," he said. "I want you to be surprised."

"Okay." Lou closed her eyes and placed her hand in Keoni's.

He guided her to the top of the hill and turned her in the direction of the view. "Kay then. Open your eyes."

THE VIEW FROM THE TOP

LOU'S EYES FLUTTERED OPEN, AND SHE GAZED OUT OVER THE CITY of Honolulu. It looked smaller than she'd expected, more like a child's drawing of a city than the actual thing. Lou had never seen a panoramic view of downtown Seattle before, but she suspected it would be much bigger, with more buildings, interstates, and of course the space needle, which looked like a giant flying saucer hovering over the buildings.

Honolulu was a single row of buildings that seemed no bigger than a line of toy blocks anchoring the horizon. Rising from both the left and right were the verdant slopes of the mountains. Above and beyond the mountains and the tiny skyscrapers were the navy sky and the turquoise sea.

The sight touched something in Lou's heart. It was the ultimate clash of humanity verses nature. She imagined what it must have looked like to stand here two hundred years earlier, and her throat clogged with emotion. Tears burned the back of her eyes.

"Heh." Keoni's voice was close. His hand settled at the small of her back. "You okay?"

Her throat constricted even more as she imagined what it must have been like to have grown up here and see this kind of juxtaposition of man verses nature on a daily basis. The beauty of Hawaii was overwhelming, but the buildings made her feel almost sick. She wished she could wipe out the buildings and see the view before it had been spoiled.

"You don't like it?" he asked.

"I'm sorry," she said. "It's just so…" She trailed off, unable to find the right words. "It's spectacular, but I kind of hate it."

She glanced up at him, hoping she hadn't hurt his feelings. His eyes widened slightly, and then he laughed.

"I've seen a lot of people look at this view, but not one has ever reacted like that before." He stared at the view as if seeing it through her eyes.

When he turned to look at her, his eyes were sad. Lou reached up to touch his swollen cheek. "Does it hurt terribly?"

"It's fine." His eyes drifted shut as she gently traced his injured cheek. When he opened his eyes again, the sadness was gone, replaced by something sharp and hungry. His gaze dropped to her mouth, and she felt a shiver of longing race down her spine, wondering what it would be like if he gathered her close and kissed her.

Lou dropped her hand and took a step back. She had nearly lost herself for a moment, but then she'd remembered. There was Paul to think of. She'd almost forgotten him. The romance and beauty of Hawaii had nearly seduced her.

She picked up her camera, fiddling with the dials until she felt her breathing was under control. She snapped a few pictures of the view, feeling comfortable again behind the camera.

When they started down the hill back to the valley, Lou had her thoughts under control. She focused on the views she'd missed on the way up, trying to memorize every detail.

Everything was lush and green. Some of the trees reached for the sky, but others broke off in different directions, stretching their gnarled and twisted roots back toward the ground.

Tombstones carved from granite and limestone marched up the

hills. Green mountain peaks rose behind the grave sites and disappeared into a thin layer of fog.

Lou looked away from the view to Keoni. His tall, strong form was almost as beautiful as the landscape. She could see the flex of his muscles beneath the thin fabric of his shirt.

Keoni turned, and Lou averted her eyes, looking down at her camera again. She tried to reassure herself that she wasn't doing anything wrong. She was simply appreciating the beauty in front of her. Keoni was like a work of art. Lou remembered Paul's advice to make sure she looked around some while she was in Hawaii, and she cringed. She didn't think he'd meant looking at Keoni.

Lou tucked her camera back in her bag and leaned through the open window of the station wagon to put it on the back seat. When she straightened, she noticed the shiny surfboards on top of the car. She couldn't imagine trying to balance on one of those over the giant waves she'd seen in the movies. The red board was at least ten feet long.

Unable to resist, Lou reached up to touch it. Her fingers barely grazed the slick surface of the board when Keoni came up beside her and grabbed her wrist.

"Don't touch my board," he said.

Lou's eyes snapped from the red surfboard to Keoni's face. She thought he might be joking, but when she saw his eyes, she wasn't so sure. She'd never met someone so hard to read.

"Why not?"

"It's bad luck."

Lou laughed. Surely, he was kidding. She looked into his eyes, glancing from his perfect left eye to the bruised and bloodied right eye. Then she looked down at his mouth. His lower lip was swollen and split, and Lou had the irrational urge to heal him with a kiss. She wanted to stretch up on her toes and kiss the cut on Keoni's mouth, to taste him.

She pictured Keoni's mouth sliding across hers, and a kaleidoscope of butterflies took flight in her belly. Her heartbeat raced.

Lou wasn't used to making the first move. She'd always allowed Paul to set the pace. But this was different. She was different around Keoni. Unable to stop herself, she rose onto her toes and brushed her lips across his in a whisper soft kiss.

She only wanted a brief taste of him, to satisfy her curiosity. Lou knew it was wrong of her, but she felt wild. A spark exploded between them, igniting something that had been buried deeply inside her.

Keoni's hand slid up Lou's arm to her shoulder. He cupped the back of her neck and held her in place as he deepened the kiss. Lou had started the kiss, and now Keoni was finishing it. It went from light and curious to hot and demanding.

His kiss was unlike any she had ever experienced. It stole her breath and weakened her knees. She melted into him, opening her mouth to his tongue. The salty sweetness of his mouth seduced her. She pressed closer to his body, wanting more.

Keoni ended the kiss with a muffled curse. "What the hell was that?"

Reality came crashing down, and Lou realized what she'd done. She'd kissed another man. The color drained from her face as she thought of Paul.

"I don't know what movies you've seen," Keoni said. "But I no Beach Boy here to show you a good time, hear?"

"What?" A flush spread across her cheeks. "I don't think that."

"I'm not some vacation fling."

Lou clamped her mouth shut, embarrassment turning to outrage. She pushed Keoni in the chest, feeling gratified at his painful grunt. "Let me go."

"Fine." Keoni took another step back, but his hand snaked around her wrist when she tried to slide past him. "You understand, yeah? This can't happen."

"You don't have to spell it out." She pressed a hand to her heated cheeks, feeling tears swell behind her eyes. "I understand."

"Kay then. Good."

"Penny will be wondering where I went," she said. "Let's go inside."

"Right behind you."

They climbed the stairs to the porch in silence. At the front door, Keoni toed off his shoes and added them to the pile of footwear at the door.

Glancing down at Lou's sandals, he said, "We don't wear shoes in the house."

Lou felt more heat flood her cheeks. She might as well be wearing a neon sign that said, "tourist."

She bent down and unlaced the ribbons of her espadrilles. It was a task that seemed to take forever. She felt Keoni's eyes watching her every move. Her fingers stumbled over the laces, and she slipped the sandals off her feet.

Keoni's eyes were dark and unreadable. She didn't know why he was so angry. Maybe he had a girlfriend too. Maybe she wasn't the only one who'd betrayed someone they loved.

The low buzz of conversation ground to a halt when Keoni and Lou walked in the house. Everyone turned to stare at them. The moment passed and everyone went back to their conversations, but Lou felt like she'd just failed an important test.

She needed to find Penny and get out of here.

"I'll get them," Keoni said, apparently feeling the same way.

He left, and Lou glanced around the room curiously. The furniture was clean, but well-lived in, and it seemed to be decorated in a hodgepodge style. It was the opposite of her parents' home in Seattle, which was cold and modern.

Keoni's parents' house was as warm and welcoming as the islands themselves. Everywhere she looked was a celebration of surfing. Surfboards leaned against the walls and hung from rafters. Surfing trophies lined a bookshelf, and contest posters decorated the walls.

Lou walked over to the trophies and saw that most of them were engraved with Keoni's name.

She picked one up and read the inscription. "Makaha International Surfing Contest 1959, First Place, Keoni Makai."

That was nearly ten years ago. Keoni had to have been just a kid when he won that trophy.

"Howzit?"

Lou turned at the greeting and found herself looking at a man who closely resembled Keoni. He was around the same height and build, but his eyes were darker, and his hair was streaked with russet.

"Hi," Lou said.

"You want a *malasada*?" He offered her a tray filled with pastries.

"What are they?"

He flashed a white-toothed grin. "Just try one."

Lou took one of the pastries and bit into it. The dough was crisp on the outside and soft in the center, still warm from the oven. The flavors of sugar and cinnamon burst over her tongue.

"You must be Keoni's brother?"

He nodded and rolled his eyes. "All my life, I get that. Same thing, all the time. Keoni's little brother." He sighed. "I never catch a break." He grinned. "I'm Kimo," he said, offering his hand.

"Mary Lou Hunter," she said.

"I think my brother has it bad for you, yeah?" He raised a dark brow.

"What makes you say that?" She took a bite of her pastry, hoping to look unaffected.

Kimo laughed and inclined his head across the room. "He looks like he wants to come over here and bust me up because I'm talking to you."

Lou glanced across the room and saw Keoni watching them with a fierce scowl.

"He's too afraid to make a move?" Kimo asked.

Lou blushed. "It's not that."

He nodded. "He has a thing about tourists."

"What thing is that?"

"I dunno," Kimo said, waving his hand in the air as if he couldn't be bothered with remembering. "But he's crazy if he doesn't make a move on you. I would make one myself, but I'm leaving tomorrow."

"Where are you going?"

"San Diego. I'm starting my advanced individual training."

Lou's stomach dropped when she realized what he was saying. "You enlisted?"

"Yeah," Kimo said, bursting with pride. "I just finished boot camp."

Lou studied his handsome face. He couldn't be any older than her brother, John, who had enlisted last year when he'd finished high school. Six months afterward, John had landed in Vietnam.

"How old are you?"

"Eighteen."

Lou nodded, feeling tears come quickly. Her knees went weak, and she suddenly felt faint. She pushed past Kimo, needing to get out of the crowded room.

"What's wrong?" Kimo grabbed her arm as she stumbled.

"I need some air."

"Come on." He set the plate down on and grabbed her hand. "I've got you."

Kimo swept Lou through the crowded living room and out the back door of the house. Once outside on the small porch, Lou sucked in deep breaths.

"Sit down." Kimo helped her sink onto a bench that ran the length of the porch.

Lou hung her head in her hands and tried to calm her breathing. Kimo squatted down beside her and patted her shoulder gently.

"Our family can be a little much," he said, rubbing her arm. "I'm sorry."

Tears fell down her cheeks, but she smiled. "It isn't that. You just remind me of my brother."

Kimo rolled his eyes, smiling with effortless charm. "I can't catch a break," he muttered. "Prettiest girl I ever saw says I remind her of her brother."

"I'm sure you don't have any trouble getting girls. But you won't see many where you're headed. My brother joined the army after high school. Now he's in Vietnam."

Lou could tell that Kimo thought he was invincible. So did John.

"That's a bummer." Kimo sat down beside her and rubbed her shoulder. "Is he okay?"

"Last I heard from him was six weeks ago. He's okay I guess."

"My family doesn't get it. They don't understand why I want to fight for my country. It's the right thing to do, though. You know?"

Lou shook her head. "It isn't right that all these boys are dying." She swiped at her tears. "Not right at all."

Kimo nodded in agreement, and they fell silent for a moment. "Maybe my brother doesn't dig you as much as I thought he did," he said, turning to look back at the house. "We've been out here for what? Two minutes? And he hasn't busted out here yet to see what we are doing."

As if on cue, the door burst open and Keoni stepped onto the porch.

Kimo threw back his head and laughed.

"What's so funny?" Keoni demanded.

"Nothing."

Kimo got to his feet and stood next to Keoni. Lou was struck by how much they looked alike. Keoni was a bit taller, but they both had the same lean build and larger-than-life presence. They had the same jawline, full mouth, and deep-set eyes.

The porch felt incredibly small, filled with Keoni's tension and Lou's fears.

"What did you say to her?" Keoni asked his brother.

"I'll let her tell you," Kimo said. His eyes sparkled with

mischief, and he leaned down to plant a kiss on her cheek. "Don't worry, eh?" he said.

Lou bit her lip, watching Kimo edge past Keoni to go back inside the house. A murderous expression crossed Keoni's face as he watched his brother.

"What?" Kimo said over his shoulder. "It might be a long time before I get to kiss a pretty girl." His laugh sounded, and the door banged shut behind him.

Keoni turned back to Lou, shaking his head. "Everything is always a joke to that one," he said.

Lou's heart broke for Kimo and his family, and for the families of every boy sent to fight in the jungle on the other side of the world.

"What happened?" Keoni asked when Lou finally looked up at him.

"Is that why everyone's here?" she asked Keoni. "They're saying goodbye to Kimo?"

"Yeah," Keoni said. "He dropped by, and word spread that he was here. It's not usually so crowded."

"My brother..." Lou started, but she couldn't find the words. She swallowed, and more tears slid down her cheeks. "My little brother..." She closed her eyes and shook her head.

Keoni took Lou by the shoulders and folded her into his embrace. She smelled the ocean in his hair, and it calmed her.

"My brother enlisted, too. I haven't heard from him since Christmas." Her voice broke. "He's all I have."

"Your parents?" Keoni asked. "Are they dead?"

Lou shook her head. "No. My parents aren't dead," she said with bitterness. "They're just absent. They're distant and selfish." She gestured to the house where Keoni had been raised by a loving family. "It's nothing like what you have here. I was more of a mother to John than our own mother ever was. And now he's gone."

Keoni's grip tightened on her shoulders. "He isn't gone," he said. "Don't think like that."

"It's terrible to feel so helpless."

"I know."

Their eyes locked, and Lou knew that Keoni understood. They couldn't stop the war. They couldn't prevent their brothers from dying.

"You must think I'm crazy," she said. "We've just met, and I'm already crying all over the place."

"It's okay." His big hand cupped he shoulder, and he pulled her close.

Lou stared over his shoulder into the backyard. It was an idyllic scene, like something out of a story book. A picnic table sat under the shade of a giant mangrove tree. A rope hammock swayed between two palms. The breeze, heavy with the scent of jasmine and honeysuckle, stirred her hair.

This was paradise. The world was a mess, but with Keoni's solid presence beside her, and the beauty of the graveyard surrounding them, the troubles seemed very far away.

The door to the house opened, and Lou turned to see Bones.

"Heh, man," he said. "Give us a song." He held a guitar by the neck and thrust it toward Keoni.

"You play?" Lou asked.

"He's terrible," Bones said, urging Keoni to take the guitar. "The only reason we ask him to play is cuz we feel sorry for him."

Keoni stood and took the guitar, pushing Bones aside. "Shut up."

They went back in the house, and Penny came to stand next to Lou. "How was the view?" She asked.

"What?"

"The view," Penny said. "Did you get some pictures?"

Lou had forgotten all about the view. "It was amazing," she said.

"Uh-huh," Penny said. She looked across the room at Bones,

who was talking to Kimo. "I can't believe we met the two best-looking guys on the island. That grass shack is looking better and better."

Keoni started to play, and the room went silent. The music he coaxed from the guitar was like nothing she'd ever heard before. It was pure and sensual and soulful. It was as if he was playing with his heart and not his hands.

Bones had lied. Keoni wasn't terrible at all. He was magnificent.

Then he began to sing. He had a smooth rich voice that sneaked into her chest and wrapped around her heart. He bent his dark head over the guitar, and his hair fell onto his forehead. The muscles in his forearms flexed as his fingers slid across the strings.

Lou stared, unable to tear her eyes away. When Keoni lifted his head, their gazes locked, and Lou felt a shiver race down her spine. It was clear to her that even a girl like her who had her entire life planned out could easily fall in love with a man like Keoni Makai.

SECRET BEACH

Hawaii Loa Ridge
   A Wednesday in January 1968

The next morning, Lou thought for sure she would sleep late, but her body betrayed her, and she woke at 7:30. She rolled over in the bed and knocked heads with Penny, who she'd forgotten was there.

"Christ!" Penny moaned, rubbing her head. "You've got a hard head, woman."

"Sorry," Lou said, sitting up in the bed.

It took her a second to realize where she was. The light filtering into the room looked different. It was brighter and warmer than it should have been. She remembered that she was on vacation in Hawaii, staying with Penny's cousin. Henry had relinquished his bed for Penny and Lou and had generously offered to sleep on the sofa.

His house was small, consisting of a tiny kitchen and living room combination, a short hall, a bedroom, and one bathroom.

What it lacked in size, it made up for in location. Two blocks away were the sparkling sands of Diamond Head Beach.

Lou swung her feet off the bed and padded across the tile floor to the window. If she leaned to the left far enough, she could just make out the blue waters of the Pacific Ocean.

She turned back to the bed and saw that Penny had gone back to sleep.

"Oh no, you don't," Lou said, marching over to the bed. She yanked the covers off Penny, forcing her to wake up. "This is our first day in Hawaii, and we aren't going to miss it."

"Ten more minutes," Penny mumbled, reaching for the covers.

Lou shoved the covers aside. "Wake up." She crossed the room to the door. "I'm going to see if Henry's got any coffee, and when I get back, you better be out of that bed."

Penny grumbled, but did as she was told. Lou blew her a kiss and slipped into the hall. She quickly used the bathroom, then tiptoed into the living room, past the sofa where Henry had spent the night. As she crept past, she saw that Henry wasn't there. The sofa was vacant, and the blankets and pillow were stacked in a neat pile.

Lou heard a noise in the kitchen, and when she turned the corner, she found Henry standing at the sink humming to himself as he filled a kettle with water.

Lou leaned against the door frame, watching him dance as he waited for the kettle to fill. He must be a morning person if he was in this good of spirits after spending the night on his sofa.

"Good morning," Lou said.

Henry dropped the kettle with a clang and then laughed at his clumsiness. "I didn't think you'd be up for a while."

"My body still thinks it's in Seattle." She eyed the kettle with eagerness. "Is there coffee?"

"There will be." He placed the kettle on the stove. "If you go outside on the lanai, you can see the tail end of the sunrise," he said. "The spectacular view is the only reason I bought this dump."

Lou nodded and took him up on his offer. She stepped out on the lanai, and immediately froze when she the view. Henry hadn't been kidding. She felt like she was standing on top of the world. Over the tops of palm trees, she could see the entire east side of Oahu. Some of the names she's seen on the map unfolded before her eyes. The jutting ridge of Diamond Head Crater glittered under the bright sun, and the turquoise waters of the Pacific lapped the sparkling shore. Unlike the view of Honolulu from Keoni's family home, this one wasn't marred by skyscrapers.

The beauty struck her so hard that she almost forgot she wasn't looking at it through the lens of her camera. As the idea struck her, she spun on her heel and nearly collided with Henry who'd just walked outside.

He sidestepped her before she took them both down, his arm whipping out to steady her. Lou's cheeks heated as she got her feet under her again. Paul was always telling her to slow down and pay attention.

"Sorry." Her voice came out in a rush. "I didn't hear you. I didn't…"

Henry cut her off with a laugh. "It's no big deal." He held her camera out to her with a grin. "Were you coming for this?"

Lou's eyes widened and she nodded. "How'd you know"

"Penny warned me you never went anywhere without it. You left it on the coffee table last night."

Lou and Penny had stayed up late the night before talking excitedly about everything they wanted to see and do while in Hawaii. Lou had been cleaning her lens while Penny droned on about Bones. She must have left her camera in the living room.

"Thanks." She lifted her camera to her face and snapped a few shots of the colorful sky. "Did Penny also warn you I'm a klutz?"

Henry's laugh rumbled. "You're not a klutz. The view has the same effect on me, and I see it every day."

Lou lowered her camera and shot a grin at Henry. He was

outgoing and friendly, just as Penny had promised. "Thank you for giving up your bed," she said.

"Mi casa es su casa." He grinned. "Since I moved to Hawaii, my relatives have come out of the woodwork."

Lou's cheeks blazed hotter. "I hope it isn't an inconvenience."

Henry shrugged. "If they all looked like you I wouldn't mind."

Lou blushed from her head to her toe and Henry laughed again. "I'm a harmless flirt," he said. "You'll get used to it." He turned and headed into the kitchen. "You want breakfast?"

Lou's stomach growled at the mention of food, and Henry laughed again.

"I'm going to make you a Hawaiian specialty," Henry said, heading inside.

"Please don't go to any trouble. I can fix a piece of toast for myself."

"No way." Henry stepped into the house. "Sit down and enjoy the view."

"Henry..."

"No arguments. The kitchen is too small for two people, and I'll get distracted trying to check you out."

When Henry was gone, Lou walked back to the table and sat down on one of the chairs. The morning was cool, but the humidity was already inching up to curl her hair and heat her skin.

Lou heard Penny's voice, and a moment later, she stepped out onto the lanai.

"Oh my God," Penny said, taking in the view. "This is unreal."

Lou stared at the lavender hued sky. The sun was a bright swatch of gold spearing across the horizon. Lou felt like she had been plucked out of gray Seattle and dropped down into a fairy tale. She sighed. "I know."

"I bet you've already taken a dozen pictures, haven't you?"

Lou nodded. "I need to slow down. Or maybe I just won't eat and spend my food money on film."

"I smell coffee," Penny said, pulling a chair out and taking a seat. "Henry! Is that coffee?"

Lou sniffed the air and detected the faint spicy and earthy scents of coffee. She loved the smell of coffee more than she liked drinking it.

"Come and get it!" Henry yelled from inside.

Penny got to her feet. "Want some?"

"Please."

Lou needed to clear her head, and she hoped coffee would help. She'd slept like a rock the night before, but her dreams had been... eventful. Most of them had featured a handsome man who played guitar and spoke with an exotic accent. She didn't think any amount of coffee could rid her mind of Keoni Makai, but it was worth a try.

When Penny came back out a minute later with two cups of coffee, Lou took one look at the coffee, which happened to be the same brown as Keoni's eyes, and blurted out her confession. "I'm a hussy."

Penny raised an eyebrow. "It's just coffee."

"I kissed him."

"Henry?" Penny sipped her coffee. "He's a terrible flirt, but I didn't think he'd move that quickly."

"Not Henry."

Penny put her mug down on the table. "I know, honey. I was just trying to lighten the mood. Don't be a bummer."

Lou glared at her best friend. "Stop joking. I feel terrible."

"But did you feel terrible when Keoni kissed you?"

Lou's body reacted instantly. Her skin tingled and her nipples hardened. She hadn't felt terrible when his lips had pressed against hers. She hadn't felt terrible at all.

Lou glanced down into her cup of coffee and shook her head. "What am I going to do?"

Penny shrugged. "It was just a kiss. Don't sweat it."

Lou wanted to scream. She'd betrayed Paul, and Penny was acting like it was no big deal.

Penny reached for her hand. "It's 1968. Haven't you heard? Women don't have to get married to have a little fun. So you kissed a guy? It's not the end of the world. Paul will never know."

Lou's chest ached. Paul might not ever know, but she would. Could she live with herself?

Before she could decide on the answer, Henry came outside with a tray of food. There was a plate piled high with sandwiches and a big bowl of fruit. He set the tray on the table and pulled out a chair.

"You can't come to Hawaii and not try spam," he said, grabbing a sandwich. "And poi." He made a face that showed what he thought of poi. "Although once is enough with poi."

Lou took a sandwich. It smelled good. She took a bite and was pleasantly surprised. "It's not bad," she said, taking another bite.

Henry had pan-fried the meat-like substance so that it was crispy on the outside. It was salty and flavorful and reminded Lou of thick bologna.

"I'm sorry I have to work again today," Henry said.

"That's okay," Penny said. "Bones and Keoni said they would show us around."

Lou put down her sandwich. "I don't think that's a good idea."

"But Keoni and Bones know all the great spots."

"We will be fine on our own. Exploring by ourselves will be fun." She gave Penny a sharp look. "We wanted an adventure."

"Didn't you like Bones and Keoni?" Henry asked.

Lou's cheeks heated and she avoided Henry's eyes.

"Lou liked Keoni a little too much," Penny said.

Henry burst out laughing. "Did he play his guitar for you?"

"Yes," Lou admitted.

Henry's eyes gleamed knowingly. "Don't feel bad," he said. "There's hasn't been a woman yet who didn't fall in love with Keoni after hearing him play his guitar."

"He sang, too," Penny chimed in.

"I'm not in love with him." Lou gave up on eating and picked up her coffee instead. "You liked Bones too."

Penny laughed. "I'll be the first to admit that."

"It's not funny." Lou felt the prick of tears behind her eyes. She'd been as bad as a faucet lately. Tears were only a blink away.

Penny and Henry shared a concerned glance. "It's okay," Penny said. "We can have fun without those boys. I'll call Bones and tell him not to come today."

"Really?"

"Yes, but only because I love you so much."

Penny grumbled as she got up from the table, and Henry laughed. "I don't have to work Friday," he said. "I'll show you some great spots. And I promise, I won't play guitar for you."

HENRY HAD WARNED THEM NOT TO GO PAST DIAMOND HEAD Beach when they got to the shore, but he hadn't told them why. Unfortunately, Lou and Penny weren't familiar enough with the beach that they could tell where one ended, and the next began.

Because of Penny's fair skin, they walked until they found an area shady enough for her to lay her towel down under a grove of palms. Lou stretched out on the sand next to her.

Lou had some Native American Chinook blood in her somewhere down the line, and she tanned easily. After a few hours in the sun, Lou was already golden brown, while Penny still looked like she'd just stepped off the plane from Seattle.

The beach was narrow, but the sand was soft and white, and the water was warm. It was a quiet beach, with only the occasional person strolling down the sand.

"Henry sure is lucky to live here." Lou flipped over on her stomach and thumbed through her magazine.

"Do you notice anything funny about this beach?" Penny asked.

Lou turned over and looked around. The beach sloped into the turquoise water at a gradual angle. She could see all the way out to an island about two hundred yards at sea.

"It's kind of quiet," she said. "I'm surprised there aren't more people here."

Penny gazed down the beach and around the corner. "Look at that," she said quietly.

Lou looked to where Penny nodded, and her jaw dropped. A man was walking toward them. He was tall and tanned with dark hair. Even from a distance, Lou could see he was completely naked.

"This is a nude beach," Penny said.

They tried not to stare as the man walked by them, barely glancing in their direction. He walked with a casual, unselfconscious gait, humming a song to himself as he strode past.

"Isn't he worried about getting burned?" Penny asked, craning her head to watch him.

They burst out laughing and then tried to regain control as another man came into sight from down the beach. Naked as the day he was born.

"This must have been what Henry was warning us about," Lou said.

The second man walked by and nodded at them politely. He seemed unconcerned about his lack of clothing.

Penny reached back and unhooked her bikini top, then tossed it to the sand.

"What are you doing?" Lou asked.

"When in Rome..." she said. "Ah, it feels so good! I've never been topless in public before. It's so liberating."

Lou lay back in the sand and closed her eyes. "No thanks," she said. She figured she'd already taken enough liberties on this trip so far.

PLAYING TOUR GUIDE

KEONI EASED HIMSELF INTO THE FRONT SEAT OF BONES'S STATION wagon.

"You look like shit, cuz," Bones said.

"Thanks, eh?"

Keoni sank against the seat and closed his eyes. His body felt even worse today than it had yesterday. The bruises on his face had darkened to deep purple and yellow, and his ribs ached every time he moved.

"I got the boat for next Sunday," Bones said.

"What?"

"For the coral dive. Next Sunday. The day after the Duke. That okay?"

Keoni leaned back in the seat and pinched the bridge of his nose between his fingers. He had forgotten all about the dive.

"Sunday's fine," he said.

His mind drifted back to Lou. He had been thinking of her all night while he worked. Good thing his job at the cannery was mindless, or he would have screwed up a hundred times.

That kiss kept playing in his mind over and over. He couldn't forget the slide of her lips across his, or the way she'd pressed against him. He couldn't let it happen again. He refused to get involved with a tourist.

"Maybe we shouldn't see them again," he said.

"What? Are you crazy? The two prettiest girls in the world want us to show them around, and you don't want to?"

With a sigh of frustration Keoni reached into his backpack and pulled out the clean shirt he'd packed before his shift. He didn't want to smell like pineapples all day. Moving slowly, he lifted his arms and pulled off his uniform shirt. His injured ribs protested with every move.

He flipped down the visor and shook his head at his disheveled appearance. Using his fingers as a comb, he did his best to arrange his hair, but it refused to cooperate.

Bones was right: he looked like shit.

There was nothing more he could do about it. No more time to argue. Bones turned into the neighborhood on the ridge, heading toward Henry's house. Keoni's heart beat faster at the thought of seeing Lou again.

Was she as pretty as he remembered, or had Keoni built her up in his mind? It didn't matter, he realized. Lou was more than a pretty face. He was attracted to more than the way she looked. He loved listening to her talk, and watching her take pictures. She was clumsy and cute and sexy as hell.

But he didn't get involved with tourists, he reminded himself. They all left eventually. They were here to take what they wanted from Hawaii, and then they left.

"Why you so wound up?" Bones asked as they stopped in front of Henry's house.

"Who says I am?"

"You're about to jump outta your skin, cuz."

"Nah," he said.

Bones laughed and smacked Keoni hard enough on the shoulder to make him wince. "You need to relax. Have some fun. Quit being so damn serious all the time. They're just a couple a girls lookin' for a good time." Bones grinned. "And we are the guys who are going to give it them."

Keoni shook his head at the blatant sexual innuendo. His cousin might not have any scruples about hooking up with tourists, but Keoni was different. He'd been burned before, and his heart still bore the scars.

He gingerly climbed out the car to the sound of laughter drifting up the hill. Turning in the direction of the sound, Keoni saw Lou and Penny walking up the hill.

They must have just come from the beach. Lou was barefoot and wearing only a few scraps of fabric that hardly qualified as a swimsuit. Her skin glowed, and her hair shined under the bright sun. Desire knotted his belly, and something spasmed in his chest.

He shouldn't have come.

When his shift finished at the cannery, he shoulda climbed into his bed instead of Bones' car. He could have slept for a few hours then walked right out his back door to Ali'i Beach. That's what a smart person who didn't want to mess with tourists would do.

But Keoni was stupid. Because instead of sleeping in his bed or surfing in his own backyard, he'd driven all the way across the island to Henry's house where the waves were shit this time of year and Lou's laugh echoed up the street to seduce him.

Lou's hair hung loose around her shoulders, a many-hued curtain of waves. She walked carefully, watching her feet more than she looked up. Absent was the camera around her neck, but Keoni was sure it was within arm's reach.

The women hadn't noticed Keoni and Bones parked in Henry's driveway yet. One of them said something that brought on another fit of giggles. Lou was laughing so hard; she stumbled and nearly fell. Keoni's chest tightened. He could hardly stand to watch. The slope of the ridge was only a few feet to her right. If she wasn't careful, she could fall straight down the rocky slope.

"Heh," Bones called to the women as they came closer. "What's so funny?"

Lou's head snapped up, and her laughter died. Her eyes widened and the healthy glow faded from her cheeks. She didn't look at all happy to see him.

Her reaction surprised Keoni. He knew he'd been rude a few times yesterday and that emotions had run high between them, but he'd thought they'd parted on good terms. He didn't think she'd be angry to see him again.

She breezed by him with barely a hello and stormed into the house, slamming the screen door behind her.

"Don't worry about her," Penny said. "She hasn't eaten lunch. She gets a little grumpy."

Keoni narrowed his eyes at Penny. "She didn't look grumpy a minute ago," he said.

Penny winced. "She wasn't expecting to see you."

Keoni crossed his arms over his chest and glared at his cousin. "I thought you made plans."

"We did," Penny said. "Don't sweat it. Just let her have a few minutes, and it will be fine."

Keoni shot a dark look at his cousin. "I shoulda gone to bed."

"Chill out, man. You can sleep later."

"I gotta work later. Some of us work, you know?"

Bones chuckled good-naturedly. "I work, cuz. I just work smart, not hard." He turned his attention to Penny. "Been down to the beach?"

Penny giggled and covered her mouth with her hand. "Did you know there was a nude beach down there?"

Bones nodded. "Sure. We call it Secret Beach. Henry didn't warn you?"

Penny laughed harder. "He did, but we weren't listening."

"He already go to work?"

"Yeah. They got a new horse, and he's the only one who can work with him." They went inside the house, and Penny turned toward the bedroom. "Give me a minute, will you?"

"Sure."

Penny to the bedroom and closed the door. Keoni heard raised voices and then a moment later Lou came out of the bedroom. She had a dress on over her bikini, but her feet were still bare. Her eyes were glassy, and her face was still pale. When she stopped in front of him, she couldn't look him in the eyes. Her gaze settled somewhere around his chin.

"Can we talk to outside?" she asked.

Keoni nodded and opened the door for her. She thanked him and then stepped outside onto the lanai.

He joined her at the railing, hardly noticing the spectacular view. His heart lodged in his throat as he looked at Lou. "What's wrong?"

Lou clasped her hands together and stared at her fingers. "It's not you," she said.

Keoni choked back a laugh. He didn't know what to say, so he stayed silent, waiting for her to finish. When she didn't elaborate, he took her hands and pried her fingers apart. "Do you want me to leave?"

She raised her eyes from their hands and met his gaze. Her eyes sparkled in the sunlight, an enchanting shade of green-blue. "No," she said. "I don't."

Keoni narrowed his eyes. He shouldn't have touched her. His hands betrayed him by lacing their fingers together.

"I should go," he said. He was tired and hungry. He could think of a dozen other things he'd rather be doing than convincing a tourist to spend time with him.

She shook her head, her eyes pinned on their linked hands. "I don't want you to go."

"Playing tour guide isn't really my bag, yeah? I'm not good with games, either. Tell me what you want, and I'll do it. You don't want me here, no sweat." He untangled their fingers and pulled his hand away. "I'll go. Just tell me straight." His voice cracked, giving away his emotions.

Lou was quiet for a long time. She looked at the view, unable to meet Keoni's gaze. "Don't go," she said.

"You sure?"

She nodded and finally turned to look at him. "I'm probably making the biggest mistake of my life, but I'm not ready to say goodbye to you. Maybe we can just be friends?" She smiled tentatively. "Can we try that?"

"Sure," Keoni said. Friends meant there was no way he would get his heart broken by a tourist again. "Friends is good."

THE GREAT KAMEHAMEHA

THE FOUR OF THEM SPENT MOST OF THE DAY TOGETHER, AND THE next after that, and then the next. Keoni and Bones showed Penny and Lou some of the landmarks that made Hawaii famous: Le'ahi Crater, the Punchbowl Cemetery, and Hanauma Bay.

Keoni did most of the driving. Lou sat up front next to him while Bones and Penny sat in the back seat. Bones pointed out places as they drove, and Keoni told stories. He told the story of Maui trapping the sun, and the tale of the youngest riddler, Kai, who used his clever tricks to avenge his father's murder.

They stopped often to eat picnics at beaches or take photographs. Penny and Bones would wander off together, getting to know each other better, while Keoni stayed with Lou.

They became friends. Nothing more.

She took pictures of everything, and they talked. They exchanged their life stories. Their upbringing couldn't have been more different. Keoni was one of five siblings, and Lou only had John. Keoni had a close relationship with his parents and everyone in his extended family, including Bones, who was his cousin on his mother's side. Lou and her parents had never been close, but now they saw each other only on holidays.

Keoni's family was poor and uneducated. Lou's father was an engineer at Boeing, and her mother was an elementary school teacher.

"Do you make up all those stories?" Lou asked as they sipped cold sodas outside a gas station.

Penny and Bones had gone in to buy some food, and they were taking forever. It was hot under the sun, and Keoni and Lou sat in the shade.

"Nah. They're true."

Lou cocked her eyebrow at him. "What about that one about the talking spear?"

"All true."

They were quiet for a minute, relaxing under the only tree in the parking lot.

"I've got somebody at home," Lou said.

"I figured."

"I should have told you earlier."

"No sweat."

"He's important to me."

"Maybe I've got somebody, too."

Lou leaned back in the grass and squinted at him in the sun. "Do you?"

"Maybe."

"But you kissed me."

He picked up a blade of grass and tore it into pieces. "I kiss a lot of girls."

It was true, but Keoni thought Lou might need to hear it. It would make her feel better. She was leaving in a few days, and they could forget all about each other. Maybe they could be pen pals. Friends.

Bones and Penny came out of the gas station with a supply of food and beer for the rest of the afternoon, and the conversation ended. The got back in the car and drove up the winding road of the Pali Highway.

Lou was quiet while Bones and Penny chatted in the back seat and Mick Jagger's voice rang over the speakers.

Keoni drove up the twisting highway, sneaking looks at Lou when the road straightened out. She had her hair tied back from her face with a colorful scarf, but a few strands kept escaping to blow across her face.

"Do you know any stories about this place?" Penny asked Keoni.

"Sure."

"Tell us one of them," Penny said.

"And don't make it up this time," Lou said.

"I never do."

"Tell the one about Kamehameha," Bones said. "It's about me."

Keoni drove through the first Nu'uanu Tunnel. When they came out the other side, the road climbed higher into the mountains. He concentrated on navigating the hairpin turns, then launched into the story about the great warrior chief who had lived two hundred years ago.

"Even though Kamehameha was not the true heir," he said, "he was favored by Ku, the god of war, and he was chosen to rule." Keoni turned onto a gravel drive that led to a parking lot and stopped the car. "But Kamehameha didn't want to rule. He wanted to live the good life. He wanted to surf and party. He didn't want to fight."

Keoni cut the engine, and they climbed out of the car. They were high on a cliff, one thousand feet above sea level. The mountains rose around them, disappearing into a lavender mist of clouds.

"What happened?" Lou asked.

"Kamehameha was attacked and forced to fight back. He found out that he was even better at leading an army than he was at partying. He got a taste for battle, and he was no longer satisfied with his small kingdom. He dreamed of uniting all the islands under his rule."

They walked together to the stone terrace that overlooked the windward side of the island. Keoni waited for Lou to snap a few photos before continuing.

"First Kamehameha conquered Kauai, then he moved on to Maui and Molokai," he said. "Oahu was the last to fall. Warriors met Kamehameha's soldiers at the base of Diamond Head, but they couldn't hold. Kamehameha drove them all the way into the mountains to this very spot."

Keoni pointed over the edge of the steep cliff. A steel railing and a bronze sign commemorating the spot kept tourists from stepping over the edge. In the distance, the windward villages of Kaneohe and Kailua spread out below them.

"The defenders of Oahu chose death over being captured by the great chief," Keoni said.

"You mean they jumped?" Lou asked.

"Or they were pushed, but they all went over." He leaned over the railing, looking down he cliff.

Lou scanned the view through the lens of her camera. Keoni grabbed her elbow, holding onto her when she got too close to the edges.

"Is it a real story?" Lou asked Bones.

"It's real," Bones said.

"When they developed this road into a highway, the construction workers found over eight hundred skulls—the remains of the men who died in battle."

"Wait," said Penny. "What does this story have to do with you?"

Bones laughed. "How many greats ago was Kamehameha?" he asked Keoni.

"Three, I think."

"He was our great-great-great-grandfather," Bones told Penny.

"So you are the descendants of a murderer?" Penny asked.

"He was a great chief."

"Who was responsible for murdering hundreds of people."

"He united the islands," Keoni said.

"Do you want to see the Old Trail?" Bones asked, offering Penny his hand.

She accepted, and once again, Lou and Keoni were alone together.

"Should I be scared?" Lou asked.

"Why?"

"You have the blood of a murderer running through your veins."

"We all do. Only difference is I can trace mine."

A gust of wind tore through the mountains, plastering their clothes against their bodies.

Lou held her scarf in her hair in place, laughing as the wind tried to rip it away.

"That was the ghosts of the dead soldiers," Keoni said as the wind faded.

Lou laughed. "You definitely made that up."

Keoni shrugged, grinning. "Maybe."

Lou's smile faded and she turned serious. "What's this rule you have about tourists?"

"Who told you about that?"

"Kimo."

Keoni shook his head. "Course he did."

"It's probably a good rule." Lou retied her scarf. "You get so many people coming and going in your life. It must be hard."

Keoni didn't answer.

"And I have Paul," she said, securing the knot.

"That's his name?"

She nodded. "We've known each other for a long time, but didn't start dating until two years ago."

Keoni grimaced. His chest hurt just thinking about Lou with another man. "What's wrong with him, eh?"

"What do you mean?"

"Something must be wrong with him, or he woulda married you already. He must be stupid."

"We're getting married soon." Lou walked along the railing. "Probably next year."

Keoni shook his head. Paul was a fool to let a woman like Lou slip away. If she were his girl, he would get a ring on her finger as soon as he could. The thought surprised Keoni. Although he wanted to get married and have a family someday, he was still young. He hadn't ever thought about settling down. Now that he had, he knew he wanted it to be with a woman like Lou. Someone curious about life, someone who shined all the time like she did.

Keoni had only known Lou for a matter of days, but he knew she was the woman he'd been holding out for. Too damn bad she was a tourist.

CHILI WATER

MAKAHA BEACH, OAHU

BEING FRIENDS WITH KEONI HAD ITS BENEFITS. LOU GOT TO SPEND time with him, get to know him, and get to know all the best spots in Hawaii. If Lou were honest with herself, she'd admit she was falling for him, but she preferred to lie to herself. It was safer.

Bones invited them to spend the day at Makaha, the beach town on the west side of the island where he'd grown up. Penny and Lou borrowed Henry's Mustang and drove across the island to meet Keoni and Bones.

Henry warned them that Makaha wasn't the friendliest place on the island. The people of Makaha were known to dislike tourists.

"Just be careful what you do in Makaha," Henry said. "There's only one way in and one way out."

"What do you mean?" Lou asked.

"There's only one road that goes to Makaha, and it's a dead end."

Lou thought about Henry's warning as she drove along the Farrington Highway toward Makaha. The road was etched in between the jagged cliffs of the Wai'anae mountain range and the Pacific Ocean. They passed one small gas station, but the rest of the road was deserted.

When they got to Makaha the first car they saw had a bumper sticker that read *Welcome to Makaha—Now Go Home!*

"Geez," Penny said, reading the bumper sticker. "They really don't like tourists here, do they?"

Lou looked up and saw Bones coming toward their car. "I don't think anyone is going to mess with us today."

Penny jumped out of the car and flung herself into Bones's waiting arms. He picked her up, and they kissed as if no one was watching. Lou glanced away and got her camera out of her bag. She started down to the beach, and Bones hollered at her to wait.

"Stay with me," he said.

"Does everybody hate tourists at this beach?" she asked, feeling a shiver of fear as she glanced around.

The beach looked harmless enough. It was quiet except for a few families and some guys with diving gear.

"Pretty much," Bones said. "But don't worry. Keoni will stay with you."

Lou nodded. She hadn't been sure if Keoni was coming today or not. She knew he'd hardly been sleeping in between showing them around the island during the day and working at night.

They walked down to the beach, and Lou spotted Keoni right away. He was standing near a picnic area next to a tall red surfboard. His hands were planted on his hips, and he was studying the waves.

It was a moment before he noticed her, and Lou took advantage of the time to study him. If not for his modern clothing, Keoni could have been a surfer from a long-ago generation. Lou imagined that Keoni's ancestors had stood in the very same spot hundreds of years ago, looking at the very same waves.

Keoni turned and saw Lou. A smile broke out over his face,

and she couldn't help smiling back. Keoni's lip had begun to heal, and he was more handsome every day.

"This is where you won the trophies," she said, coming to stand next to him.

"You looked at my trophies?"

"You're not embarrassed, are you?" Lou asked. "You should be proud."

"I couldn't care less about contests."

"Why?"

"Someday contests are going to ruin surfing for everyone."

"How do you mean?"

"Hawaiians have a rich tradition of surfing competitions," Keoni said. "Chiefs would compete against each other, and the people would gamble on who would win. Warriors would settle a fight before it began by having a contest."

"So what's the problem?"

"It's hard to explain."

"Try."

He was quiet for a moment, studying the waves. "Hawaiians have had everything stolen from us. Our land, our culture, our language." He ticked off everything his people had been robbed of his voice rising with each item. "But no one can take surfing."

Lou's eyebrows drew together. She didn't understand. "Surfing contests celebrate the sport."

"That's the tricky part. What if I go up to Sunset on Saturday, and I want to surf?" he asked. "I can't because the beach is closed for the contest."

"Ahh."

"You see?"

"Yes."

"The more popular surfing gets, the bigger the chance we have of it being stolen," Keoni said.

Lou pursed her lips, thinking. "You think you can do something about it?" she asked.

Keoni shrugged. "I'm going to try."

"How?"

"I don't know."

Lou smiled. "You'll think of something."

"How'd you figure?"

"Because you're smart."

"Hah!" Keoni laughed. "I didn't even graduate high school."

"That doesn't matter," Lou said. "You're smart where it counts. Not in the classroom, but out here." She gestured around them. "The people love you, Keoni. They will listen to you."

"You think so?"

"I know so. This whole week, everywhere we go, people call your name and treat you like a celebrity. You're the most popular person on the island."

"Nah."

"It's true." She curtsied low. "I'm honored to be in your presence."

He laughed and pulled her upright. "Is that what you want with your pictures? For people to know your name?"

Her chest tightened. She'd never really thought about it before. She just knew she loved taking photographs. "No," she said, deciding. "When I take pictures, I see what people don't notice. I want people to see that." She laughed, realizing it didn't sound as good out loud as it had in her head. She tried again. "I want to show people something they've never seen before. I want them to look at something they've seen a million times and think it's new."

Their gazes collided, and Lou studied Keoni's brown eyes, seeing the gold sparks around the irises that she hadn't noticed before.

"Keoni!" called a voice from down the beach. "That you, man?"

Keoni pretended he didn't hear, but Lou poked him in the chest, refusing to let him off the hook. "See? Everyone knows you."

Keoni rolled his eyes and turned to look up the beach where a group of guys were sitting around a picnic table.

"Your public awaits." Lou curtsied again, grinning.

"Stop that." Keoni grabbed her elbow and hauled her to her feet. He put his arm around her shoulder and led her toward the group. "A quick hello, and then I want to catch some waves."

The men at the picnic table were thrilled to see Keoni. They were an intimidating bunch, but friendly because she was with Keoni.

"I can't believe they passed you over for the Duke," one of the heavily muscled divers said.

"Next year."

"You diving today?"

"Nah, just some surfing. Nate, Kawika, Danny—this is Mary Lou. She's from Seattle."

Everyone was silent for a long moment as they looked at Lou. Finally, she broke the awkward silence by asking what they were eating.

They looked her up and down for a second before answering.

"Fish and poi," Kawika said. "There's plenty."

Lou thanked them and tried some of the freshly grilled fish. It was the most delicious thing she'd ever tasted, and she told them as much.

"What's poi taste like?" Lou asked, remembering Henry's recommendation that she try it at least once.

"Try some," Keoni said, offering her the bowl.

Lou dipped a piece of bread into the paste-like substance and took a bite. She paused before swallowing. She would have spit it out if it hadn't been too rude. Poi tasted a lot like she imagined wallpaper paste must taste.

"You don't like it?" Keoni asked.

Lou shook her head and forced herself to swallow. "Sorry," she said.

"No problem," Keoni said.

"Can I try some of that stuff?" she asked, pointing to a jug that they'd been passing around the table.

"Better not," he advised.

"Why not?"

"It's hot," Danny said. "Not for tourists."

Lou's eyes narrowed. "I can handle it."

Danny shrugged and handed Lou the jug. There weren't any cups, so she had to put her mouth to the jug and take a swig just like the guys. Everyone stared at her as she tipped the jug up and took a big gulp.

A moment later Lou's face turned red and tears started pouring from her eyes.

"Turn it off," she gasped, fanning her face. "How do I turn it off?"

"The poi." Keoni handed her a piece of bread dipped in poi.

Lou crammed the bread into her mouth and chewed, then took the bowl and scooped up poi with her hand, trying to put the fire out.

"That's what the poi's good for," Danny said, laughing.

"You could have warned me." Lou glared at Keoni.

"I tried." Keoni took the jug and tipped it back. "You didn't listen."

The guys all got another laugh as they passed around the jug, and Keoni led Lou away.

"How about that surfing lesson now?" he asked.

Keoni had been trying to talk Lou into a surfing lesson all week, but she kept putting him off. She was afraid she was going to be terrible at it. She didn't want to disappoint him.

"Maybe," she said.

Keoni got his board and peeled off his shirt with careful movements. Lou stared at his chest where it was stamped with purple bruises. "Are you okay?"

He touched his palm to his ribs and nodded.

"What the hell did you do to yourself?"

"It was a very good day."

Lou's gaze flew up to meet his. Her mouth was still on fire from the chili water, and some of the heat had burned into her chest. She couldn't remember ever feeling so angry. "You could have killed yourself."

Keoni's shoulders stiffened. "I know how to handle myself."

"You're no better than Kimo and John," Lou said. "You think it's a joke."

He shook his head. "I know the risks."

"You just choose to ignore them."

"What do you care?" Keoni asked, the volume of his voice rising. "In a few days, you'll never see me again. You don't have to worry about me."

"I won't."

"'Kay then," Keoni said.

"Go on," Lou said. "Go surf. I want to take some pictures anyway."

Keoni grabbed his board and started off, then changed his mind and turned back to her. "I'm sorry, yeah?"

Lou's shoulders sagged, and she glanced up at Keoni with the ghost of a smile. "I'm sorry, too. I shouldn't have yelled."

"That was nothin, hear? You oughta see my mom let loose on my brothers." Keoni whistled through his teeth. "She could wake the dead."

Lou didn't laugh at his terrible cemetery joke. "Go surf, Keoni," Lou said. "I'll take some pictures of you."

His smile twisted. "Something to remember me by."

Lou raised her camera to her face and watched Keoni walk away through the viewfinder. She didn't need a picture to remember him by. His image was etched in her mind, and on her heart.

THE RESCUE

Lou adjusted the lens on her camera, trying to get all of Makaha Beach into one wide shot.

Makaha was a long way from the crowds of tourists at Waikiki Beach. Except for the divers they'd shared food with and a family having the picnic, the sparkling sands of Makaha were deserted. This was truly unspoiled Hawaiian paradise. The dry, rugged slopes of the Waianae Mountains rose high above the shoreline, looking like fierce guardians of the bay, and the blue Pacific stretched as far as she could see.

Everywhere Lou looked, she saw the natural beauty of the island. To the north, she could see the westernmost edge of the island, where the peak of Ka'ena Point loomed over the sea. To the south, there were sand and palm trees.

In the ocean, there was Keoni.

Lou took a dozen pictures of Keoni, trying to capture what made him so intriguing. He was in his natural element in the ocean. He surfed without effort, making the impossible look easy.

Lou lowered her camera and stared out at Keoni with her own eyes. She had to admit to herself that she was enchanted with him. It was impossible not to be. Keoni was easy to talk to, and he made

Lou laugh even when he wasn't trying. He was a family man who loved to tell stories about Hawaiian culture, play his guitar, and spend every moment he could in the water. Lou would have traded in everything her parents gave her for the love she knew Keoni's family shared. Even though they didn't have a lot of money, the Makais were rich in love.

Lou wanted the same thing for herself someday. She wanted a close-knit family filled with love and security. She and Paul had planned on having that together, but after meeting Keoni, Lou wasn't so sure she could go back to that plan. No matter how hard she tried, she couldn't stop her attraction to Keoni. What did that say about her relationship with Paul? How could she want Keoni if she was truly in love with Paul?

Lou went back to where she'd left her towel, took off her sundress, and stretched out in the sun. A million thoughts swirled in her head, but she didn't want to focus on any of them. She wanted to forget everything for a while, and let the Hawaiian sun work its magic on her.

She pushed aside her conflicting thoughts and enjoyed the ocean breeze and the magnificent sight of Keoni on the waves. His body gleamed with sleek muscles, and he moved with precision and grace. He surfed fast and turned hard, then transitioned off the top of the wave, stalled, and disappeared into the deep blue channel of the barrel.

Lou sat up straighter, holding her breath until he sped out of the tube safely. The red surfboard flashed in the sun as he zoomed toward shore.

Lou started to exhale, and then her breath caught as a wave broke violently against the steep shoreline and doubled back, heading straight for Keoni.

Her palms went damp, and her heart lurched as she braced herself for Keoni to fall.

But he didn't. Instead of wiping out, he turned disaster into opportunity. Crouching down low on his board, he grabbed the sides with both hands and flipped into the air. In an incredible aerial feat, Keoni let the wave spin him upside down. He hung suspended in the air for an impossible moment, his body curled tightly into a ball. Then, in one fluid motion, he arched and landed on the incoming wave. His board landed on the water in a graceful kiss, and he zoomed back out to the ocean.

Lou jumped to her feet and clapped, completely enthralled by Keoni's skill. She didn't doubt Keoni would change the world of surfing. With talent like that, he was destined for greatness.

Lou ran to the edge of the water to wait for him, bursting with joy. She wanted to throw her arms around him and feel the energy of his body next to hers. Lou stopped herself just before she splashed into the water. Her excitement had almost made her forget all the reasons she couldn't be with Keoni.

But now the realization that she wasn't free to throw herself into his arms came crashing down on Lou, killing her joy.

Lou turned her back on the shore, clenching her fists at her sides. How was she going to bear being around Keoni for the next few days?

It would be torture. Impossible. Being near him was just too tempting. She should have said goodbye to him long before now. Lord knows, she'd tried. Every time they were together, Lou felt herself being drawn closer and closer to Keoni as if pulled by an invisible magnet.

She waded into the water and tilted her face to the sky, watching a lone seagull. She didn't realize she was breaking a cardinal rule in Hawaii by turning her back on the ocean. She didn't even know she was in danger until a rogue wave crashed over her and pulled her under the water.

One moment, Lou had been looking up at the sky, then the next she was eating a mouthful of sand. She managed to let out a startled scream before she was dragged under the water.

For a moment she was too shocked to react, and then adrenaline shot through her veins, and she started to fight back. She kicked wildly against the current. She was a good swimmer, but she was used to the water of Lake Washington, which didn't surge with a fraction of the power of the Pacific Ocean. Striking out at the wave determined to drag her out to sea did nothing but exhaust Lou, and use up the precious air in her lungs. If she could just claw her way to the surface, she could suck in a breath and scream again, hoping to grab Keoni's attention. He had been surfing nearby, but it had happened so quickly that Lou couldn't be sure he had seen the accident.

Her lungs started to burn with the need for air, and she knew she didn't have time to think, she needed to move. But which way was up? She couldn't be sure.

The waters of Makaha, which had seemed brilliantly translucent from the shore, were surprisingly black underneath. She had been sucked into a bowl-shaped depression in the sea that teemed with spiky coral. Another wave crashed over her, spinning her upside down and dragging her over the sharp coral.

Salt water filled her nose and mouth, and the bitter taste of fear clogged her throat. The roar of the ocean was suffocatingly loud, and Lou felt as if she was lying on the tracks as a freight train zoomed over her.

Her mind was fuzzy, but she had enough sense to realize she might die. It had been years since Lou had prayed, but she felt the words forming in her mind.

Please, God, don't let me die.

She was too young. She was only twenty-four years old, and she hadn't done half the things she'd planned to do. She was going to marry Paul, and live in a charming brick bungalow by the water.

Keoni's face came to mind, and Lou became even more confused. She didn't know what she wanted. Only one thing was certain. She didn't want to die.

As the last of the air in her lungs trickled away, Lou kicked desperately for the surface. She was too disoriented to know for sure if she was heading in the right direction, but she had to try. Down to her last breath, she would try.

A thin trickle of light filtered through the blackness, and she swam toward it with every last ounce of will in her body. A hand shot through the light, and strong fingers grasped her wrist. Lou was yanked through the water with enough force to pull her arm from the socket, but pain was the least of her worries. She needed air.

A moment later, she had it. At the surface of the water, Lou opened her mouth and gulped down the fresh, fragrant air.

"Hold on," Keoni yelled over the noise of the waves.

Lou didn't need to be told twice. She was too spent to do anything but cling to Keoni, and he had to drag her dead weight through the waves on his own. He swam through the current with the strength of several men, quickly stroking to safety. He fought through the shore-break, then half carried, half dragged Lou to shore.

When they made it through the waves, they collapsed on the sand in a heap. Their arms and legs were entangled, and Lou's long hair snaked around Keoni's chest and back, binding them together. Lou was crushed under the heavy weight of Keoni's body, making it hard to breathe. When he tried to roll off her, she clung to him, burying her face in his shoulder.

"Don't leave me." Her voice sounded hoarse and desperate.

Their chests heaved together as they fought to catch their breath. Keoni pulled back enough to examine her face. His hand splayed over her cheek.

"Are you okay?"

The adrenaline that had flooded Lou's body moments ago disappeared, and she began to shake. She was too shocked to answer, and she was suddenly freezing cold.

Keoni rolled off her and pulled her into his lap, rocking her like a child. He stroked her hair and whispered in her ear, his voice sounding just as scared as she felt.

"You're fine, Lou. Just breathe," he said. "Can you do that for me, *nani*? Just breathe?"

Lou nodded into Keoni's shoulder and sucked in a deep breath. She smelled the tangy scent of the ocean on Keoni's skin and felt the puff of his breath on her neck. His body was warm and solid, his hands firm as they held her tightly.

"You're okay."

Keoni kept repeating the words until they finally sunk in, but still, it was a long time before Lou wanted to move.

She clearly remembered the last thing she had thought of before she had almost given up on life. It had been the details of Keoni's face. The deep-set, coffee-colored eyes that crinkled in the corners when he smiled. The mouth that, even damaged, was so sensual that she couldn't stop thinking about kissing it. The proud nose. The high, noble cheekbones. The dimple that winked in his cheek when he flashed his crooked smile. Lou recalled everything about Keoni's face as if she had been looking at him for years.

Keoni threaded his fingers through Lou's hair, massaging her scalp and gently releasing the tangles. His quiet strength seeped into her bones.

He'd saved her. He was a hero.

A shiver of longing raced down Lou's spine, and before she could change her mind, she lifted her face and brushed her lips across Keoni's injured mouth.

The contact was brief but electrifying.

Lou started to pull away, but Keoni didn't let her. His hand tightened at the back of her neck, and he lowered his mouth to hers. Lou froze for a moment as a burst of white stars exploded behind her eyes. Then she kissed him back.

HEROES DIE HARD

HE'D BEEN HOLDING BACK FOR DAYS, BUT NOW THAT HIS MOUTH was finally on hers again, he couldn't stop

Her hands slid into his hair, and she pulled him closer, deepening the kiss. It was the signal Keoni had been waiting for. The tenuous control he'd clamped on his desire snapped, and in less time than it took to drop in on a wave, the kiss went from exploratory to explosive.

Lou gasped, and her lips parted. Keoni licked the inside of her bottom lip, and she licked him back. He rolled onto the sand, bracing himself above her.

The sudden movement made a riot of pain shoot through his ribs, but Keoni didn't care. He finally had Lou's mouth under his, her body pressed against him. He'd been wanting to do this since that brief kiss they'd shared at the graveyard.

Her lips were soft and firm, and her tongue slid against his in an inviting dance. Their mouths fit together as if they'd been made to kiss.

Keoni felt a satisfaction deep inside his soul, and he knew they had been born to find each other. He hadn't thought he believed in soul mates, but kissing Lou convinced him otherwise.

Keoni tasted the metallic tang of blood and realized his mouth was bleeding. He pulled back, pressing his hand to his lip.

He rolled onto his back. The moment was ruined.

"Sorry," he said.

Lou was silent, and he could hear her gasping for air. He was such a jerk. She'd nearly died, and he'd taken advantage of her vulnerability. He pinched the bridge of his nose between his finger and thumb, sighing deeply.

"Are you okay?" she asked. Her voice was still shaky.

Keoni dropped his hand from his face and looked up at Lou. She was bent over him, staring at the blood on his mouth.

"I'm alright." It was her who'd almost drowned. He just had a busted lip. "Are you okay?"

Lou nodded, her eyes hazy and heavy-lidded with desire. A blast of lust shot through Keoni.

"You saved my life. I owe you my life."

Keoni was startled and then disappointed. Is that why she'd let him kiss her like that? She thought she owed it to him. He felt the hot rush of lust turn to ice in his veins. He sat up so quickly that he felt lightheaded.

"Keoni?" Lou sat up beside him and put her hand on his back. "What's wrong? You're a hero."

Keoni squeezed his eyes shut. "Don't call me that."

"Why not? It's true. Bones told me you've saved dozens of people. You're famous for it."

Keoni tried to block the memory of Eddie's body, floating in the ocean facedown, but it crept past his defenses and played out in his mind. He flinched when Lou's hand slid over his shoulder.

"Keoni? What is it?"

"Nothing."

"You have that look on your face."

"What look?"

"The one you get before you go away for a little while," she said.

The care in her voice made his heart ache. He softened and turned to her. "It's nothing."

Keoni wouldn't talk about Eddie's death. The events of the day were for himself only. It was his punishment to remember them in silence. If he shared them with someone else, even someone like Lou, then the pain might lessen. Keoni didn't want the pain of losing Eddie to lessen. He needed the grief. He needed to remember his failure.

Lou seemed to sense his resistance, and she leaned her head on his shoulder, giving him the same advice he'd given her when he'd pulled her from the ocean's grasp: "Just breathe," she said.

Keoni felt himself smile, and he tipped his head to rest against hers.

"I'm trying," he said.

They were quiet for a long time, resting their heads together and watching the waves. After a while, Keoni felt calmer. He turned to Lou and pressed a soft kiss to her lips. It was feather-light and meant to soothe, but it rekindled the fire that hadn't been extinguished from their first kiss.

Lou pulled away too soon. "What have we started?" she asked.

"Something that's bound to end."

There was an edge to his voice, and a bitter taste in his mouth. He'd gone and fallen for her, he realized. He'd fallen for a tourist. It was something he'd promised himself he'd never do again.

He stared out at the ocean. The waves looked calm now. That was Makaha for you—the waves were some of the most unpredictable on the island. A few minutes ago, they'd tried to suck Lou out to sea, but now they looked as calm as glass.

"I guess we should just quit now," Lou said.

"'Kay then."

"It's for the best." She got to her feet.

Keoni stood up, clenching his hands into fists to keep from touching her.

"Is that it, then?" Lou looked up at him, confusion in her eyes.

"Yeah." He narrowed his eyes at her. "I'll never understand women. I just told you what you wanted to hear, and now you're angry."

Lou's jaw clenched. "You're right. It is what I wanted to hear. Maybe I should just stay away from you. I only have a few more days anyway."

"Four days."

"You're counting."

Keoni raised one eyebrow. "Yeah. So?"

She came forward and put her hand on his chest. At first, he thought it was to push him away, but then her hand softened on his bare skin. She fingered the necklaces at his throat. "I don't think I can stay away from you, Keoni. I've been trying all week. I do have a favor to ask."

Keoni would have done anything for her. "I already saved your life, remember?"

"I do." Her throat worked as she stared up at him. "I don't want to be scared of the ocean," she said. "Do you think you can give me that surf lesson now?"

Keoni's gaze snapped from Lou to the ocean. He'd completely forgotten about his surfboard during the rescue. He scanned the waves, and saw a flash of bright red floating in the waves.

Keoni realized at that moment that he was probably in love with Lou. He'd never forgotten his surfboard before.

THE SURF LESSON

EVERYBODY KNEW KEONI NEVER LET ANYONE TOUCH HIS surfboard. His surfboard was his most-prized possession. The ten-foot-long big wave gun had been specially crafted to handle the monster waves of the North Shore. It was called *The Himalaya* in honor of the fourteen-thousand meter mountain.

Of all the boards Keoni had ridden in his life, *The Himalaya* was his favorite. The board sang over the surface of the water, responding to him like an extension of his body. He only had to think where he wanted to go and the board went.

"You ready?" He asked Lou.

She wet her lips and nodded at him.

Keoni wanted to fold Lou in his arms and keep her safe, but it was better that she get back in the ocean as soon as possible. She needed to face her fears. It was the only way to be rid of them. Fear was the most debilitating disease.

Keoni laid his board down on the sand and told Lou to lie on top of it. He stepped back and held his breath as she lowered herself onto the Himalaya. Keoni had never allowed anyone to get this close to his board before. Lou lay on top of it with her belly flush to the slick surface and Keoni felt his heart stop.

She looked perfect.

Lou pushed up on her elbows and looked at him over her shoulder.

"Is this right?" she asked.

Keoni nodded, not trusting himself to speak.

"I feel funny doing this on the sand," she said. "Shouldn't we be in the water?"

Hiking up his shorts, Keoni squatted down beside her. "Try listen," he said. "This is the best way to learn."

He'd given hundreds of surf lessons over the years, and he always started everyone off the same way. They learned the mechanics of paddling and popping up on the sand first. When they had that down, they graduated to the water.

Keoni showed Lou how to paddle. "This is the most important part. You have to pull through the water with the right amount of caress and force."

Lou looked over her shoulder at Keoni, her eyebrows drawn together in concentration. She was giving it her all, taking the lesson seriously. When she could paddle to satisfaction, Keoni told her to stand aside so he could demonstrate popping up.

Lou's eyes went wide. "I'm never going to be able to do that," she said. "I told you I'm horrible at anything that requires coordination. I almost drowned just walking on the beach."

"That's because you turned your back on the ocean," he said. You never turn your back on the ocean. It's the first rule of living in Hawai'i."

"You were watching me?"

Keoni nodded. He always kept one eye out for a dangerous situation, but he'd been watching Lou because she was gorgeous. As soon as she'd peeled off her dress, Keoni had spotted her and decided it was time to take a break from surfing.

Keoni showed her how to pop up again, this time breaking it into four motions. After a few tries, Lou got the hang of it. She was proving to be a quick learner.

"You said you weren't athletic."

She shook her head. "I'm not."

Keoni lifted the Himalaya up from the sand, and tucked it under his arm. "You look like a dancer when you take pictures," he said.

Lou stopped walking and stared up at him. "What?"

"You look like a dancer. The way you move. It's like a sensual dance."

Lou's cheeks turned red. "You think so?"

Keoni swallowed hard and nodded. She couldn't have been more beautiful than she was right now. He wanted to grab her again and kiss her, but he resisted.

"Time to see if you can do that on the water," he said.

He led her into the waves. Her teeth chattered as they waded into the water. The waves were calm, but both of them knew how quickly that could change.

"I'm scared," Lou said.

"That's okay. You should be."

Lou glanced sharply at him.

"The ocean is dangerous. Don't forget that. A little bit of fear is good." He pointed at the surfboard. "Now get on."

Keoni held *The Himalaya* steady while Lou climbed on. Once she had her belly pressed to the board and was floating, Keoni showed Lou how to balance her weight on the board, and how to turn. He stretched over her so that his front was pressed to her back, and he went over the paddling motions once again.

"The key is paddling," Keoni said. "You have to paddle hard. Get ahead of the wave so it can lift you. Let the ocean do the work."

"What do you mean?" She turned and looked at him over her shoulder.

Their faces were close enough to kiss, but Keoni was all business. He took Lou's hand and let it hover over the surface of the water. The warm waves pushed against their palms.

"You feel that?" he asked.

"The water?"

"No, I mean the energy. The power."

They were both quiet as the ocean undulated beneath their joined hands. The only sound was their breath and the crash of the waves.

After a moment, Lou nodded. "I feel it."

Keoni heard it in her voice that she did. She was almost ready.

"Now you just have to wait for the right wave."

"How will I know?"

"You just will. Trust the ocean to tell you," he said. "If you fail, try again. But don't try hard. Try easy."

Lou's eyebrows pulled together. "What does that mean?"

"Sometimes you gotta let go," he said. "Don't try so hard. Instead, you gotta try easy."

Keoni gave the board a little push to start Lou off, and then stepped back. He crossed his arms and watched as she paddled over the shore break into the open water.

His heart was in his throat as he watched her form and technique. He'd taught her all that could be taught in a first lesson. Now the waves of Makaha needed to cooperate. This wasn't the ideal place to give a surf lesson. Makaha was too unpredictable. There were four sections where the waves broke, and Keoni had steered Lou into the easiest one, but that didn't mean she would stay there.

It would have been much easier to teach Lou how to surf at Queen's Beach in Waikiki, where the waves were long and gentle, but he didn't have the luxury of choice. She'd been scared half to death by the ocean, and she needed to face it as quickly as possible, before it paralyzed her forever.

Keoni was a good teacher, but he had quit giving lessons years ago. Surfing was too personal to Keoni. To him, it wasn't a sport— it was so much more. Keoni felt like he was selling a little piece of his soul every time he taught someone how to stand up on a wave.

But he didn't feel that way watching Lou. Looking at her wet body pressed against the slick surface of his surfboard, Keoni was jealous of the surfboard. He wished her body was flattened against him.

She crouched over the board and slid her right foot forward, and Keoni's heart raced. She looked so damn sexy on the waves.

She popped up on the board, and Keoni's heart squeezed. She was doing it. She was a natural, just like Keoni had known she would be. It broke his heart to watch the smile spread across her face, knowing he would never see her again.

Fuck that, Keoni thought. *Fuck never seeing her again.*

He couldn't let that happen.

Lou hopped off the board and ran to him. She threw her arms around him and he pulled her close, lifting her off her feet.

"That was amazing!" She buried her face against his neck.

"You were amazing." He pulled back and kissed her the way he'd wanted to do for a week. When she moaned and pulled him closer, Keoni pressed against her, letting her feel what watching her surf had done to him.

Lou gasped, and Keoni took full advantage, plunging his tongue into her mouth. Lou's arms tightened around his back and she kissed him back, meeting each thrust of his tongue.

Keoni remembered they were at a family beach and pulled back. "Let's get outta here."

Lou's eyes were heavy-lidded and her breath came fast. "Where?"

"Bones lives just up the street." He grabbed his board and reached for her hand.

But the moment was broken. Tears filled Lou's eyes, and Keoni knew she'd changed her mind. She'd remembered her life back on the mainland and the man waiting for her.

Keoni cupped Lou's cheek. "Do you love him?"

Every breath was torture as he waited for Lou to answer. Finally, she shook her head.

"I don't know anymore." She took a deep breath and let it go. "I had my whole life planned out, then I met you." She smiled sadly, a tear falling down her cheek. "You weren't supposed to happen." She slid her arm around his neck and hugged him. "But when I thought I was going to die the only face I wanted to see was yours."

Keoni leaned down and touched his forehead to Lou's. In Hawaiian culture, touching faces and sharing breath was the essence of life, the purest way to show love.

Keoni drew in a breath, and as he exhaled, Lou breathed him in. It was too late to stop trying to love her. Keoni realized he'd started falling for Lou the moment he'd slipped the lei around her neck at the airport.

He was going to be a mess when she left, and it was going to be sweet torture to be around her in the meantime, but he couldn't say goodbye. Not yet.

CHANGE OF PLANS

As NIGHT FELL, THEY SPREAD OUT BLANKETS IN THE SAND, STOKED a fire, and played music. They ate fresh fish Bones pulled from the ocean and washed it down with beer. Keoni played his guitar, and Bones sang along in a deep melodic voice.

Lou put aside her problems and let the Hawaiian sunset work its magic on her. Penny sat next to her as the sun sank into the sea, and Lou felt like they hadn't talked in weeks. There was so much to tell her best friend. So much to confess.

"I tried chili water," Lou said.

Penny's nose scrunched up. "With or without beans?"

Lou leaned back on her elbows and gazed at the lavender-hued sky. She would have taken a picture, but she was completely out of film. She'd have to stop at a store and buy more tomorrow, which meant she'd be eating canned food for a while when they got home unless she figured out another way to pay rent.

"Not that kind of chili," Lou said. "It was some sort of spicy water. And tasted poi, too. And I almost drowned, Keoni kissed me, and I surfed."

Penny rolled onto her elbow to face Lou. "Back up and say that again."

"Poi isn't that bad." Lou pulled a face, remembering it wasn't that *good* either.

"I don't give a flip about the menu items. You almost drowned? Lou! What happened?"

Lou picked up a handful of sand and let it trickle through her fingers. "Did you know you weren't supposed to turn your back on the ocean?"

"Around here?" Penny gestured at the crashing ocean a dozen feet away. "Anything can happen."

Lou nodded. It was true. In Hawaii, anything seemed possible. "He saved me." Lou cut a glance at Keoni, who was strumming absently on his guitar. He lifted his gaze from the strings and caught her eye. The look he gave her made her heart swell painfully. "When I said he was a hero, something strange happened."

Penny leaned in. "I want to know about this kiss," she said. "How was it?"

The memory of Keoni's mouth on hers—his tongue in her mouth, his hands in her hair—made her shiver with longing. "I felt it everywhere," she said.

Penny laid back and let her eyes drift shut. "I love those kinds of kisses."

Lou hadn't known those kinds of kisses existed. They didn't with Paul. His kisses were gentle and sweet, but they didn't send tingles down her spine or make her toes curl. Her heart ached thinking of Paul, but it hurt worse to think of saying goodbye to Keoni.

She rolled onto her side to face Penny. Her friend was always there for her. Penny never judged. She never scolded. She let her talk for hours about photography without complaining.

"What about you?" she asked Penny. "What did you do today?"

Penny glanced across the fire at Bones and sighed. "We're in love."

The ache in Lou's heart spread through her chest. "You've only known each other a few days."

"When you know, you know."

"What about Joe? What about Seward Park?" *What about our plan?* They were supposed to grow old together as neighbors and best friends.

Penny sat up and wrapped her arms around her knees. "I feel like I did that summer in New York before the accident. I feel like my old self again. He makes me feel alive."

"And Joe doesn't?"

Penny shook her head. "Not like Bones. There's something about him." A ghost of a smile drifted across Penny's lips. "Look at him, Lou. He's so…"

Lou looked across the fire at Bones, who was laughing at something Keoni said. He held a ukulele, strumming it absently. It should have looked ridiculous for such a big man to be playing such a small instrument, but it didn't. Nothing about Bones was ridiculous.

"He's so?" Lou prompted.

"Dangerous." Penny whispered the word as if Bones might hear it from across the fire. "He makes me feel like I could do anything I wanted. I haven't felt that way in a long time."

Lou draped an arm across Penny's shoulders. "I know."

Penny had had a promising career as a ballerina until an accident had almost taken her life. Now, she didn't dance anymore, she taught lessons instead. Penny's life was steady and safe, but apparently that wasn't enough.

"Joe doesn't make me feel the way Bones does."

"Maybe he will again." Lou thought of Paul's safe kisses. "Maybe you just needed a reminder of how good things can be and you two can find passion again."

Penny cut her eyes at Lou. "Are you talking about me? Or yourself?" Anger vibrated in her voice. "You haven't exactly been playing it safe with Keoni."

Lou's shoulders tensed. The swelling in her heart grew painful. "I'm not the one saying I'm in love after a week."

"Love doesn't have a timeline, Lou." Penny's eyes flashed in the darkness. "You can't plan everything."

"You really mean this?" Lou asked. "You would really throw away everything for him?"

Tears glistened in Penny's eyes. "It's not about throwing something away. It's about wanting more. Deserving more. Don't you want that?"

A coil of anger broke free in Lou's chest. She didn't know what she wanted anymore. That was the problem.

"Can I steal you away for a walk?"

Lou looked up and saw Bones standing over them. He held a hand out to Penny, and she gracefully rose to her feet.

"We'll talk more later," Penny said.

"Okay."

Bones and Penny wandered off, leaving Lou and Keoni alone again. Keoni was busy with his guitar. He adjusted the strings and started playing a new song. He strummed a few chords and started singing.

His voice sent a rush of longing straight to her core. She could easily see herself falling for him if she didn't have her life in Seattle. She gazed at Keoni across the fire, wondering how many women Keoni had seduced with his music, his smile, and a surfing lesson. He'd said he wasn't good at games, but it seemed like he was playing one. Was she a game to him?

When he finished playing, he fished two beers out a cooler and came to sit next to her. Lou watched Penny and Bones stroll hand-in-hand in the distance.

"Is he in love with her?"

Keoni shrugged. "I don't know."

Lou felt the sharp spear of anger. "Love isn't a game."

Keoni sighed. "Yeah, I know that."

"Maybe you should tell your cousin."

"Kay then." Keoni popped the top on his beer and drank.

"Does he really love her?"

Keoni turned to look at Lou, his eyes almost black in the darkness. "I'm not a mind reader."

Lou looked directly into Keoni's probing eyes. It would be so easy to get lost in him, to let herself fall. But she couldn't. She looked away. "Tell him to be careful."

"What else should I tell him, eh?" Keoni's voice rang with temper.

"She can't just forget her life in Seattle to come out here and marry Bones," Lou said. "It's ridiculous."

Keoni reached out and took Lou's hand, lacing their fingers together. Her heart jolted so hard she almost put her hand to her chest to stop the pain.

"Why not?" Keoni asked, tugging her hand into his lap.

"Because it's ridiculous."

"Yeah." He blew out a frustrated breath. "You said that already."

"I didn't come here to have vacation fling." She jerked her hand from his.

"We weren't talking about us." He pinched the bridge of his nose and squeezed his eyes shut.

"You kissed me."

"You kissed me back. More than once."

Talking about the kisses they'd stolen made Lou think about how good they'd felt. Even though she was angry and confused, Lou craved another kiss from Keoni. She wanted to press her body to his and feel the hard ripple of his muscles under her fingertips.

She shivered as desire raced through her.

"Cold?" Keoni asked.

Not at all. She was burning up.

Keoni broke some twigs in half and fed them to the fire. Sparks danced into the sky.

He sat back and sipped his beer, seeming lost in thought. He had that look on his face again—the pained expression that Lou had referred to earlier. She studied his profile, appreciating the strong lines of his face. He had a straight, proud nose, full lips, and a square jawline under the scruff of his beard. He was so handsome; it was hard to believe he didn't have a girl.

"Why don't you have a girlfriend?" Lou asked.

"Who says I don't?"

Lou smiled. "If you had a girlfriend, you wouldn't be spending all your time with me."

"Maybe I like you."

Maybe she liked him, too. "Answer the question."

Keoni took a long pull from his beer. "I want somebody special." His throat worked as he swallowed. "I want somebody who isn't afraid to show how she feels. Somebody brave, who can face her fears. Somebody kind, who looks out for her best friend." Keoni reached up and brushed a strand of hair behind Lou's ear. His fingers curled around her neck. "I want somebody whose laugh lights up my world."

"Why don't you date tourists?" she asked.

"I fell in love with one."

"What happened?"

"She broke my heart."

"Is that what makes you so sad sometimes?"

"No." The answer came so quickly, it felt like a slap.

The grief-stricken look on his face made Lou's stomach tighten. "So that one girl ruined tourists for you?"

"She did."

"What was her name?" Lou didn't want to know but she had to ask.

"Claudia." The way Keoni said her name made it sound like an exotic flower.

"Is your heart still broken?"

Keoni didn't answer. He stood and doused the fire with sand. "It's late," he said. "It's time you should go."

Keoni started off down the beach toward Bones and Penny. Lou watched his retreating back and knew he was right. She didn't belong here. She was just a tourist with a ticket home, and it was almost time to go.

THE DUKE KAHANAMOKU
INVITATIONAL SURFING CONTEST

A Saturday in January 1968

Keoni sat on his surfboard, letting the waves roll under him. The last time he had paddled out to the lineup at this beach was nearly a year ago when he'd thrown a lei into the waves in memory of Eddie Alvarez.

Eddie hadn't wanted to be buried in the ground. He'd lived his life for the ocean, and that's where he belonged after death. Almost two years ago, these waters had stolen his best friend's life.

Keoni hadn't saved him. He'd saved a soldier at Waimea Bay, an elderly man at Waikiki, and Lou at Makaha. He'd saved so many people, he didn't even remember them all. People did stupid things in the ocean. They swam out too far. They underestimated the power of the waves. They turned their back on the ocean.

Eddie had done none of those things. Born in the Niu Valley, Eddie had been raised to swim, dive, sail, and surf. Just like every other kid growing up in Oahu, Eddie had learned to swim before he could walk and ride a surfboard before a bike.

The waves had been calm the day Eddie died. Much calmer than they were today, on the morning of the 4th Annual Duke Kahanamoku Surfing Invitational. Keoni couldn't blame the waves for Eddie's death. And he certainly couldn't blame Eddie, who was the best surfer Keoni knew. That left one person to blame for the tragedy—the one who'd been riding the wave next to him. The one who hadn't saved him.

Keoni caught a movement from the corner of his eye. His head snapped to shore, and he saw Declan paddling toward him.

Keoni's chest tightened. His stomach clenched.

He remembered the accusation Declan had hurled at him the night of Eddie's memorial almost two years ago.

Why didn't you save him?

Keoni had asked himself that question countless times over the past two years, but he still didn't have an answer.

"HOWZIT?"

Declan shook his head. His eyes were haunted. "I can't do this."

Keoni took one of the leis from Declan and fingered the soft petals. "You have to. For Eddie."

Declan shook his head. Tears filled his eyes. "I'm sorry."

Keoni squinted at Declan. "For what?"

"I'm sorry for saying you should have saved him. I know you couldn't."

An invisible fist squeezed Keoni's heart. He'd never forgotten Declan's accusation. Even though Declan had been wasted when he said it, Keoni knew he'd meant it. He knew it was true. "It's alright."

"I can't do this," Declan repeated, staring at the waves with glassy eyes.

Keoni didn't blame Declan for pressuring out on these waves. It was almost a relief that he hadn't been chosen for the contest. It would be torture to win on the waves that had taken Eddie. But it would also be sweet revenge.

Keoni cleared his throat. "You don't have a choice," he said.

Declan's gaze snapped up to meet his. His Adam's Apple bobbed as he swallowed hard. "I know."

Keoni smiled despite the pain that stabbed his chest. "So, you better win. You hear? You better kick some ass." He spotted more surfers paddling toward them. "We've got company."

Declan dashed a hand under his eyes and straightened his shoulders. By the time Keoni's brother Tau and Bones joined them, Declan looked to have pulled himself together.

Declan handed each man a lei. They formed a circle, joining hands just as they'd done at Eddie's wake.

Keoni said a few words about Eddie, and then they placed the leis in the ocean and watched them float away.

No one spoke. There was only the crash of the waves against the shore and the cry of birds overhead.

Eventually, it was time for Declan to check in with the other contestants.

They rode the surf back to shore. All except Keoni, who sat by himself in the lineup until the last possible moment.

He stared out at the sparkling sea, waiting for the hard lump in his chest to soften. All his life, the ocean had been his place of refuge. He understood the ocean more than most people. He saw the patterns in the waves and felt the vibrations of the ocean in his heart.

A wave that looked like a bump in the distance suddenly exploded against the reef, creating the perfect hollow pipeline as it closed out.

Keoni's heart leaped. The wave was pure perfection. It had been sent down from the gods, and it was coming straight for him.

Keoni paddled hard to get ahead of the wave, but it caught him quickly and lifted him. He popped up, sliding his feet under his body and crouching low over the board as the wave roared beneath him.

The wave doubled in size, growing stronger as it hurled toward shore. Keoni dropped in on the steep wave, bent at the knees halfway down the line, and stalled his surfboard by stamping down on his back foot. He leaned sideways and scraped his hand along the face of the wave, slowing his speed. He made the big bottom turn, and with a snap under the lip of the wave, he maneuvered the long nose of the surfboard into the most dangerous section of the wave.

The wave formed a barrel around him, just as Keoni had intended. For a few moments, the outside world fell away. His fears, his worries, his disappointments were eclipsed by the blue-green wall of water that surrounded him. It was a religious experience, getting tubed inside a wave. Everything moved at once, yet everything stood still as the roar of the wave filled his ears.

Inside the turquoise barrel of the wave, time stood still. The brilliant light at the end of the tunnel mesmerized Keoni. If he died at that very moment, it wouldn't be a bad way to go. The realization that Eddie had felt the same eased some of Keoni's pain.

He glided out of the barrel to a deafening cheer from the crowd. Usually, Keoni would have paddled out to the lineup again for another wave, but today wasn't that day. There was a contest about to start, and he hadn't been invited.

It was tempting to stay in the water—partly to prove a point, but partly to play lifeguard. Sunset Beach was serving up some unpredictable surf today, and some of the contestants had never surfed waves in Hawaii before. They had no idea how heavy it could get.

In the end, Keoni paddled toward shore. There was an all-women's exhibition before the contest, and Keoni wanted to watch from the shore. Maybe with Lou. Maybe holding her hand and sneaking one more kiss before they both remembered they were just friends.

Keoni strode out of the water, his mind already on Lou and how he would find her in the swollen crowd. He tucked his board under his arm and turned his head as he heard a woman call his name. He smiled, hoping to see Lou, and froze as he saw the crowd surge around him. In an instant he was surrounded by fans.

Keoni pushed through the crowd, determined not to lose the lightness in his heart created by the wave. He made his way through the press of his admirers, bearing their attention with patience. He paused to say hello to those he knew, shook hands, and received hugs.

The crowd grew, and people he'd never seen before yelled his name. Papers and pens were shoved at him. They wanted to get his autograph and take his picture.

Embarrassed by all the attention, Keoni scanned the crowd for a way out. His eyes lit on the tallest person on the beach—Bones. His cousin stood out in the crowd, but so did the two women beside him. Penny's bright hair caught every eye, and one look at Lou in that tiny white bikini made most men stop in their tracks.

Lou caught his eye and raised one eyebrow. Keoni laughed, knowing what she would say about his celebrity status.

"Heh! Bones!" Keoni yelled over the noise of the crowd.

Bones jerked his chin at Keoni and smirked.

Keoni waved him over. "A little help?"

Bones shrugged his big shoulders as if he couldn't be bothered. But a moment later, he changed his mind and decided to take pity on Keoni. Bones marched through the crowd, pushing people out of the way to get to Keoni.

The tight crowd peeled back as Bones bulldozed his way through. One look at Bones was enough for most people to move. Bones grabbed Keoni's shoulder and ushered him through the crowd.

"Get back," Bone growled. "You want beef?" he asked a stubborn fan refusing to make way.

They made their way through the crowd and joined Penny and Lou who'd found a perfect spot to watch the exhibition.

"Some crowd, huh?" Lou asked. "They all seem to love you."

Keoni smiled. "I'm related to half of them."

She lifted the ever-present camera from around her neck and fiddled with the buttons. "I got some good pictures of you on the waves." She glanced up at him. "You were amazing. Why aren't you competing?"

Keoni's gut clenched. "I wasn't invited."

"Why not? You're probably better than any of the contestants."

Keoni shook his head. "It's starting." He pointed to the women standing at the shore with boards tucked under their arms.

There was a loud cheer, and then the unthinkable happened, Declan paddled out onto the waves.

"Is that a dog?" Lou asked, lifting her camera to zoom in.

Keoni peered at the waves. A smile broke out over his face. The pep talk he'd given Declan must have worked, because he was hamming it up for the crowd with a dog on the end of his surfboard.

The crowd went wild as Declan rode the waves with a small white dog perched on the end of his board. Keoni wondered what the hell his old friend was up to, but then he noticed Lou's smile, and he forgot about everything else. When she was taking pictures, she became an even more beautiful version of herself.

Tomorrow they had to say goodbye. Keoni didn't know how he was going to keep his hands off her on their last day together. Somehow he had to try.

BREAKING THE RULES

THE HORN SOUNDED ANNOUNCING THE BEGINNING OF THE
competition, and everyone turned their attention to the surf.

The magazine and television reporters jostled to get the best
spots as the men paddled out to the lineup. A helicopter hovered
over the bay like a giant fly.

Keoni pointed to the numbered jerseys the contestants wore.
Declan's was number five. "Keep your eyes on him."

Lou popped up on her toes to get a better view.

"It's all about wave selection," Keoni said, explaining how the
judges scored points.

"Your friend is pretty good," Lou said.

Keoni nodded. Declan was doing everything right. He was
snapping and going straight off the lip, and he got barreled at the
end of the heat.

He's going to win, Keoni realized with sudden certainty. Declan
was going to win.

Keoni's chest puffed with pride for his childhood friend.
Declan had won plenty of contests in his surfing career, but
winning the Duke was like winning a gold medal at the Olympics.

"Geev'um, Declan!" Keoni yelled, holding up his fist in the shaka sign. "Geev'um da lights!"

Declan's head came up when he heard the Pidgin expression, and he beamed at Keoni.

When the contest was over, the judges took their time tallying the scores, but in Keoni's mind, it was clear who had won. There may have been a few surfers who caught better individual waves, but Declan had shown them all up by picking the best waves of every set.

The judges took the stage and tapped the microphone to get everyone's attention.

"Third place belongs to Bobby Carter, and second place goes to James Johnson." There was a dramatic pause as the director teased the crowd. "Let's give a cheer for the winner, Hawaii's own Declan Bishop!"

Keoni stood back and watched one of his oldest friends take the stage. Bikini-clad girls presented him with leis and showered him with champagne.

"I would like to dedicate this win to my brother, Eddie Alvarez, and to my man, Keoni Makai, who would be standing in this spot right now if he would have been invited."

Declan pointed to Keoni in the crowd, and everyone turned to look at him. Keoni raised his hand in the shaka sign, and the crowd began to chant his name.

The directors looked at each other, shifting uncomfortably on the stage. After Declan's speech, it would be impossible to ignore Keoni in the future. Declan had looked out for Keoni in his moment in the spotlight, and that was enough.

"Are you okay?" Lou asked.

"Not really," he said.

"What's wrong?" She drew him away from the buzz of conversation. "Is it Eddie?"

Keoni froze. He couldn't bring himself to talk about Eddie, not even with her.

"You're trying so hard to blame yourself for something that had nothing to do with you. You need to let go."

"You don't know what you're talking about," he said.

"I watched you before the contest. I saw that look on your face. You know the one."

Keoni knew.

"And then Declan's dedication." She put her hand on his arm. "Is this where it happened? Is this where he died?"

Keoni's heart thundered in his chest. He couldn't breathe. He felt like he'd been pummeled with a heavy wave. The entire day he'd been hanging by a thread. He didn't want to hang on anymore.

Lou raised her hand and brushed a tear from his cheek. Keoni hadn't realized he was crying. It had all been too much today. The contest. Declan. Lou. He couldn't take it anymore.

"It was my idea to come here that day." Anger twisted his words. "He wanted to go to Patterson's, but I made him come. If I would have listened to him, he would still be alive."

"Do you really believe that?" Lou's voice was like a hard slap. "Do you think you're that powerful? That you control who lives and dies?"

His throat was too clogged with tears to answer.

"It wasn't you who killed Eddie," Lou said. "It's damned egotistical of you to think so."

Keoni's mouth dropped open. He'd never thought of it like that before.

"You have to let go of your pain." She touched his chest right above his heart. "It's the only way you can heal."

Keoni flinched, his muscles going stiff under her soft touch. What if he didn't want to heal? What if he liked his pain and guilt?

Lou poked Keoni in the chest. "You want to be miserable your whole life, blaming yourself for something you couldn't help?"

Keoni watched tears spill down Lou's cheeks, and he felt like she was stabbing him in the heart. He couldn't stand to see her cry.

"What about Kimo, and John, and all those other boys in Vietnam?" she asked, crying freely now. "Are you responsible for their lives, too?"

Keoni pulled Lou against his chest. She was trembling. He held her tighter, and they clung to each other, both of them crying openly.

Keoni knew he wasn't supposed to cry. He was the descendant of mighty warriors and ruthless chiefs. He was supposed to be strong. Crying was weak, but the tears wouldn't stop. After two years of being repressed, once started the tears wouldn't end.

Keoni cried. He cried for Eddie, and for the children he would never make. He cried for Kimo, and John, and all those other poor boys fighting a war that made no sense. He cried for Lou, because he wasn't ready to say goodbye.

He slid his hands into her soft hair, memorizing the feel of her body against his. Would he ever want a woman as much as he wanted Lou? Would he ever meet someone who sparkled as much as she did?

His tears stopped as a wave of passion filled him. He could feel the soft curve of her breasts pressed against his chest, and his body betrayed him. Lou pressed closer and lifted her face to his. Their mouths found each other's.

This kiss was hot and hungry. When they came up for air, they were both panting.

His mouth traced a path of kisses along her jaw to her neck. He was tired of resisting her. He gave in.

"Come home with me."

Lou shivered in his arms, and for a moment Keoni's heart stopped. He was sure she was going to say no.

"Yes."

The steadiness in her voice was enough to convince Keoni to let go of any lingering doubts. A smile broke over his mouth. "Go tell Penny," he said.

Lou hurried off to find Penny. When she drew her friend aside,

Bones made eye contact with Keoni and gave a single shake of his head. Keoni lifted his shoulders in a shrug, he knew his cousin well enough to read the judgement on his face.

Bones walked over to Keoni, scowling. "What's going on?"

Keoni frowned. "I'm living a little. Not taking things so serious. Just like you said."

"You breaking your rule?"

Keoni's shoulders tensed. "It's my rule. I can break it."

Bones narrowed his eyes at him. If Keoni didn't know Bones, he would be intimidated by the fierceness of his expression. "Don't be late tomorrow. Be at Henry's at 6:00 a.m."

Keoni had almost forgotten about the coral dive. He sighed. "That early?"

"Yeah. You got beef with that?"

Keoni watched Lou walk across the beach toward them. He wished he had more than one night with her. He wasn't going to waste time arguing with Bones about when they were leaving in the morning.

He pushed by Bones and went to join Lou. "See you tomorrow."

His mind was already on tonight and what he was going to do with Lou.

A NIGHT WITHOUT SCARS

LOU AND KEONI WERE QUIET ON THE DRIVE FROM SUNSET BEACH to Hale'iwa.

Lou tried not to think about the future or all the reasons she shouldn't be with Keoni, but it was impossible.

She barely knew him.

She was leaving the next day.

One night with him was never going to be enough.

Paul.

Keoni reached over and took her hand, lacing their fingers together. When he touched her, the reasons she shouldn't be with Keoni were hard to remember.

He squeezed her fingers, and Lou squeezed back. He took his eyes off his road for a second to give her a look that ignited a fire inside her.

The road stretched on for miles, weaving between the tall cliffs of the mountains and the cascading waves of the Pacific Ocean. Finally, they came upon the sleepy town with a few storefronts and a gas station. Keoni turned onto a street lined with tiny houses. Surfboards, boats, and canoes lay strewn across the small front yards.

Keoni pulled to a stop in the driveway of a green cottage with a wide front porch.

"This is it."

His voice was unsure, and Lou wondered if he was having second thoughts. Her stomach clenched, and her heart beat wildly. It was now or never. Lou leaned across the gearshift and cupped his jaw. The scruff of his beard tickled her fingers.

She shifted closer. "I have a whole list of reasons why I can't be with you."

His eyes flashed up to meet hers. "So do I." He lifted his hand to cup her cheek, drawing her closer. "I don't do this," he said. "I don't bring women here. Ever."

A stab jealousy pierced Lou's chest. She hadn't given much consideration to Keoni's past lovers, and she didn't want to think about it now. Nothing was going to ruin this night between them. It was all they had.

She leaned closer and pressed her mouth to the scruff of his beard. The noise he made encouraged her to slide her mouth along his jaw to his ear. "Take me inside?"

Her voice ached with longing. Keoni turned his head and captured her mouth in a lingering kiss. When they parted, he rested his forehead on hers for a long moment. Their heavy breathing filled the tiny space of the car.

Finally he let her go and reached for the door. Lou waited for him to come around to the passenger side and open her door. He took her hand and helped her from the car, holding it tightly as they walked toward his house.

A porch stretched across the front of the house. The white wood gleamed in the moonlight, and flowers burst from planters.

Keoni stopped Lou outside the front door and knelt down at her feet. He untied her sandals and slipped her shoes off her feet before kicking off his own and setting them beside hers. Lou glanced at the shoes sitting side by side in front of the door, and her heart squeezed. Even though they were so different, the shoes looked right together. They belonged. Just like she belonged with Keoni. Even if it was only for a night.

Keoni took her hand and led her into his house. As soon as they were inside, Keoni pulled her into his arms. Any lingering doubts vanished as their mouths met.

Now that she was barefoot, he seemed so much taller. She had to come up on her toes to kiss him. He met her halfway. Bending his neck, he kissed her with a tenderness that chased away all her fears.

He kissed her slow and sweet, until her body hummed with pleasure. Lou grew impatient with the soft kisses. She wanted more. Fisting her hand in his shirt, she yanked him closer.

Keoni flinched and suppressed a groan of pain. Lou remembered his injuries and ran a soothing hand down his chest.

"Sorry."

He took her hand. "It's alright."

"Does it hurt too much?" Her doubts surfaced again. Maybe he was changing his mind.

He squeezed her fingers. "I'm fine." A smile ghosted the corner of his mouth. "Come see why I picked this house," he said. "You'll wish you had your camera."

He led her down the dark hall, and they stepped into a bedroom. The room was dark except for a sliver of moonlight sneaking in through the curtains. As her eyes adjusted to the darkness, Lou made out a double bed covered in a quilt and a small dresser. It was a tidy space, but hardly worthy of a photograph.

"You want me to take a picture of your bed?"

Keoni chuckled and dropped her hand. He crossed the room to the window and shoved aside the curtains, revealing an unobstructed view of the navy sky, glittering sand, and undulating sea.

"It's dark now," he said, "but you get the idea."

Lou stepped closer, pressing her face to the cool glass that was the only thing separating her from paradise. Keoni could roll out of bed in the morning and walk right out onto the beach.

Keoni came up behind her and swept her hair from her shoulder. He brushed a kiss to her neck, his lips bringing a shiver to her skin. "Do you like it?"

Lou melted against him. "I love it." She wasn't talking about just the view. She was talking about the man who embodied the spirit of the islands.

"Me too." His voice was a hungry growl as his lips skated along her skin.

Lou turned away from the view to look at the man who had captured her heart. Their eyes locked as she undid the top button of his aloha-style shirt. She pressed her lips to the strong column of his throat and felt the quickening of his breath.

"You smell like the ocean."

He smelled divine. Like man and salt and sweat. She wanted to lick him all over, but she'd get to that. She undid the next button and kissed a path to his collarbone.

He sucked in a breath as her tongue dragged along his heated skin. Each button she undid revealed a little more of his perfect body—muscled chest, taut stomach, and finally a thin trail of hair that disappeared under the waistband of his shorts. Lou's fingers slid along each delicious ridge of his smooth muscles. Mindful of the bruising along his ribs, she touched lightly.

"You should be more careful."

"I'll try," he said in a gruff voice.

She glanced up from the tantalizing view of his naked chest to his face. His jaw was tight, and his eyes glittered like onyx.

"You won't." The words fell from her lips without a filter, and she smiled to temper them. "You don't know how to be careful."

Lou knew enough about Keoni to know that he could no more try to be careful than a volcano could try to stop erupting. He wasn't the type to be careful; he was the type to risk his life for a stranger.

She slid her hands up his chest and pushed the shirt from his shoulders. It fell to the floor, and her eyes took in the feast of his beautiful body.

This wasn't the first time she'd seen him without his shirt, but it was the first time that she could touch him, and even taste him if she wanted. Her mouth watered at the thought, and she bent her head to sample him.

She kissed the top of his chest, running her tongue over the soft curling hair. He tasted like the ocean. She kissed lower, letting her lips glide over his finely sculpted muscles.

"What happened here?" She kissed the raised skin of a half-moon scar at the top of his hip.

"I don't remember." He curled his hand around the back of her neck and pulled her up his chest.

Lou didn't believe him, but she didn't push the subject. This wasn't a night to quiz each other or lay their scars open. This night was once in a lifetime. She wouldn't waste it.

She reached up and unzipped her dress, letting it fall to her waist. The bikini she'd spent almost a week's paycheck on had been worth every penny. The way Keoni looked at her made her feel like the most beautiful woman in the world.

Gathering her courage, she looked up to meet his eyes. "Touch me."

Keoni's eyes darkened, and he reached up to undo the straps of her bikini. Lovingly, he cupped her breasts. "You're perfect, Lou. Absolutely perfect."

She knew it wasn't true. She wasn't perfect. No one was. Especially not her. Pushing aside the dark doubts that swam to the surface of her mind, she sank into the pleasure of Keoni's touch.

He flicked his thumbs over her nipples, and she forgot her doubts. He bent and kissed her. She kissed him back, her tongue tracing the groove of his lower lip. He groaned and eased back.

"I want to go slowly with you," he said. "I want to take my time with you."

"But we don't have time." She pushed her dress over her hips.

"So impatient." His smile flashed as he watched her wiggle out of the bikini bottoms.

He pulled her against his chest, and Lou wrapped her legs around his waist. He carried her to the bed and lay her down on the colorful quilt, then reached over to switch on the bedside lamp.

She blinked against the harsh light. "What are you doing?"

"I want to see you."

Keoni stood at the edge of the bed, gazing down at her. His eyes blazed over her naked body. Lou knew she should be embarrassed, but she was too turned on to care. She was glad Keoni had turned on the light, because now she wanted to memorize every detail of him.

Her gaze devoured him slowly. The surf shorts hung low off his lean hips, revealing the deep V of his hip bones and the line of hair that thickened beneath his navel. Her eyes traveled up over the muscular wall of his chest to his face. His body was glorious, even with the scars and bruises, but his face was even better. Dark eyes, proud nose, full lips, and smooth skin tanned to a glowing bronze —he was a work of art.

The dimple in his cheek winked as he smiled.

"What are you smiling at?" she asked, coming up on her elbows.

He shook his head. "How'd I get so lucky?"

"Take those off." She pointed to his shorts.

Keoni did as he was told. Unbuttoning his shorts, he slid them over his hips. Lou lay back on the bed and took in the sight of him. He was even more beautiful naked than she had imagined.

He lowered himself to the bed, covering her body with his. He kissed her gently. Lou could kiss Keoni for days. He was an amazing kisser. He kissed her deeply, his tongue demanding a response from hers.

They couldn't get enough of touching each other. Lou slid her hands down Keoni's back, feeling the rise of the muscles on either side of the valley of his spine. Keoni groaned as she pulled him closer. She slid her hands along his tight abdomen down the soft trail of hair that thickened into a coarse mound of curls. She circled her fist around the length of him. He was hard and thick, and his skin was soft as silk.

His eyes drifted shut and he managed to laugh even as he moaned. "You're not afraid to go for what you want, eh?"

Lou had never been so bold in her life, but she wasn't going to stop now. She stroked him until he was hard as steel. Until he groaned and thrust against her.

He took her mouth in a fierce kiss, his hands gliding down her body to touch every inch of her. As he pushed a finger through her slick folds, Lou gasped and arched against him. His thumb slid over her swollen clit, and she cried out in pleasure. He tore his mouth from hers and kissed a hot path across her breasts. Sucking her nipple into his mouth, his fingers worked inside her.

Lou's world came to a standstill as wave after wave of pleasure crashed over her. She needed to touch him. Lou disentangled her hands from the pillow she'd been gripping and reached for Keoni, but he rolled off her and disappeared for a moment. When he came back to the bed he had a foil packet in his hand.

Lou's eyebrows rose as she watched him tear it open with his teeth. "I thought you didn't bring girls here?"

"I don't," Keoni said. "But I'm not a virgin." He started to roll the condom over the wide head of his cock, and then he stopped and looked at her. "Do you want to stop?"

"No," she said, shaking her head. "Don't you dare."

Keoni didn't hesitate. He rolled the condom on in one swift motion. The bed creaked as he knelt between her thighs, balancing his weight with his hands on either side of her head. They looked into each other's eyes, and Lou was glad the lamp was on. She watched Keoni's eyes as he guided himself inside her, filling her slowly, one inch at a time.

It was almost too much. She was glad Keoni was setting the

pace and going slowly. When they were completely joined, Lou bit her lip to keep from crying out.

"You okay?" His lips were near her ear, and the rasp of his beard scraped her jaw.

"Yes." Her voice was strangled. She took a breath and tried to relax as her body pulsed around him.

Keoni chuckled, and Lou realized how desperate she must have sounded.

"Don't laugh at me," she said, reaching up to scrape her fingers down his back and urge him closer.

"Jesus, Lou," he growled, as her hips rocked against his.

He buried his head against her shoulder and they moved together, slowly at first and then with helpless desperation.

"Look at me," Keoni demanded.

Lou hadn't realized her eyes were closed, and she opened them to see Keoni's soft brown eyes gazing down at her. The look in his eyes undid her. She gave herself to him, holding nothing back. He set a brutal pace and she met it with abandon.

Lou stared into Keoni's eyes, feeling herself go to an unknown place that was so full of pleasure it bordered on pain. She cried out as Keoni drove into her, relentlessly crushing the tenuous hold she had on her control. The sound of her own voice raised in a passionate cry surprised Lou. It was enough to make her spiral into climax. Pulses of sheer ecstasy washed over her. He drove into her until she was completely spent, and then began to speed up again, driving her to another orgasm before giving himself over to his own pleasure.

NO ORDINARY DIVE

WHEN KEONI GOT BACK FROM TAKING CARE OF THE CONDOM IN the bathroom, he paused in the doorway to his bedroom to look at Lou. She lay naked on his bed, her brown hair spread on his pillow like billowing silk. The sight of her made him hard again even though he'd just had her. He could have her a million times and still want more.

He hoped the smile she was wearing was because of him, but if it wasn't, he was going to fix that.

She opened her eyes and looked at him. Her smile faltered as she raised up on her elbow to look at him. "What are you doing over there?"

He leaned against the door frame, hoping he looked more casual than he felt. "Looking at you," he said.

"You gonna come back ta dis bed, or what? Eh?" Lou asked in a funny voice.

Keoni chuckled at her attempt to imitate his accent. "I don't sound anything like that."

Lou scooted over to make room for him in the bed, patting the sheet next to her. "Yes you do."

Keoni went back to the bed and claimed the spot next to her.

He wound a strand of her soft hair around his finger. "I love your hair."

Lou reached up and ran her hands through his hair. "I love yours, too." She winced when she saw the gash on his forehead. "Another scar?"

He bent to kiss her. "I guess."

Lou sighed and pulled him closer. Her lips opened under his, and when their tongues met, Keoni struggled to keep it slow and casual. He could drown in her kiss One night together would never be enough, but it was all they had.

She sucked his bottom lip into her mouth and ran her tongue along the deep groove of the cut. A rocket of pleasure burst inside him, and he couldn't hold back. He slanted his head and took over the kiss. He kissed her hard, thrusting his tongue into her hot mouth until she moaned.

He had never been so turned on by just kissing a woman before, but this time he wasn't going to rush.

She pouted when he eased back. "Where are you going?"

He rolled to his feet, pulling her with him.

"I want to show you something."

"Do I need to put on clothes?"

Keoni's eyes wandered over her naked body. "Absolutely not."

"K'den," she said, grinning.

She was making fun of his accent again, but Keoni didn't mind. He could code switch at any time to sound like he was from the mainland, but he didn't need to be anyone other than himself with her.

He took her hand and tugged her up from the bed. "You want to see it, or what?"

"I want to see everything." She clutched his shoulders, pulling him against her.

"You've already seen me at my worst. My face was a real mess that first day at the airport."

"I thought you were…" She paused, searching for the right word. "Majestic."

A laugh burst from his mouth. He'd thought she was going to say dangerous or crazy. Not majestic.

"What?" Lou slapped him on the shoulder. "It fits you."

"You think I'm majestic?" Keoni asked. "With a face like this?"

Lou pushed his hair from his face, running her fingers lightly over the gash on his forehead that should have been stitched up a week ago.

"Yes."

Keoni cupped her chin and tilted her face up to his. "You need glasses, or what?"

Lou's gaze roamed over his face. "I can see just fine." She smiled flashing the dimple in her cheek. "Now what did you want to show me?"

"The bathroom." He tugged her down the hall.

"The bathroom?"

"If you think the view from my room is good, wait till you see the bathroom, eh?" He exaggerated his accent just enough to make her laugh.

She giggled and followed him into the darkened bathroom.

"Close your eyes," he said.

"You love this, don't you?" she asked. "You love showing me new things."

Nothing could be truer. It had been one of the best weeks of Keoni's life, sharing Hawaii with Lou. He'd been able to see his home through fresh eyes. For the first time in his life, he thought he really understood the spirit of aloha. It meant more than a greeting and an endearment, it meant unselfish sharing. He wanted to share everything with Lou.

"Close your eyes, Lou. You're going to love this."

She closed her eyes and Keoni switched on the light. He walked over to the glass door of the shower.

"Okay then. Open up."

Lou opened her eyes and looked first at Keoni, then behind him to the outdoor shower. Her mouth dropped open, and her eyes widened.

The bathroom was the real reason Keoni had rented the tiny house. It was a small square room with only a sink and a toilet on one wall, but the other wall was made up of a glass door that led to an outdoor shower.

Keoni opened the glass door and stepped out onto the wood-planked floor. He curled his fingers at Lou to join him.

"You are so lucky to live here," Lou said.

"We Hawaiians have a saying about that."

"What is it?" Lou asked.

"'Lucky we live in Hawaii.'"

Lou burst out laughing.

Keoni was going to miss that sound. She'd enchanted him with that sweet laugh, and it would be so hard to forget.

"Come here."

She stepped closer and peeked around at the space. "Can anyone see us out here?"

"No."

Bamboo trees and banana plants formed high walls around them, and the sky was their ceiling. He turned on the tap and wrapped his arm around Lou's waist while waiting for the water to heat.

When it was warm, he drew her under the spray and massaged his hands through her thick hair. She sighed and tilted her head back, letting his fingers work over her scalp.

"Have I told you I love your hair?"

Lou smiled and tilted her head back. "You can tell me again."

"I love your hair."

He reached for a bar of soap and lathered it between his hands. Lou's eyes popped open and she plucked the soap from his hands.

"Ah," she said, inhaling deeply. "This is why you smell so good. Coconut soap."

"My sister Miriam makes it by the truckload. She's always giving it to me."

Lou scrubbed the soap over his chest. "Tell her thank you for me."

They started to kiss again as Lou ran her hands over Keoni's body, washing him thoroughly. He took the soap and washed her with the same attention to detail she'd given him. Then he shampooed her hair with the coconut shampoo—also made by Miriam.

When they were both clean, Keoni wrapped Lou in a towel and took her back to his bed where they made love much slower this time and dozed off in each other's arms.

Later in the night, Keoni woke up and covered them with the quilt. He lay on his back, and Lou propped herself up on one elbow beside him and traced her finger down his bearded cheek.

"Can you turn on the light?" she asked.

Keoni reached over to turn on the bedside lamp. He blinked at the sudden brightness and pulled Lou back into his arms, settling himself against the pillows. "You don't want to sleep?" he asked.

She shook her head against his chest and pushed the quilt down so that she could trail her fingers along his skin.

"I think the rumors I heard about you might be true," Lou said.

Keoni could feel her smile against his shoulder. He reached up and took her hand, lifting it to his mouth for a kiss. "What rumors?"

"I heard you were a descendant of a god."

Keoni laughed softly and pushed Lou's damp hair off her cheek. "That isn't a rumor."

She lifted her head and looked at him. "Are you saying it's true?"

"Of course. Do you want to hear the story?"

Lou laid her head back on his shoulder, chuckling. "Is this another one of your made-up stories, Keoni?"

"Do you want to hear it, or what?"

Lou nodded and ran her hand across his belly, making him lose focus. "Tell the story."

"A long time ago…"

"Oh, boy," she muttered.

Keoni pulled her tighter against his chest. "Try listen," he scolded, stilling her hand. "A long time ago, the goddess Pele came down to Maui for a swim in her favorite pond. She happened to see a warrior chief training for battle at the top of a waterfall, and she fell in love with him." Keoni swallowed hard as Lou's hand dipped lower under the sheet. He cleared his throat. "He felt the same about her, and they spent a few precious days together. When Pele had to go home, the warrior chief wanted to ask her to stay, but she was a goddess, and he was only a man. He knew he couldn't."

Lou's hand stopped, and she lifted her face to look at him. "Did he let her go?" Her voice was quiet, and tears sparkled in her eyes.

Keoni cupped her cheek and pressed a kiss to her forehead. "He had to. But he told her that he would wait for her if she wanted to come back."

"And then what happened?"

"She came back."

They fell into a deep silence. Lou rested her hand on the flat of Keoni's belly, and he worked his fingers through the tangles in her damp hair. Her breathing became so regular that Keoni thought she might have fallen asleep.

"Keoni?"

"Yeah?"

"That story doesn't explain how you're descended from the gods."

"Sure it does." Keoni kissed the top of her head, smelling his shampoo in her hair. "The warrior chief was my great-great-great-great-grandfather."

Lou laughed and shook her head against his chest. Keoni

pulled her tighter against him, and a few minutes later she drifted off to sleep in his arms.

~

KEONI WAS USED TO STAYING UP ALL NIGHT, WORKING THE LATE shift at the cannery. He held Lou as she slept, savoring the feel of her warm body pressed against his. Keoni didn't think he would fall asleep with Lou in his arms, but the last week finally caught up with him, and he drifted off to sleep.

The sun on his face woke him with a start. Lou was curled against his side, and her body was so warm and soft that he closed his eyes again, drifting off briefly before he was awakened by a feeling of cold dread in his belly.

Keoni turned toward Lou, intent on waking her slowly when he realized the cause for the sinking feeling in his gut. He sat bolt upright and looked at the clock on the nightstand.

It was 6:30. He'd overslept. He should have been at Henry's a half hour ago. Keoni jumped out of bed and ran down the hall. In the kitchen, he yanked the phone off the wall and dialed Henry's number.

Leaning his head against the wall, Keoni waited for an answer. "Come on. Come on," he begged.

The phone rang, but no one answered. Keoni slammed the phone down, nearly knocking it off the wall.

"What's wrong?" Lou stood in the hallway wrapped in one of his quilts. Her voice was sleepy, but her eyes were alert. "Is everything okay?"

Keoni took one look at her and felt his heart stop. Lou was beautiful in the morning, with her face naked of any makeup and her hair in a mess of waves that his hands had created. The quilt slid off one shoulder, revealing her bare skin.

"Nothing to worry about, *nani*," Keoni said. "I'm late is all. I messed up." He walked down the hall and stopped in front of her.

He kissed her and pulled the quilt tighter around her shoulders. "Can you get dressed real quick?"

Her eyes turned serious. "What's going on?"

"Don't worry." He kissed the top of her head and shooed her into the bedroom.

They gathered their clothes from the floor of his bedroom, dressed quickly, and were in his car headed south in less than ten minutes.

Keoni drove straight to the marina, hoping to catch Bones and Henry there. He sped through the country roads toward Honolulu, once again pushing the VW Bug to its maximum speed. When he peeled to a stop next to Bones's truck at the marina, it was 7:30.

They'd made it in record time, but it was still too late. The boat slip was empty. Keoni balled his hands into fists.

Clyde Ho, a man Keoni had known since junior high school, was washing down a boat in the next slip.

"Bones gave me a message to tell you," Clyde said, shutting off the water and straightening. His eyes darted to Lou as she came to stand beside Keoni on the dock. "But I shouldn't say it with a lady present."

"Fuck," Keoni muttered.

Clyde smirked. "That's pretty much what he said."

"He left without me."

"Sure did," Clyde said.

Keoni glared at Clyde, then turned away to stalk down the dock. "I cannot believe he would do something so stupid."

"What's going on?" Lou asked.

Keoni took a deep breath and then sighed it out. He reached for Lou's hand. "Bones left without me."

"Where did he go?" Her eyebrows drew together and she peered into the distance.

Keoni looked up at Clyde, who was observing them with interest. He pulled Lou closer. "Come on, I'll tell you over breakfast."

At that moment, the bright side of the situation became clear: Keoni could spend more time with Lou.

First, he took her to his favorite place at Waikiki for breakfast. While they sipped coffee and waited on pancakes, Keoni told Lou about the dive. Usually, he wouldn't share the details with anyone. Not even Henry knew all of it. But Keoni figured it didn't matter because he would never see Lou again. The realization depressed him but made it easier to unburden his guilt about missing the dive.

"This was no ordinary dive," he said, keeping his voice low in case anyone else was listening.

Lou stopped stirring her coffee and focused on him. "What do you mean?"

"We were hunting for black coral. It's very rare and grows at the bottom of the ocean. The jewelry stores pay top dollar for it. They turn it into fancy bracelets and earrings that cost a fortune."

Lou leaned closer. "What aren't you saying, Keoni? Is it dangerous?"

Keoni fell silent as the waitress brought their food. He had been starving a minute ago, but as he looked at the plate, all he could think about was Bones on the dive—alone. Bones should have waited for him. It was never a good idea to go on a dive solo. Diving that deep without a partner was reckless.

"Bones is the best diver I know," he said, more to reassure himself than for Lou's benefit.

Keoni thought back to the first time they'd found the black coral. It had been an accident. The depth finder on their boat was on the wrong scale, and they thought they were at 200 feet. It wasn't until they came up that they realized they were closer to 300 feet.

Keoni pushed his food around on his plate. "It's like an alien planet under there that deep," he said, his voice hushed.

"I'd love to see it."

Keoni smiled at Lou. He bet she would love that. The tall trees of bright coral, the strange-looking fish, and the rocky bottom of the ocean that looked more like a mountaintop than the deep sea would have blown her mind.

"I wish you could," he said.

They exchanged a sad smile. They both knew the chances of it ever happening were little to none. Lou had never been on a dive before, and diving that deep was for experts only. Managing the time without air, the heavy equipment, and the threat of predators were too much for all but the most experienced divers.

The ball of dread that had woken Keoni that morning grew.

"Bones should have never gone alone," Keoni said.

"But he's not alone. Henry's with him."

Keoni shook his head. "Henry isn't good for anything but driving the boat."

Lou pushed her plate aside. "This is all my fault. I kept you up all night."

Keoni pushed his plate aside and leaned across the table to kiss her. "I kinda liked the way you kept me up all night." Guilt coiled in his stomach, but he pushed it away. "At least I get to spend more time with you."

Lou's lips curved in a smile, but her eyes were flat.

Keoni leaned back in his seat and pointed to her plate. "Eat," he said. "You're gonna need it."

PATTERSON'S POINT

AFTER BREAKFAST, KEONI TOOK LOU TO PATTERSON'S, WHERE he'd learned to surf. It was a small break near the foot of Diamond Head, named after the people who used to live there.

She stood barefoot on the soft sand in the same clothes she'd worn the night before, looking out at the ocean. The waves were thick and dark blue, with peaks that jumped up at random and crashed down with a violence that made Lou shudder.

She was still shaken by the experience of almost drowning at Makaha. She shifted closer to Keoni, seeking his protection. She felt safe with him nearby, as if nothing bad could happen to her.

"This is where I first met Declan Bishop." He pointed out to the whitecaps beyond the reef that spilled into the turquoise sea.

"What was he like?" Lou was curious about the champion surfer who'd charmed the crowd with his surfing dog and wowed them with his skills on the waves.

Keoni laughed. "He was short and skinny."

"That isn't what I meant."

They walked along the shoreline under the shadow of Diamond Head Crater and sat under the cover of a palm tree on a grassy patch.

"Do you want to know the real story of how Diamond Head got its name?" he asked.

"Do I have a choice?"

"There's always a choice."

"Henry already told me the story." At Henry's insistence, they'd spent an afternoon climbing to the top of the crater. Henry had promised the tough climb was worth the view, and he'd been right.

"Not the one for tourists," Keoni said. "The real story."

Lou tensed at the way Keoni said the word *tourist* like it was dirty. She was just another tourist to him after all. A knot tightened in her belly, and she suppressed a wave of sudden tears.

"It wasn't named because the sailors thought the sparkles in the crust were diamonds," Keoni said. "A long time ago…"

Lou forgot her sadness as Keoni spun his story. She could listen to him talk for hours. The flow of his deep voice mesmerized her. She loved the soft subtle way he elongated his vowels, giving them the proper attention they deserved. Keoni told a story the same way he kissed her, the same way he played guitar—with his soul.

"The prince was determined to find his bride. He decided to go to every island and search for the most beautiful woman," Keoni said. "He took a double-hulled canoe with forty men to navigate the seas. Every time he dropped anchor, he lost a few men."

"Did they get attacked?"

"No. Nothing like that." He lay back in the grass, and Lou settled against him, using his arm for her pillow.

"What does this have to do with Diamond Head Crater?"

He chuckled. "Try listen. I'm getting there."

Lou sighed and snuggled closer to him, breathing in the scent of coconut on his skin. She wished she had swiped a bar of his soap to take home with her. In a few hours, she would be boarding a plane back to Seattle. She would never see Keoni again.

She trailed her hand down his arm and linked their fingers.

Even though she was as tanned as she'd ever been in her life, her skin was pale next to his. She would miss the feel of his hands sliding over her skin.

"The men were tired of sailing, tired of eating fish, and tired of each other. They all hoped their prince would find a wife, and Oahu would be their last stop before home."

"You're making all this up as you go along, aren't you?"

Keoni gave her a smile that made her heart skip. She would miss that smile so much.

"It's a true story."

"Sounds made up to me."

She brought his hand to her lips and kissed the calloused pads of his fingers one by one. Keoni's eyes flashed to hers, gleaming darkly. "Do you want to hear the story, or what?"

"Not really." Time was running out. "I'd rather you kiss me."

BY THE TIME THEY MADE IT TO HENRY'S HOUSE, IT WAS afternoon. Lou only had a few hours before she had to catch the evening flight back home. She was determined to spend every last minute with Keoni, soaking up every detail about him.

"Come in?" she asked when he walked her to the door.

Keoni gave her a tight smile, but he nodded and followed her inside. Bones's car was in the driveway, but he and Henry weren't back from the dive.

"They took Henry's car," Penny said, coming into the house from the lanai. She was dressed for traveling in a ruffled shirt and jumper. Her makeup was flawless, but did nothing to hide her red-rimmed puffy eyes.

Lou took one look at her friend and knew she'd already told Bones goodbye. "Are you okay?"

Penny darted a look in Keoni's direction and tears filled her eyes.

Keoni cleared his throat. "I'm going to check with the marina and see if the boat is back yet." He gave Lou's hand a squeeze and went into the kitchen to use the phone.

Lou drew Penny out to the lanai. She swallowed the lump in her throat, knowing she was going to look worse than Penny when she had to tell Keoni goodbye.

They walked over to the railing that looked out over Diamond Head Crater.

"How was it?" Lou asked, already dreading the moment she would kiss Keoni goodbye.

Tears glistened in Penny's eyes. "Samuel dumped me."

Lou's eyebrows shot up. "What do you mean?"

Penny's full mouth thinned to a flat line. "I offered to stay here with him. To marry him like he wanted."

For a brief moment, the skittering of Lou's heart came to a screeching halt. "What? Have you lost your mind?"

Penny sniffed back tears. "He said he didn't mean it. He didn't really want to marry me. He was just having a good time."

Keoni came out onto the lanai, his expression worried when he saw Penny's tears.

"It's gonna be okay." Lou put her arm around Penny and pulled her close. "You'll get back to Seattle and forget all about that big oaf."

"He's not an oaf." Penny lay her head on Lou's shoulder. "He's the best thing that ever happened to me."

Lou cringed. She could remember Penny saying that about the last three men she dated, including Joe. Lou had thought Penny would finally settle down with a steady guy like Joe.

"You're all the same, aren't you?" Penny's words flew across the lanai at Keoni. "You act like you're in love just so you can get what you want from us."

The color drained from Keoni's face, and his eyes flashed to Lou. Without a word, he went back inside the house and closed the door behind him. Lou tried to console Penny for a few more minutes, but there wasn't anything she could do or say to make her friend feel better. It was going to be a long flight back to Seattle with both of them nursing bruised hearts.

Lou went inside and found Keoni sitting on a stool in the kitchen. He flinched when she laid a hand on his shoulder.

"Is that what you're going to do, Lou?"

"What are you talking about?"

"Are you going to go back to Seattle and forget all about me?" He didn't give her a chance to answer. "This is why I don't date tourists." A bitter laugh escaped his mouth.

"You knew I was leaving today. Nothing has changed. Except now Bones has broken Penny's heart. He said he wanted to marry her, but when she offered to stay, he changed his mind."

Keoni looked away, but not before Lou saw the flash of guilt cross his face.

"You knew this would happen, didn't you?"

Keoni shrugged. "Bones is never going to marry a *haole*. A tourist." He spat the word like it was dirty.

Lou winced. "Is that how you think of me? Just a good time?"

Keoni pushed back from the counter so fast he almost knocked over the stool. A thundercloud of emotions darkened his face, but before he could answer, the front door flew open, and Henry burst inside.

It was clear from Henry's pained expression that something horrible had happened.

"Bones is missing!" he said.

ONE MORE NIGHT

THE BLOOD DRAINED FROM KEONI'S FACE. "WHAT DO YOU MEAN 'missing'?"

Henry paced back and forth along the short hall. His bright hair stood up all over his head. His wild eyes met Keoni's and he swallowed , and his eyes were wild when they met Keoni's.

"He's gone."

Keoni closed the space between him and Henry in two long strides. Grabbing Henry by the shirt, he yanked the shorter man up to eye level. "What happened?"

Henry shook out of Keoni's grasp. "Cool it, man. Choking me ain't gonna change nothin'."

Penny came in from the lanai. "What's going on?"

"Bones is gone," Keoni said. His voice was somehow calm despite the volcano erupting inside him.

"Do you mean…" Penny wobbled on her feet, and Henry rushed to catch her before she could faint. Her face blanched as white as the sand at Kauna'oa Beach. "Do you mean he's dead?"

Henry fired an accusing gaze at Keoni. "Where were you, man?"

Keoni's throat burned. He felt like he'd just been tossed off his board by a wave he hadn't seen coming. A heavy weight crushed his chest, and he couldn't breathe. His heart slammed, trying to break free of his ribcage. A buzzing noise filled his head, blocking out every sound but the wild beat of his pulse as he relived the moment of Eddie's death. He saw every grizzly detail as if it was happening all over again—his friend's blue lips, the dark hanks of wet hair stuck to his face, the lifeless brown eyes.

Then, he felt Lou's hand on his. She linked their fingers and squeezed his hand hard. Her touch yanked him back to the present.

"He was with me." She pressed against his side, supporting the burden of his weight. "This is my fault."

The buzz in his head faded, and the thin line of red behind his eyes grew faint. He drew in a deep breath and smelled the coconut shampoo in her hair. She slipped her arm around his waist and guided him to a stool. Her hand stroked his back in soothing motions.

"Maybe he isn't dead," Lou said. "We have to hold on to hope."

Penny sobbed against Henry's chest. Keoni lifted his head and stared at her. He'd assumed Penny and Bones were just having fun, but maybe it was more than that. Maybe she really did love his cousin.

Lou rubbed his shoulder, standing close enough to absorb some of his pain.

"What happened?" Keoni asked, pinning Henry with his gaze. "Tell me exactly what happened."

"When you didn't show up," Henry started, and then stopped abruptly when he saw Keoni's face harden.

"Go on," Keoni said through clenched teeth.

"When you didn't show up, we waited for a few minutes. Then Bones got impatient. He was convinced you weren't going to show." Henry's eyes darted to Lou and then back to Keoni. "Anyway, we set out for Shark's Ridge. The weather was clear, if a little windy. It was a perfect morning for a dive." Henry paused and swallowed hard before continuing. "Bones said he was going deep, at least 250 feet. With a single tank of air and such a deep dive, he could only stay on the bottom for about ten minutes. I waited, counting down the minutes."

"Why didn't you go after him?" Penny cried, banging her fists against Henry's chest.

Henry grabbed her wrists, holding her back. "You don't understand. It would have been suicide for me to go down after him. I don't know what I'm doing diving that deep. I was only there to drive the boat."

Keoni gripped the counter, his knuckles turning white. It had been his job to dive with Bones. Henry was right, going after Bones would have been like jumping off a ten-story building.

"Did you look for him at least?" Penny asked.

"Of course I looked for him. I searched for an hour. Then I called the Coast Guard. They've got boats out there now."

"They'll find him," Lou said. The confidence in her voice left no room for doubt. "We need to stay positive. No good comes from worrying over something we don't know is true. It's better to stay hopeful, don't you see?"

Keoni's eyes locked with Lou's, and he knew without her saying the words that she was thinking of John and Kimo. Their brothers needed them to stay positive. It was all they could do.

Keoni put his arms around Lou and pulled her to stand between his legs. He held her against his chest, offering comfort and taking some of his own.

"Don't give up," she said, hugging him tightly. "Promise you won't give up yet."

Keoni nodded against her shoulder. He inhaled deeply. Smelling Miriam's coconut soap on her skin calmed his racing heart.

"I promise."

Lou squeezed him tighter, giving him her strength. Keoni held on, wrapping his arms around her slim waist and pulling her closer.

What was he going to do without this woman? He felt a wave of despair wash over him. He couldn't bear to say goodbye to her. Not now. Not with Bones missing.

"We should get to the Keaukalani's," Henry said. "I told the Coast Guard to call there first."

Keoni's mind whirled with what they should do next. He realized there was nothing they could do except wait. It was going to be hours of torture. He took another deep breath and nodded, determined not to show his misery. He would stay positive, and Lou would help him. Bones's parents would need his strength.

Keoni reached for Lou's hand and laced his fingers through hers. Thank God she was here. He couldn't do this without her. "Thank you," he said.

Lou smiled sadly, tears swimming in her eyes. "Of course."

Her smile spurred him into action. He grabbed his keys off the counter and hopped off the stool. He was nearly to the door when he realized Lou wasn't with him. He turned around to look at her, and when he saw the stricken look on her face, he knew. "You're not coming."

Lou shook her head, tears streaming down her cheeks.

Keoni strode back across the room and stopped in front of her. He knew that Penny and Henry were staring at him, but he didn't care. He humbled himself in front of all of them. "I need you," he said. "You can't leave now."

She bit her lip and shook her head again. "I have to go, Keoni. My flight leaves in a few hours."

"Forget the flight. Get another one. Stay with me, please." He was begging, but he didn't care.

Lou's eyes skittered away from his, and he knew. She was leaving.

"Let's talk outside," she said.

"No." The single word fell like a hammer crushing all his hope. He couldn't believe she would do this to him. She knew how Eddie's death had almost killed him. "I don't want to go outside. I want you to come with me. Give me one more night. Just until we know."

Lou's face paled, and the line of freckles stood out on the bridge of her nose. "I have to go home," she said. "We have to say goodbye."

Keoni gritted his teeth. She may as well have slapped his face. "I guess you got what you wanted, didn't you? A vacation fling?"

"Keoni, don't be like this. I would stay if I could, but I have to get home. I have a job, and a family."

"And a man." Keoni spat the words out. "Don't forget about him."

"I haven't." Her voice was dangerously quiet.

"I'm not asking for forever," Keoni said, trying one last time. "Only for tonight."

Lou shook her head. "I can't give that to you."

"That's it, then? This is goodbye?"

She nodded. Tears streamed down her face, but she didn't move to wipe them away. Keoni hated to see her cry even more than he hated the thought of this being goodbye. He grabbed Lou around the waist and pulled her against his chest so hard that pain seared through his sore ribs. He crushed his mouth to hers, thrusting his tongue between her teeth. She gasped in surprise, but her lips parted as she kissed him back hungrily.

Keoni abruptly ended the kiss, leaving them both gasping for air. He took a step back, and glared down at her, taking in the delicate features of her face one more time. Her green-blue eyes were wide, the lashes fringed with unshed tears. Her mouth was parted, and pink from the crush of his brutal kiss. The dimple that winked in her cheek when she smiled was nowhere to be found.

"Goodbye," he said.

Not waiting for Henry, Keoni stormed out of the house. He yanked open the door to his car, got in, and sped off toward the Keaukalani's house, where he would wait helplessly to find out if he had killed another one of his best friends.

WET ROSES

LOU AND PENNY BARELY SPOKE ON THE FLIGHT HOME TO SEATTLE.
Penny stared ahead at the seat in front of her. She was no longer
crying, but she looked like she had just survived a war. Her hair
hung limply around her face, and her eyes were red and swollen.

Lou had never seen Penny look so devastated before. Penny
was always well-dressed and effortlessly stylish. She had a natural
grace from her years of dancing that Lou had always envied. Now
she looked like a crumpled version of herself. Broken.

Reaching across the seat, Lou linked her fingers with her
friend. She couldn't offer much comfort other than her touch. She
was just as miserable as Penny. She couldn't get Keoni's devastated face out of her mind. He'd looked so lost, so hopeless and
guilty.

She had changed her mind the moment he'd walked out the
door. She'd gone after him, but it had been too late. He had already
peeled out of the driveway. Lou watched his VW Bug disappear
down the road, stirring up a cloud of dust in its wake.

She had gone back inside and shoved her clothes into the suitcase without folding them. Henry had taken them to the airport on

his way to the Keaukalani's, promising to call with any news of Bones.

"I can't believe he's gone," Penny said, her voice cracking.

They were the first words either of them had uttered in more than two hours. Lou squeezed Penny's fingers and said, "Stay strong."

"I can't believe it," Penny repeated, staring at the seat back in front of her with glazed eyes.

Lou turned away and stared out the window at the dark sky for the duration of the flight.

When the plane touched down, they disembarked like robots. The weather was terrible. It was rainy, cold, and windy. A thick fog obscured the view of Mt. Rainier in the distance. Lou couldn't help comparing it to the warm, fragrant air that had greeted them in Hawaii.

They trudged through the airport and collected their luggage, bundling up in their coats and jackets before they went outside to catch a taxi.

"Do you think Henry called yet?" Penny asked, her eyes brightening with hope.

"Maybe," Lou said.

Penny and Lou both knew that if Bones didn't turn up by tonight, the chances of him surviving were slim.

Lou pulled her hood over her head as they walked out of the airport into the cold night. The Seattle–Tacoma Airport wasn't nearly as busy as the Honolulu terminal. Only a few cars idled at the curb.

Lou gasped when she spotted a familiar Ford Fairlane at the curb. Her mouth dropped open as the door swung open and a man in a black overcoat and hat climbed out.

"Paul!"

Penny looked to the curb where Paul stood. "What's he doing here?"

"I don't know. I guess he wanted to surprise me." Lou grabbed

Penny's arm as she was about to wave in Paul's direction. "Give me a minute will you?"

"What do you want me to say?"

"Nothing," Lou hissed. "Just tell him I've gone to the bathroom."

Lou left her bag on the sidewalk and went back inside the warm airport. She threw off her hood, splattering rain all around her, and strode straight to the restroom.

"Deep breaths," she whispered to herself.

The woman at the sink next to Lou gave her a funny look and hurried out of the restroom without drying her hands.

Lou sighed and pulled her emergency makeup kit from her bag. She looked terrible. Her hair was a mess, and there were dark circles under her eyes. When she looked into her own eyes, she saw someone she didn't recognize. Someone who'd cheated on her boyfriend, and didn't regret it. The only thing she regretted was leaving Keoni.

She looked away from her reflection, choking back a sob. She yanked a brush through her tangled hair, smelling the coconut shampoo from Keoni's shower. She touched powder over her nose and forehead, then dabbed on some lipstick, all without meeting her own eyes in the mirror.

What was Paul doing here? She hadn't asked him to pick her up. Closing her eyes, Lou bent her head over the sink and tried to work out a plan. She needed a plan. She always had a plan. The moment she'd deviated from it, all hell had broken loose.

Steeling herself to face Paul, Lou washed and dried her hands, straightened her posture, and went back out into the airport. She cobbled together a thin plan. She would tell him she was exhausted and needed rest, and then she would crawl under her covers and figure out the rest in the morning.

Lou saw Paul right away. He was standing inside the doors of the airport smoking a cigarette. His eyes swept over the crowds with a look of disdain. He hated traveling and despised the airport. It was a huge sacrifice for Paul to show up here.

She studied him as if seeing him for the first time. He was a tall man with an imposing air of authority, dressed impeccably in a black raincoat that she knew covered an expensive suit. His face was half hidden under the brim of a wool hat that sparkled with raindrops.

Lou's heart squeezed. Had she ever really loved him? Or had she just loved the idea of him? He was smart and ambitious, handsome and strong. But he didn't make her laugh, and he didn't kiss her as if it was the only thing in the world he wanted to do.

Their eyes met over the crowd. A smile broke out over his face, and he pulled a bouquet of drenched flowers from behind his back. He dropped the cigarette to the ground, crushed it under his shoe, and strode toward her.

Lou reminded herself that Paul Sullivan was everything she had ever wanted in a man. She smiled back and went to greet him.

"The flowers got a little wet," Paul said. "Sorry about that."

The roses were wilted under the weight of rain. They smelled like wet wool and were a far cry from the fragrant lei Keoni had slipped around her neck in Honolulu. Lou lifted her face from the bouquet and allowed Paul to brush her cheek with a kiss. When he tried to linger, Lou turned her face and buried it against his collar.

"What are you doing here?" she asked, holding back tears.

Paul eased her back and looked at her from under the brim of his hat. "You aren't happy to see me?"

"Of course I am." Her head ached with the effort of trying to smile. "It's been a long day, and I'm tired."

"Of course." The cheer returned to Paul's voice. "Penny looks like someone's been beating her with a stick. Both of you girls need some rest."

Lou let Paul lead her through the airport.

"You'll never guess where I had dinner tonight," he said.

"Where?" Lou fixed her hood over her hair as they walked outside.

"Dr. Martin's," Paul said.

Lou had no idea who Dr. Martin was and she realized she didn't care. "Really? That's wonderful."

"It is! I think he can get me a position with Judge Sodderman this summer."

Paul led Lou to the car and opened the passenger door for her. Penny was already in the back seat. Lou turned to look at Penny as Paul walked around the front of the car.

"You okay?" Lou asked.

Penny shrugged and looked out the window. She didn't say a word the entire ride home.

When they arrived at their apartment, Paul carried their luggage upstairs for them.

"Geez," he said, struggling with the heavy suitcases. "These weigh a ton."

Lou didn't invite Paul in for a drink. If he was disappointed, he didn't show it.

"I'm too tired," she said. "I'm sorry."

Paul pulled her into his arms. "I'll see you tomorrow."

"Tomorrow?"

"It's Monday," Paul said.

"Oh, yes. I forgot." On Mondays, they went to Jefferson's. "I'll meet you there." She kissed his cheek and pushed him into the hall.

When he was gone, they went into the kitchen to call Henry. He didn't answer, so they sat down on the sofa to wait. They were too exhausted to sleep.

"Are you going to tell Paul about Keoni?" Penny asked.

"I don't know." Lou stood up and paced the room. "What about Joe?"

A bark of laughter escaped Penny's mouth. "I can't be with Joe anymore."

"Penny! You don't mean it."

Penny glared at Lou. "Of course I do."

"At least think about it for a few days."

"Oh, come off it, Lou!" Penny said. "You don't care about me and Joe. All you care about is living out your plan no matter what the cost."

"That's not true."

"Of course it is. You could have had two weeks with Keoni if you wouldn't have been so stubborn."

"I wasn't being stubborn," Lou said. "I was trying to be faithful."

The words came out harsher than Lou had intended.

Penny flinched as if Lou had struck her. "Guess you didn't try hard enough."

Hot tears spilled down Lou's cheeks, and she turned away. A moment later, she felt Penny's arms around her.

"I'm sorry," Penny said. "I didn't mean to make you cry."

"I know." Lou hugged Penny back. "I'm sorry too."

"Do you love him?"

Lou knew Penny wasn't talking about Paul. She was talking about Keoni.

Lou nodded. Yes, she loved him. Yes, her heart was broken. But at least Keoni was alive. She would never see him again, but at least she knew he was safe, at least for now. She couldn't imagine the pain Penny was feeling, wondering if the man she loved was alive.

MOLAKA'I

THE LIVING ROOM OF THE KEAUKALANI'S HOUSE WAS PACKED WITH people, but hardly anyone was speaking to each other. Everyone gathered around the kitchen table, drinking strong coffee and staring hopefully at the phone.

Bones had been missing for over eight hours. The sky was growing dark, and they had only a few more minutes of search time before they had to give up.

Keoni finished the song and started playing Otis Redding's hit again. Thoughts of the last time he'd played the song on the beach with Lou filled his head. He remembered the way she had looked at him from across the fire.

Keoni's hands stilled on the guitar as he thought of what she must be doing right now. It wasn't as if she'd ever given him anything but mixed signals. She'd reeled him in with a glance or a casual touch only to push him away. He'd resisted her, telling himself she was off-limits because she was a tourist. If he would have listened to his instincts, he wouldn't be nursing a broken heart as well as guilt right now. But he'd ignored his gut, fallen for Lou, and now she was gone.

Keoni was left picking up the pieces, just like when Claudia had left six years ago. Keoni had only been nineteen years old when he'd met Claudia and fallen in love with her. He'd always blamed his stupidity on youth, but he was a man now and had no one to blame but himself.

"Play us another."

Keoni dragged himself back to the present and looked up at the woman demanding a song. It was hard to believe Ryla was the same little girl who had chased puppies around at parties at the graveyard. She'd grown up, blossoming into a beautiful woman overnight. Ryla was the same age as his Kimo. At nineteen years old, she was no longer a child. Dressed in a slinky dress with a plunging neckline, she sure didn't look like one. She wore stage makeup and flowers in her hair. Keoni figured she must have come straight from a gig.

"What do you want to hear?" he asked. His heart wasn't in another song, but he figured he should keep busy while they waited on news about Bones.

"Anything you want." Ryla sat down on the floor at Keoni's feet and waited while he adjusted the strings on the guitar.

He strummed the opening chords of a traditional Hawaiian folk song, and the quiet buzz of conversation ground to halt as they both began to sing. They had always made a good team. Ryla's sweet soprano voice blended effortlessly with Keoni's deep baritone.

"Another?" she asked.

Keoni nodded and adjusted the strings for another song. Playing guitar and singing usually took his mind off his troubles, but tonight nothing could.

If only he'd been on the dive, Bones would have never gone missing.

Keoni stopped playing in the middle of the song and pinched the bridge of his nose to clear his thoughts. Lou had told him he was egotistical thinking that he could save everyone. She'd said he was no more responsible for Eddie's death than he was for Kimo's safety in Vietnam. He wished Lou was here now to tell him again, to hold him and give him her strength.

He felt Ryla's hand on his arm, and he opened his eyes to look at her.

"Don't stop," she said, squeezing his arm. "You're making everyone feel better with your music."

Keoni hadn't realized he'd stopped strumming. His mind was so full of doubt, he couldn't focus. He stared into Ryla's dark eyes, feeling lost. She had a rare beauty that matched her exquisite voice. With her full mouth and dark eyes, Ryla looked exactly like the drawings of the Hawaiian goddess Pele.

Why couldn't Keoni have fallen in love with Ryla instead of Lou? It would have been so much simpler. Ryla was equally as beautiful as Lou, maybe even more so. She was kind and loyal. She loved her family as much as Keoni loved his. And she was Hawaiian. She would never leave the islands and abandon her home. Keoni had known Ryla since they were kids, and even though he was older than her, it wasn't by that much. They were both adults. It could have worked.

Instead, he'd fallen in love with a woman who refused to give him even one more night. When he needed her most, Lou had disappeared.

Keoni glanced up at the clock on the kitchen wall. Time crawled as they waited for word. Once darkness fell, his chances of being rescued were slim to none.

The shrill noise of the phone ringing pierced the tension in the room. Auntie K snatched the phone off the wall before it could ring twice. She held the phone to her ear, and the tears started flowing before she even said hello.

Keoni's uncle pried the phone from his wife's hand. "Hello?" he asked, his gruff voice crackling.

The entire room went still. Except for Auntie K's crying, there wasn't a sound.

"Oh, thank God, son!"

Bones was okay. Cheers of relief filled the room as Bones's friends and family hugged each other.

"Keoni," his uncle said, waving him over to the phone. "Bones wants you."

Keoni was at his uncle's side in two long strides. Tears streamed down his face as he took the phone.

Bones's voice came booming over the line. "Howzit?"

"You're alive, then?" Keoni cried openly and didn't care who saw. Half the people in the room were bawling, and the other half were opening cabinets and finding the stash of booze the Keaukalanis had in their cupboards.

"I'm alive," Bones said.

It was enough for Keoni just hearing his voice. "I'm sorry I was late."

"It's not a problem. I get to keep all the cash myself, eh?"

"We thought you were dead," Keoni said, feeling the initial euphoria give way to despair. He'd let Bones down, and he would never forgive himself.

"Did they leave?" Bones asked, the bravado in his voice disappearing.

"Yeah, they're gone, brother."

"Kay then," Bones said. "Good."

Keoni didn't agreed. He would have given anything to have Lou's arms around him right now.

Arrangements were made for Bones to be picked up in Moloka'i. He'd ended up swimming nearly five miles to get to the island after coming up from his dive to find the current had pushed him out of sight of Henry and the boat. Still wearing his wetsuit, he'd walked down the road. He stopped at the first payphone he found and called home.

The Keaukalanis were ecstatic over Bones's miraculous reappearance. Those not going on the rescue mission to retrieve Bones from the small island off Maui decided to throw an impromptu party that began with cups being filled from a jug of swipe, the potent homemade liquor that Hawaiians were famous for.

Henry came over to hand Keoni a cup, and they toasted to Bones's life.

"Do you want to call, or should I?" Henry asked.

"You," Keoni said.

They drank to Bones. Keoni gulped half the contents of the cup in one long sip, then put it down with a gasp. The brew was so strong that it stung his throat as he swallowed. His eyes watered and his chest burned as the liquor spread through him. He took another sip and felt pleasantly numb all over.

"Easy with that," Ryla said, prying the cup from his hand to take a sip.

"I can handle it." He took the cup from her and drank deeply as if to prove a point to both of them. "You're the one who should be careful. You're half my size."

"I'm not a little girl anymore," Ryla said, taking the cup from his hand. "In case you didn't notice."

Keoni's gaze dropped down her body. Her silky dress displayed the smooth skin of her shoulders and a daring amount of cleavage. He noticed.

Keoni took another long swallow of the swipe. It was already going to his head. It had been one of the longest days of his life, and he was thankful that it would soon be over. He'd lost the love of his life, but at least Bones wasn't dead. At least he didn't have another death on his hands.

"You want to get drunk?" he asked Ryla. Without waiting for an answer, he refilled the cup from the jug of swipe and held it out to her.

"It's been a rough day." She took the cup and raised it to her boldly painted mouth.

"The worst." He took the cup and took another long swallow.

His throat burned, and his stomach protested. He hadn't eaten since that morning, so he was already halfway to plastered after two cups.

"How's Kimo?" Ryla asked.

Keoni winced. "He's alright, I guess."

There'd been no word from his brother since he'd left for San Diego. But Keoni didn't think that was unusual. He wouldn't officially start worrying about Kimo until he was fighting in Vietnam.

His mind wandered to Lou and her brother, John. Lou hadn't heard from her brother in a month. Was he still alive? Keoni shoved the thought of Lou away with another long sip of swipe.

Warmth spread through his body. He didn't know if he felt drunk or sick. He pushed up from the sofa and hurried to the bathroom before he could be sick. Once he'd closed the door, he turned on the faucet and splashed his face with cold water. The room was spinning, but he wasn't sure if that was due to the swipe, his relief over Bones, or his heartache.

If only he could get through tonight, there was no way tomorrow could be any worse. Lou was gone, but it wasn't the end of the world. Bones was alive.

He told himself everything was going to be okay, but he knew it was a lie. It would be a long time before he felt right again.

Keoni stepped into the hall and went back to the living room where the volume of noise had risen while he'd been in the bathroom. It was a chaotic scene, everyone talking and laughing at once. Keoni's head spun with the noise. He leaned against the wall and closed his eyes.

"You okay?"

Keoni opened his eyes and saw Ryla staring up at him. "It's too loud." He squeezed his eyes shut and pinched the bridge of his nose. His head ached, and his heart was broken.

Ryla opened the door to Bones's old bedroom and pulled Keoni inside. "Take a breath," she said. "Sit in here for a minute."

Keoni went into the room that Bones's younger brothers now

shared. The room brought back memories of Bones as a child. They had been kids when Keoni's parents had moved their family to Oahu from Maui. Keoni and Bones had been instant best friends and partners in crime. As a kid, Keoni had spent as much time in this room as he had his own.

The posters on the walls were different, and the trophies lining the shelf were for baseball and track instead of football, but the room still looked the same. It was crammed with furniture and sports equipment. A bunk bed lined one wall, and a single bed was shoved against the window on the other side of the room.

Keoni sank down on the single bed, letting the mattress take the burden of his weight. He sighed and leaned his head into his hands, feeling the prick of tears behind his eyes.

Ryla sat down beside him, and handed him the cup of swipe. They passed it back and forth between them until it was empty.

"Why are you so upset? Everything turned out okay."

"I guess."

"I know what's eating you," she said.

"Yeah?"

"It's not your fault," she said. "Eddie's death was an accident."

"I know." For once Keoni was glad the subject was Eddie. It was better than Lou. The pain of losing her was still too fresh, while the pain of losing Eddie was old and familiar.

"You drunk yet?" she asked.

"Yeah."

"Me, too. Now I have the courage to do this."

She leaned forward and kissed Keoni on the cheek, leaving a smear of red lipstick.

"What was that for?"

"I just wanted to see what it was like to kiss you."

He stood up and paced the short distance to the door. He turned around to tell her wasn't interested, but the day had been too full of emotion, he couldn't hurt Ryla.

She looked so young and vulnerable sitting on the bed staring up at him. Her eyes were huge and dark, made up to look smoky and dramatic for the stage, but there was an innocence in them that touched his heart. She was gazing up at him adoringly, and Keoni searched for a way to tell her that they could never be more than friends.

Ryla leaned forward to place the cup on the floor, and Keoni glimpsed down her dress. He wasn't too drunk to respond to the display of her tanned flesh. His heart sped up, and the blood rushed to his crotch.

He looked away and put his hand on the door to leave.

Ryla stood up from the bed and walked toward him. "Don't tell me you never thought about it before, Keoni. You and me? We're perfect together."

"You're too young."

Stopping in front of him, she raised her chin defiantly. "I'm nineteen," she said. "I've been up on a stage half my life. I was never young."

Keoni remembered the rumors about Ryla Aikau. They said she was a descendant of the goddess Pele. With her long mane of dark hair, bronze skin, and sensual mouth, Ryla looked a lot like the drawings of the fiery goddess of volcanoes. And she sang with a voice that was blessed by the gods, like the mysterious sirens of the sea.

Ryla was beautiful and sexy, but Keoni had never thought of her as anything other than a kid. The way she was looking at him now, she didn't seem like a kid.

She was standing so close that he could smell the spicy scent of her perfume. His eyes dropped from her mouth to her chest, and he watched the swell of her breasts rise as she took in a deep breath.

The seductive scent of Ryla's perfume weaved a spell over Keoni. He pictured the two of them together in an embrace, her curvy body pressing into his. His body responded immediately, and he reached for her.

She wanted to know what it was like to kiss him? Keoni thought. Maybe he should show her.

Keoni cupped the back of Ryla's neck, pulling her closer. The small sound of pleasure Ryla made as their lips touched encouraged him, and Keoni leaned into the kiss. Crushing his mouth to hers, he felt some of the tension he'd been holding all day finally release.

He couldn't help wishing it was Lou's mouth he was kissing, but he pushed the thought away. He plunged forward, giving Ryla a kiss she wouldn't soon forget.

She tasted sweet, like pineapples and swipe. She opened her lips for him, and he swept his tongue inside her mouth.

He dropped his hand from the base of his neck to spread over the smooth skin of her exposed back. Ryla moaned and wrapped her arms around his waist.

Keoni ended the kiss and took a step back, regaining control. He was dizzy from the swipe, and more than a little drunk, but his senses were slowly coming back.

This was Ryla, he thought. Sweet little Ryla.

"That was some kiss," she said.

"I gotta go." Keoni gripped the doorknob.

"Wait," Ryla said. "You can't kiss me like that and then leave."

There was a noise from the other side of the door. Heavy footsteps were coming their way. Keoni froze and didn't relax until the footsteps continued down the hall to the bathroom. He released the breath he'd been holding and took Ryla by the shoulders.

"This isn't going any further," he told her, looking into her eyes. "I'm drunk. Hell, you're drunk, too."

"I'm not drunk," she insisted. "I've been drinking swipe since I was a kid. I know how to drink."

More footsteps sounded in the hall. Ryla pressed closer to Keoni and reached around behind him to turn the lock on the bedroom door, making sure they wouldn't be interrupted now.

"I've had a crush on you forever," she said. "Every girl in

Oahu does." She smiled up at him. "You're everyone's hero. You're handsome as sin, and you surf like the gods. But that's not why I like you. You wanna know why I like you?"

Keoni didn't really want to know, but he got the feeling Ryla was going to tell him anyway.

"Because you're never satisfied," she said. "The best isn't good enough for you, Keoni. You want more for yourself. You want more for Hawaii."

Keoni closed his eyes and leaned against the door. He had no idea what Ryla was talking about. The alcohol swam in his head, making his thoughts muddy.

Why did everyone insist on calling him a hero?

Ryla pressed her mouth to the hollow of Keoni's throat where the shark's tooth necklace rested against his skin. His pulse jumped against her lips.

"We're alike, you and me." She trailed her lips up his neck.

"Ryla." His voice was hoarse with warning.

"I like it when you say my name like that." Her lips moved across his jaw. "Say it again." Her mouth hovered over his. "Kiss me again."

Desire flooded his body as her breasts brushed his chest. His mind was clouded, but his body knew what to do. Ryla felt his growing erection against her belly and pressed herself against him.

"Oh, hell," Keoni muttered.

He kissed her again. He'd intended for it to be a quick and final kiss, but when Ryla opened her mouth and slid her tongue against his, Keoni's body responded without his mind's permission.

He ground his hips against her soft belly and moaned. Ryla moaned in response, and the sound drove a spear of lust through him.

Ryla slid her hands down Keoni's back and stole under his T-shirt. Her fingernails raked over his skin as she yanked the shirt over his head.

Ryla took a step back, letting her eyes drift over Keoni's naked chest. Her eyes came back to his, and then she reached up to the knot that cinched her dress. She tugged the knot loose, and the dress fell to the floor.

Keoni's eyes dropped to Ryla's chest. Her breasts were full, and round, tipped with pebble-hard pink nipples. Her waist was tiny, and her skin was tanned all over as if every inch had been kissed by the sun. She was naked except for a pair of white panties that looked like something a schoolgirl would wear. The panties lent Ryla a touch of innocence, and Keoni remembered how young she was. She had a woman's body, but Ryla was still a girl.

Ryla reached up on tiptoe and kissed Keoni's throat. She trailed her lips lower over his chest, lingering over the fading bruises on his ribs. Then, she dropped down to her knees in front of him.

Ryla unzipped Keoni's fly and tugged his shorts down over his hips. His cock sprang up between them, and Ryla's eyes dropped down to look at it. She wrapped her hand around the base and looked up at him with a wicked gleam in her eye.

Ryla looked incredibly sexy on her knees in front of him with his hard cock in her hand. Keoni's mind flashed to Lou, and guilt flooded him. He wished it was Lou kneeling in front of him, stroking him.

What was Lou doing right now? Keoni wondered. Was she with her man in Seattle? Keoni shuddered to think of it.

Ryla's mouth closed over the tip of Keoni's cock, and he forgot everything. She swirled her tongue around him, licked him as if he was a delicacy that she couldn't get enough of.

Keoni groaned and leaned back against the door. His hands came to Ryla's head. He meant to push her away, but her mouth felt too good. He pulled her closer.

Ryla took him deeper. She wrapped her hand around the base of his cock and sucked him into her mouth until her lips met her fist. Keoni gasped as he felt his cock strike the back of her throat. He looked down and watched Ryla moving up and down the hard length of his cock. It was enough to make him go insane.

Those white panties were just for show. There was nothing innocent about Ryla. She knew exactly what she was doing. She stroked and sucked Keoni at the same time until his knees weakened, and he had to lean against the door for support.

Lou had never put her mouth on him. They hadn't had time.

They had wasted so much time.

Keoni imagined it was Lou swirling her tongue around his cock and taking him deep into the back of her throat. He imagined it was Lou's blue-green eyes looking up at him with adoration and lust. Keoni remembered the way Lou had looked, lying on his bed after they'd made love the first time, and it was enough to send him over the edge.

He felt a flash of guilt that he was picturing Lou as he rocked against Ryla's mouth, but it wasn't enough to make him stop.

Grabbing the back of her head, Keoni drove himself deep inside her, crushing the flowers that were woven into her hair. The terrible events of the day disappeared as he thrust harder. A shudder spasmed through his entire body, and he pulled back.

"I'm going to come." His voice raspy with need.

Ryla yanked him closer, working him with her mouth and fist. The sight of her brightly painted lips wrapped around him made him lose control.

It was agony and ecstasy all at once. It was guilt and pleasure to the point of pain. Tears clogged his throat as Keoni poured himself into Ryla's mouth.

This was Ryla.

He'd known her in pigtails and bobby socks for Christ's sake, and he'd just fucked her mouth while thinking of another woman the entire time.

Ryla sat back on her heels and looked up at Keoni, her eyes glistening with satisfaction. Bones's old bedroom smelled of sex and gardenia flowers.

Keoni ran his hand through his hair and reached down to grab his shorts. He pulled them up and buttoned them swiftly with one hand.

"I gotta go," he said.

Reaching behind him, he unlocked the door. Ryla was still sitting on the floor when he opened the door and slipped out.

MOMENT OF WEAKNESS

SEATTLE, WASHINGTON
A Monday in February

EVEN THOUGH LOU ARRIVED EARLY AT JEFFERSON'S, PAUL WAS already there. He sat at their usual table with one leg crossed over the other. His body was turned to look at the sailboats on Lake Washington, giving Lou a view of his handsome profile.

Paul had the coloring of his Irish family: black hair, fair skin, and brilliant blue eyes. He wore his thick hair combed back from his face, kept in place with a touch of pomade. His square jaw was always scraped clean of scruff. He had a straight Roman nose and a stern mouth that hinted at his sensible nature.

Paul was always dressed impeccably. He claimed dressing the part was halfway to getting the job. Tonight, he looked dashing in a navy suit, white shirt, and precisely-knotted striped tie. A white square of silk peeked from his breast pocket.

Lou handed her coat to the hostess and smoothed a hand over the waist of her skirt. She hadn't had time to change after work.

Her skirt and jacket were well-cut, if a bit boring, and she'd tied a scarf in her hair to add some flair to the outfit.

Butterflies took flight in her stomach as she walked the short distance across the restaurant to Paul's table. He saw her coming and crushed his cigarette in the ashtray, then pushed back from the table. His white smile flashed and he leaned down to kiss her cheek.

"Sorry, I didn't think I was late." Lou's smile wavered as she glanced at the dirty ashtray and half-empty cocktail glass on the table. Paul had been here a while.

Paul pulled back her chair. "You must still be on island time."

Lou's first day back to reality had been anything but smooth. After getting the call from Henry that Bones was safe, Penny had taken a Valium and gone straight to bed. Lou had stayed up late, lying in bed unable to sleep. Guilt weighed heavy on her soul, preventing her from sleep.

The worst part about the guilt was that it wasn't over cheating on Paul, but rather for leaving Keoni.

Lou saw how hard waiting for news had been on Penny, who'd only known Bones for a short time. Keoni had known Bones his whole life. They were inseparable. Add in Keoni's guilt over Eddie, and Lou could imagine how low Keoni must have felt last night. He'd needed her, and she hadn't even been willing to give him one more night.

She hadn't slept more than a few hours, and she'd been a zombie all day at work. Her body was in shock from the time difference, lack of sleep, and missing Keoni.

A few weeks earlier, she hadn't even known him, but now she had to figure out to live without him.

All day at work, she'd been distracted. She'd made mistake after mistake and had been called into her boss's office at the end of the workday. He'd given her an earful, and she'd left near tears.

The only good thing to happen all day had been when she'd stopped by Pacific Camera on her lunch break. She'd dropped off her film and Mr. Tollison had promised his son would develop it right away.

"Lou?"

"Yes?"

Paul lit a cigarette and studied Lou across the table. "You haven't been listening to a word I've said, babe."

Lou snapped her focus back to Paul and forced herself to pay attention. Paul was her future. He was the husband she'd always wanted—handsome, a good provider, reliable and steady. He was a man like her father. A man who could be counted on.

"I've had a hard day." She reached across the table for the bowl of peanuts. "I didn't even eat lunch."

Paul watched Lou take another handful of peanuts with a raised eyebrow. "You don't want to spoil your dinner." He looked pointedly at the bowl of peanuts.

Lou chewed the peanuts slowly and then pushed the bowl away. "What were you saying?"

Paul took a long drag off his cigarette. "I don't think I can swing the Puget Sound this summer." He exhaled a stream of smoke and smiled at her. "I promise I will make it up to you. I'm telling you, getting a shot to intern for Judge Sodderman is going to launch my career."

Lou coughed into her fist and waved away the stream of smoke in the air. After nearly two weeks in the clean Hawaiian air, the layer of smoke clinging to the ceiling made it hard to breathe. Even though this was a classy place with a live pianist, plush chairs, and a wall of windows overlooking Lake Washington, it felt stale and musty compared to the fragrant air of Oahu.

"You won't be working much longer at that job. When we get married, you can quit and focus full-time on being Mrs. Sullivan." Paul lifted his glass to her and drank.

Lou's stomach clenched and her mouth dried out. The peanuts in her mouth tasted like sand. She swallowed roughly.

When the waitress came to the table, Lou ordered a beer before Paul could order her usual martini with a twist.

"What kind?"

A cold, crisp Primo would wash away the bitter taste in her mouth, but Lou was pretty sure it wasn't on the menu at a fancy place like Jefferson's.

"Something light," she said.

Across the table, Paul's eyebrows raised. "I didn't know you liked beer."

Lou shrugged, a gesture she'd picked up in Hawaii. She hadn't known it either. It was one of the things she'd learned about herself while in Hawaii. She also liked hiking, surfing, and tall, tanned, heroic Hawaiians, but she could hardly admit that to Paul.

"I just wanted to try something different." She took a single peanut and searched for a safe topic, one that would alleviate the concern on Paul's face.

The surefire way to get him talking was to ask him about himself, so she did.

Paul launched into a summary of his day, which sounded even worse than hers. He happily filled her in on the details of his day, which included filing, copying, and running back and forth to the courthouse in the heavy rain. Paul was a junior employee at a prominent law office. Until he passed the bar, his work would consist of the grunt jobs no one else wanted to do. Paul insisted he didn't mind the tedium of his days. He considered it paying his dues.

The waitress brought her beer and Paul's Old Fashioned. When she was gone, Paul began a story about how he'd walked in on one of the secretaries crying in the break room. He'd been trapped for ten minutes listening to her sniffle over a reprimand by one of the partners.

Paul looked past Lou's shoulder and nodded his chin at someone behind her. He always saw someone he knew at Jefferson's. Lou suspected it was part of the reason for their standing date on Monday's. It wasn't so much that he wanted to have a nice dinner with Lou, but more about everyone else knowing he belonged in the upper-class world of a luxurious restaurant like Jefferson's.

"Who was crying in the break room?" Lou's mind was still stuck on Paul's story. She'd been reprimanded today too, and she knew how humiliating it was to be raked over the coals by her boss.

Paul's attention shifted back to Lou. "What? Oh. I can't remember her name. She works for Franklin." He smiled. "That man is a hard ass. I can't wait to have my own secretary to make cry in the break room."

Lou's brows drew together. "That isn't very nice."

"I suppose not." He grinned and took a swallow of his drink. "It's true, though."

Lou studied Paul, noting the light in his eye when he spoke of the future. "Why do you want to be an attorney?"

Paul's forehead creased and he set his drink down with a clink of glass. "What kind of question is that?"

"I was just wondering."

His blue gaze burned bright in the dim light of the restaurant. "We've spoken of this many times."

"Not that I remember."

"My father is an attorney, and my uncle, too. You know that."

"That doesn't answer my question." Lou leaned her elbows on the table and searched Paul's eyes. "*Why* do you want to do it?"

The corner of Paul's mouth lifted in concern. "Are you okay?"

"I'm fine." Lou leaned closer to Paul and reached for his hand. "I just want to know what makes you tick. What turns you on?"

Lou's heart pumped in her chest as she thought of taking pictures on top of the hill at the graveyard. Capturing the perfect photograph felt a lot like flying. Did Paul feel like that about practicing law?

Paul's lip curved in a smile and he squeezed her fingers. "Your work isn't supposed to turn you on."

Lou wasn't sure she agreed. Her job at the bank paid the bills, but it wasn't something she wanted to do forever. It wasn't her life's dream. Her passion.

Paul cleared his throat and pulled his hand away as the waitress came back to the table. She replaced the half-full ashtray with a clean one and asked if they were ready to order.

"Do you want the usual?" Paul asked, raising an eyebrow at Lou. "Or do you want to try something different again?"

Lou realized she wasn't in the mood for her usual chicken marsala. "Do you have any specials?"

The waitress recited the chef's specials. Lou ordered the fresh catch, and Paul stuck with the filet mignon. After she left with their orders, Lou took a long sip of her beer. It was tarter than Primo, but just as cold and crisp.

Lou put the glass down and looked expectantly at Paul. He still hadn't answered her question.

Paul held her gaze for a beat and then smiled tightly. His lips thinned and his eyes narrowed. "I hope you'll feel back to yourself for dinner with the judge Wednesday night."

"Back to myself?" Lou took another long sip of her beer and sat back in her seat. "What do you mean?"

"I mean recovered from your trip." Paul took a long drag off his cigarette. "You seem a touch frazzled."

"Frazzled?" Frustration coiled in Lou's belly. She'd been up all night thinking of another man. Frazzled was hardly the word. "I've had a hard day is all."

"And your hair, babe." He made a circular motion in the vicinity of her head. "What's going on with your hair?"

"My hair?" Lou patted the thick waves, her frustration flaring into anger. "What's wrong with it?"

Paul squinted at her through the cloud of smoke. "I haven't seen you wear it like that in years."

She'd hadn't had time to wash and set her hair, so she'd tied it up in a scarf at the back of her neck. The damp weather had teased her waves into curls that framed her face.

Lou pushed a wayward strand behind her ear. "You don't like it?"

"It's not that I don't like it, babe. It just isn't you."

Paul's words struck a chord in Lou. It wasn't just her hair that was different. Everything about her was different. A wave of guilt washed over her again. Not for cheating on Paul, but for leaving Keoni. Another wave quickly followed the first. She should feel guilty for betraying Paul; not betraying Keoni.

She took a deep breath and closed her eyes. When she opened them again, she was met with the blue steel of Paul's penetrating gaze. He'd asked her a question, but she couldn't recall it. She couldn't think of anything except the woman she'd discovered in Hawaii and the man she'd left behind.

"I slept with another man." The words tumbled out before she could stop them. She covered her mouth with her hand, but it was too late. She couldn't take back the words.

The color drained from Paul's face. His mouth flattened to a thin line, and two red splotches bloomed on his cheeks. His blue eyes blazed brighter than sapphires.

The waitress came back with their salads. She took one look at Lou and Paul, who were engaged in a staring match, and hurried off.

Paul finally broke eye contact with Lou and crushed his cigarette out in the ashtray. Lou tensed, bracing for Paul's reaction. He wasn't the type for public outbursts, but the bomb she'd just dropped was enough to turn his world upside down.

Her heart banged against her ribcage, and a bead of sweat formed on her brow as she waited for his response. This wasn't how she'd expected to break the news of her infidelity. If Lou were honest with herself, she would admit that she hadn't planned to tell Paul about the affair at all. She'd hoped to plow on with her life, unaffected by her visit to Hawaii. But, it hadn't been that easy.

Paul finally broke her gaze and reached for the roll of silverware to his right. He unrolled the cloth napkin and spread it over his lap, then picked up his fork.

Lou's mouth fell open when Paul calmly began to eat his salad. "Did you hear me?"

He glanced up from his plate. "I heard you, babe."

Lou's vision blurred at the edges as a spear of rage pushed behind her eyes. Tears threatened, but she pushed them back. She stared at Paul as he chewed and swallowed.

"You should wear your hair up when we go to dinner Wednesday night." He speared a cucumber and raised the fork to his mouth.

Fury broke lose inside her. "I just told you I let another man touch me, and you want to talk about my hair?"

"Keep your voice down." Paul flicked a gaze over Lou's shoulder, then narrowed his eyes at her. "You had a moment of weakness," Paul said. "I forgive you."

Lou cleared her throat. "Moment of weakness?"

Paul pointed his fork at her. "You took some of your little pictures and got caught up in a fantasy."

"My little pictures?"

"It's going to be okay. I forgive you."

Tears pricked the back of her eyes, but she sniffed them back, unwilling to cry.

"I probably shouldn't ask, but who was the guy?"

Lou shook her head, not ready to talk about the details. "He's a surfer."

Paul's eyebrows shot up. "A surfer? That's not a job."

"Well, no, it's not his job," Lou said.

"Do you need to have a college degree to be a surfer?" Paul joked. "Or even graduate from high school? This guy sounds like a loser."

"He isn't a loser. He saved me from drowning. The ocean is very dangerous."

Paul leaned back in his chair, studying Lou. "So, he rescued you. You were scared and confused. I get it now. I really do, babe. But I'm not going to let a vacation romance ruin all our plans."

She should have been happy with his words, his easy forgiveness. But a warning bell sounded in her head as she watched Paul calmly eat his salad.

"Have you had a 'moment of weakness,' Paul?"

"Everything will be fine once we're married." He waved his fork in the air toward her salad. "I told you those peanuts would spoil your appetite."

Lou scraped her chair back from the table and stood. Without a word to Paul, she hurried toward the exit. She burst outside and gulped in a lungful of chilly air. Her coat was at the hostess stand, but she didn't mind the cold. Her cheeks blazed with temper, and her chest felt too tight. Each breath brought a cold, sharp clarity to her situation.

"Lou, wait." Paul came up behind her and took her elbow. "You can't just walk out on me like that."

Paul's voice sounded broken. She could only imagine the damage her abrupt exit and his ensuing chase had done to his reputation.

She gazed up at him, unsure of everything. She'd never seen Paul angry. She'd never seen him anything other than calm and reasonable. He was too smart to let his emotions take control. She'd thought she wanted to spend her life with Paul, but now she was questioning if she'd ever really loved him. All she knew was that Hawaii had changed everything. Keoni had changed everything.

She shivered and wrapped her arms around her shoulders. "I can't go back to the way things were."

"I agree." Paul's hands closed over her upper arms and he pulled her closer. "We can start over."

He bent his head and kissed her with a passion she didn't know he had in him. His lips coaxed hers open and his tongue teased hers. He tasted of cigarettes and whiskey.

Lou clutched Paul's shoulders for balance as his mouth devoured hers. Paul usually kissed her with expert precision, but this kiss was different. It was raw and full of emotion.

Paul broke the kiss to bury his head in her neck. "I can't lose you." His raspy voice broke her heart. "Don't leave me."

Lou hadn't known Paul felt so deeply. This was a side of him she'd never known. Confusion blurred her thoughts. She didn't know what she wanted anymore. She couldn't promise Paul that she would go back to the way things had been, but neither did she want to give up on her future.

"I'll try," she said, pulling back to look at him.

Paul clutched her tightly. "I'll try, too. I'll do whatever it takes."

Lou sucked in a deep breath of cool air. "Okay."

He clutched her hand and brought it to his mouth. "Will you come inside and finish dinner? We can pretend none of this happened."

Her heart lodged in her throat. She didn't think she could do that, but she allowed Paul to lead her back inside to their waiting food.

She'd made a promise to Paul, and this time, she'd try to keep it.

NOTHING TO LOSE

Keoni dreamed of sharks.

They circled him in a figure-eight pattern, swimming closer with each pass. They were above, below, and all around him. He was surrounded. The sleek predators slid through the water, strong and graceful.

He reached out to touch them, stretching through the water in a graceful arc. A loud ringing pierced the air, waking Keoni from his dream. He woke up with a start and fell to the ground with a thud. His eyes popped open, and he wasn't sure where he was.

Maybe hell? Because his head hurt so badly, it felt like someone was stabbing him in the brain with a hot poker. He blinked to clear his vision and saw nothing he recognized. After a moment, he realized that the pointy wooden thing next to his face was the leg of the coffee table, which must mean the furry material under his cheek was the shag carpeting on Bones's living room floor.

The ringing persisted, and Keoni clutched his head as a rocket of pain speared through him.

When he saw the black high-heel shoe in the hall, the memories from the night before came flooding back. He and Bones had gone out. Again.

Keoni worked five nights a week at the cannery, but every night he'd had off had been spent out with Bones. They'd gotten wasted at every bar in Honolulu and been kicked out of more than a few.

In the two weeks that Lou and Penny had been gone, Bones had hooked up with any girl who'd been willing, but Keoni had sworn off women. After what happened with Lou and then Ryla, he needed a break from the fairer sex.

He sat up and hung his head in his hands until the room quit spinning. Waking up on the floor was nothing to be proud of, but it was a hell of a lot better than where he'd woken up a few nights earlier—with his head hanging over the toilet.

The shrill noise started up again, and Keoni realized two things in quick succession. The phone was ringing, and no one was going to answer it.

The room spun as he pushed to his feet and stumbled into the kitchen, where he snatched the phone off the wall.

"What?"

"Hey, Keoni? That you, mate?"

Keoni winced at the level of excitement in Ian's voice. "Yeah," he grunted.

"It's Ian."

"Yeah, I know. Who else says 'mate'?" A quick glance at the stovetop clock told him it was almost 4:00 a.m. "Why you calling so early, man?"

"It's a storm," Ian said. His voice was feverish. "My house is shaking."

Keoni's brain cleared enough for him to realize what Ian, who lived a mile from Waimea Bay, was saying.

"Waimea's heavy?" He asked the question just to be clear, but he already knew the answer.

"Yeah, second time this month. It's a fucking miracle."

"I'm coming," said Keoni.

"Hurry up."

Keoni replaced the phone on the wall and then picked it up again. He slapped the wall, turning on the light in the kitchen. The bright light momentarily blinded him, but he was able to stumble over to the fridge and grab the piece of paper that was pinned to the side with a hula girl magnet.

A dozen names and numbers were written on the paper, and Keoni took a moment to find the one he wanted. He dialed the number, and after a dozen rings, Rabbit picked up.

"What the fuck?" Rabbit growled.

Keoni didn't bother with greetings. "Waimea's heavy."

"Yeah?"

Keoni could practically hear the hard-on in Rabbit's voice. Big waves struck Waimea Bay once or twice a season, but never this close together.

Keoni hung up the phone, trusting Rabbit to call the next person on the list. That's how the hotline worked. One surfer called the next. By sunrise, they would all be lined up at Waimea Bay with their boards.

Keoni went to the bathroom and scoured the medicine cabinet for a bottle of aspirin. He tossed aside spare toothbrushes and shaving cream cans until he found what he wanted.

"Eh, what's the matter you?" Bones called from the door of his bedroom.

Keoni looked up and saw Bones's big body filling the door-frame. He wore a pair of boxers, and his hair was wild, curling almost to his shoulders.

"I'm going to Waimea," Keoni said. "You wanna come?"

Bones was instantly alert. A grin spread across his face. "Hell yeah."

Keoni started ransacking the medicine cabinet, throwing bottles into the sink and onto the counter.

"What you looking for?"

"Something to make my head stop spinning," Keoni said.

Bones shoved him out of the way. "Here." He grabbed a bottle of aspirin and popped it open, spilling a few of the white pills into his Keoni's hand.

"What's going on?" came a woman's voice from the hall.

Keoni cringed at the sound of her voice. The memories of the night before came flooding back. He and Bones had gone to Legends last night. It was a bar in downtown Honolulu where mostly locals hung out. They had run into a few girls they'd known in high school, then they'd all come back to Bones's house to drink more. Keoni was already wasted when they'd switched from beers to shots of liquor.

"Go back to bed," Bones told the girl.

"Only if you're coming back with me." She sashayed into the hall and linked her arm with Bones's. "Hey, Keoni."

Keoni swallowed a few of the aspirin and met her eyes in the mirror before looking away. "Heh, Lelani," he said.

Lelani's eyes roamed over Keoni's naked chest and then flashed back up to meet his gaze. The sleepy look was gone, replaced by something predatory. "You can come, too," she said, giving Keoni a sexy smile.

"Don't make A," Bones told Lelani. Grasping her shoulders, he spun her back toward the bedroom. "Go back to bed unless you want to come to Waimea."

Lelani yawned, stretching her arms over her head. She was wearing one of Bones's T-shirts, and it rose up to mid-thigh as she stretched. She gave him a meaningful look over her shoulder. "I'll be in bed."

Keoni pinched the bridge of his nose between his thumb and index finger. "I need to wake up."

Bones went down the hall into the kitchen. "I've got instant coffee."

"It'll do."

Keoni splashed water on his face, and brushed his teeth with one of the new toothbrushes in the cabinet. He ran a hand over his beard and finger combed his hair.

He looked like shit, but at least his face had healed. The bruise under his eye was only a faint yellow memory, and the split in his lip was history.

Lou wouldn't think he was majestic now with his bloodshot eyes and sallow skin.

He pushed the thought of Lou from his mind, vowing to never think of her again. Fat chance that was when he couldn't go more than a few hours without his mind conjuring her up. She even haunted his dreams.

He shuffled down the hall to the kitchen and sank onto the stool at the counter. Bones looked as bad as Keoni felt. It didn't work any better to bury your sorrows in the body of another woman than it did to drown them in a bottle.

"What the hell are we gonna do, cuz?" Keoni asked, burying his head in his hands.

Bones turned his back on Keoni and scooped coffee into cups. "We're going to have coffee and surf Waimea Bay."

The forced cheer in Bones's voice grated on Keoni's last nerve. The prospect of big waves at Waimea should have had Keoni jumping out of his skin with excitement, but he felt nothing. He'd been dead inside since Lou left. He didn't even know if he could muster the energy to drive up to the North Shore.

His whole life had revolved around surfing and making a name for himself on the waves. Normally, he wouldn't have even waited for the water to boil for coffee before racing off to Waimea Bay, but today he could barely slide off the stool.

If only Keoni hadn't gone to the airport that day to get Lou, none of this would have ever happened. He tried to blame Henry, but he knew it wasn't his friend's fault any more than it had been his fault when Bones had gone missing on the dive.

There was nothing Keoni could do about losing Lou. She was gone, and he'd have to live with it. He wished he could have found that spark with a local girl, but none of them had ever seemed right.

And now he had Ryla to avoid. He'd messed everything up pretty good.

"Shit," Keoni said, banging his fist on the counter. He suddenly didn't care to wait for coffee. He wanted to plunge himself off one of those waves at Waimea.

"Calm down, brother."

"I'm outta here." Keoni jumped up from the stool.

"Where you going?"

"I dunno." Keoni grabbed his shoes and shirt from the floor.

"I never saw you like this before." Bones stared at Keoni while he pulled on his shirt and wrestled on his shoes. "You really love her, eh?"

Keoni sank to the sofa, giving up on his shoe for the moment. "Yeah. I do."

Bones sat down on the chair across from Keoni and leaned his elbows on his knees. "Maybe you didn't try hard enough."

Keoni glared at Bones. "You're the one already making time with another girl."

In a flash Bones was up from his chair. He grabbed Keoni by the neck of his shirt and yanked him off his feet. Keoni and Bones hadn't fought since they were teenagers, back when they were matched in size. Since Bones had shot up six inches and gained fifty pounds, they hadn't laid hands on each other. It wouldn't have been a fair fight.

Bones's face turned a deep shade of purple, and a vein throbbed in his neck. Keoni steeled himself to fight his cousin, knowing he would be lucky to get in a single punch. Bones was going to crush him, but part of Keoni craved the pain. Physical pain would be better than what was going on inside his body.

Bones dropped Keoni back to the ground as quickly as he'd jerked him up. He stalked across the room, stopping at the window with his fists clenched at his sides.

"It was never gonna work with Penny and me," Bones said. "Pops woulda killed me if I brought home a *haole* girl like her."

Bones came from an old Hawaiian family that placed value on their culture above all else. Bones's mother, Keoni's aunt, could trace her lineage back to Kamehameha, but his father could go one step further. Uncle K. was a descendant of the first wave of Tahitians to settle on the island.

Growing up in the Keaukalani household meant you respected Hawaiian culture. Bones could dance the hula, speak fluent Hawaiian, and recite lessons from the old gods and goddesses.

Most Hawaiians, like Keoni who was part Portuguese on his father's side, were *hapa*—mixed with another race. Bones was as pure Hawaiian as it got, and his family meant to keep it that way.

Penny, or any other *haole,* would never be welcome at their dinner table. One of Bones's cousins on his father's side had been disowned for marrying a Japanese girl. The family moved on as if the kid never existed.

Keoni's family wasn't like that. They would love Lou if they got to know her. She would charm them just as she'd charmed Keoni. They would fall in love with her, same as him.

Keoni eyed Bones in the kitchen. His cousin was standing at the sink clutching the counter with white knuckles. Penny had meant more to Bones than he'd ever admit, otherwise he wouldn't be trying so hard to erase her from his mind by nailing everything in a skirt.

Keoni went to stand beside Bones at the counter. "We are a couple of fuck ups, yeah?"

Bones cut his eyes at Keoni. "You more than me."

Shame broke over him like a crashing wave. He hunched his shoulders, cheeks burning. "What do you mean?"

"You blew it with her."

Keoni's shoulders sagged with relief. For a second, he thought Bones knew about Ryla. "I know," he said. "I messed up bad."

Bones spooned instant coffee into the mugs. "What did you do?" He raised an eyebrow at Keoni. "Other than let her get on a plane?"

Keoni cringed. "I messed around with somebody, and I feel like an asshole."

Bones narrowed his eyes at Keoni. "What the hell did you do?"

Keoni's mouth went dry thinking about that night with Ryla. He was dying to get it off his chest, maybe the guilt would lessen.

"The night you went missing, I drank too much swipe and hooked up with..." He couldn't finish. He shook his head and raked a hand through his hair.

"Who? Not Kaliah?"

Bones looked ready to snap Keoni in two if he'd messed with his sister.

"Nah, man. Not Kaliah." He clenched his jaw. Ryla was just as bad as Kaliah. Keoni thought of both girls like sisters.

"Who then?"

Keoni pulled in a deep breath and sighed. "Ryla."

"Jesus. Ryla is like a sister. She's just a kid."

Keoni shook his head, trying to banish the image of Ryla's wet mouth wrapped around him. "I was drunk."

"Too drunk to fuck?"

"We didn't... Never mind. It doesn't matter. I can't believe it happened."

Bones raised both eyebrows. "Ryla's a cool chick, but she's like fifteen, isn't she?"

"Nah, man." Keoni grimaced. "She's way older than that. Same age as Kimo." Keoni remembered Ryla as a ten-year-old, tagging along on bike rides to the beach. She and Kimo had been best friends, and Ryla had eaten more meals at his family's table than anyone else Keoni could remember. He scrubbed a hand over his face. He'd never get over the guilt.

"Does anyone else know?" Bones asked.

"I don't think so." He was pretty sure he'd gotten out of the bedroom without anyone seeing him, but that didn't mean Ryla hadn't told anyone. "I can't ever look at her again."

"Was it that bad?"

Keoni winced. "Yeah."

Bones laughed. "Bummer, man."

Regret flared in his chest. "Yeah."

"You know what you gotta do?"

"I already asked her to stay, and she shot me down. She has this whole plan for her life. I don't fit into it."

Bones shrugged and stepped around Keoni to get to the sink. "So make her fit into yours." He said it as if it were the easiest thing in the world. As if Keoni was an idiot for not having thought of it himself. "Lou could be happy here. You could be happy with her. Your parents are always telling you to settle down. Why not with a girl like Lou?"

Regret flared in his chest. "It's too late."

Bones poured hot water into the mugs and stirred. "Only if you give up."

The words seemed wise beyond Bones's capabilities. What if he'd given up too easily? What if his past was keeping him from his future?

Keoni's stomach clenched when he thought about the giant mistake he'd made with his little brother's best friend. "What about Ryla?"

"That girl has been mooning over you forever, man. Remember when she used to follow us around like a little puppy? It wasn't me she was always staring at."

Keoni barely remembered Ryla as a kid. He'd never paid much attention to her other than when they were singing together.

Bones made a zipping motion across his lips. "Don't speak a word of it to anyone." He smirked. "Ryla probably realized pretty quick you weren't all she thought you'd be."

"Fuck off." Keoni took a long sip from the mug Bones handed him. The strong coffee zigzagged straight to his aching head. His thoughts churned as he tried to sort out everything Bones had said. One thing stood out the most. Keoni might not fit into Lou's plan for her life in Seattle, but she could fit into his life here.

He suddenly knew what he needed to do. Gulping down another sip of hot coffee, he marched into the living room and found his keys.

"You going to Waimea without me?" Bones nodded his chin at Keoni's keys.

"Nah." For the first time in his life, Keoni didn't care about surfing. He didn't care about anything but reuniting the woman he loved. "I'm going to the airport."

"What the fuck, brah? That's loco."

Keoni's mouth thinned into a disapproving line. "You just told me to do it."

"Not when Waimea is heavy. It might not happen again for another year."

Skipping the big waves at Waimea Bay was a sacrifice Keoni was willing to make.

"I gotta go," he said, reaching for the door.

"Wait." Bones hurried from the room. When he came back, he handed Keoni an envelope. "Take this."

Keoni opened the envelope and saw it was full of cash. "What's this for?"

"I made a shitload a dough offa that dive."

Keoni's eyes widened as he counted the bills. "I can't take this."

Bones snorted. "How else you gonna pay for a flight to Seattle? You got a money tree I don't know about?"

Keoni shoved the envelope back at Bones. "Don't worry about it, brah. It's not your problem."

Bones crossed his huge arms across his chest, making his biceps bulge. "Just take it. You can pay me back on the next dive."

Keoni had some money saved up, but a plane ticket to the mainland would pretty much wipe him out. He swallowed roughly and tucked the envelope in his pocket. "Thanks, eh?"

"Anytime, man." Bones grabbed Keoni by the shoulders and pulled him close. They touched foreheads and noses, sharing the same breath in the ancient Hawaiian tradition of *honi* that pre-dated handshakes. "You're my brother," Bones said hoarsely.

Keoni clapped a hand on Bones's shoulder. "I know."

Bones released Keoni and headed back down the hall. "Take a shower," he said over his shoulder. "You look like shit."

FIFTY DOLLARS FOR THE PAIR

SEATTLE, WASHINGTON
A Tuesday in February

LOU LEFT THE BANK BY THE BACK DOOR AT LUNCH, HOPING TO
avoid Paul. She didn't have time to deal with him today. Her
photographs were ready at Pacific Camera, and she barely had
enough time to get across town, pick them up, and get back to
work.

She didn't have time for lunch, much less time to deal with
Paul.

He'd changed in the two weeks since Lou had been back home.
He was making a real effort to show Lou he was devoted to her.
They'd gone to dinner twice, he'd called every day, and had taken
to surprising her on her lunch hour to see if she was free for a bite.

Lou knew he was trying, but the effort felt forced. Her heart
sped up as she spotted a Ford that looked like Paul's parked a few
cars down from Bertha on the street. When she saw it was a
different model, her shoulders relaxed.

She climbed behind the wheel of her car and took off toward

the camera store. The pictures she'd taken in Hawaii were ready, and she couldn't wait to see them. She'd spent all night lying awake in anticipation of seeing them. She wanted to see all the pictures of Hawaii, but most of all the ones of Keoni.

Even though she'd committed his face to memory, she didn't trust herself to get everything right. Seeing Keoni again was going to rip her heart out, but Lou was looking forward to the pain. She wanted to see his face again no matter what the cost.

Mr. Tollison greeted Lou with a warm hug, and then dragged her over to the inspirational wall of photos.

"I told you the black and white would be perfect." He pointed to a place on the wall.

Next to a black-and-white photograph of Mt. Ranier capped in snow hung the stark image of Diamond Head Crater in a silver frame.

Lou's mouth dropped open and she clutched Mr. Tollison's hand. She remembered the moment she'd taken the photograph on her last day in Hawaii.

Keoni had never finished that story about how Diamond Head got its name. Lou's cheeks turned pink remembering how Keoni had kissed her under the shadow of the crater.

Tears sprang to her eyes. "I made the wall."

The older man laughed and patted Lou on the back. "You made the wall, dear," he said.

She had to tell John! She had to tell Keoni!

Her heart sank as she realized neither one of those options was possible. She could tell Paul, but he wouldn't understand how much this meant to her. Paul thought of her photography as nothing more than an expensive hobby.

Mr. Tollison walked behind the counter. "I'm going to pay you for that photograph," he said.

He pulled out two envelopes and slid them across the counter. One envelope was large and thin, the other was small and flat.

He nodded at the thinner envelope. "I want to buy that one, too."

Lou slid the photograph out of the envelope. Her heart lodged in her throat when she saw it was an action shot of Keoni surfing at Sunset Beach the morning of the Duke contest.

Keoni's body was turned toward the wave. He was leaning so far forward on his board that he was nearly horizontal. It was an impossible position, but Keoni made it look effortless. He had one hand splayed against the base of the wave as if in a caress, and the smile on his face was pure joy.

"It will be the first color photo I've ever bought," Mr. Tollison said.

Lou nodded, too stunned to say anything. The magnitude of Mr. Tollison's words warmed her heart. Keoni was stunning in the photograph. He was exactly as she'd remembered him. She'd thought maybe she'd exaggerated him in her mind, but she hadn't.

In the photograph, Lou had not only managed to capture the vibrant colors of the ocean and Keoni's excellent form, but she'd also conveyed his intimate relationship with the ocean.

Lou studied the picture with a critical eye, hardly believing she had been the photographer. It was perfect.

"I can offer you fifty dollars for the pair for my display wall."

"Fifty...did you say fifty dollars?" Lou's tongue tripped over the words. "Are you serious?"

"It's an investment," he said. "I think you could be famous one day." He tapped a finger to the photograph of Keoni. "You should submit this one to *Outdoor Magazine*. I think they'd buy it for a lot more than fifty dollars."

Lou's mouth dropped open. "You think so?"

He smiled. "I know my stuff. I have a contact there if you're interested in submitting."

A smile split her face from ear to ear. "I'm interested."

Her gaze drifted back to the wall where her photograph hung

for all to see. She wanted to burst out laughing and cry at the same time.

This was the best moment of her life, but the person she wanted to share it with most was hundreds of miles away.

~

LOU WENT BACK TO THE BANK ON A CLOUD OF HAPPINESS. EVEN the rain didn't bother her.

She went in through the employee entrance at the back and headed straight to the bathroom where she planned to lock herself in and look through the rest of the photographs. Miraculously, she still had five minutes on her lunch break.

"Mary Lou?"

Lou stopped and saw Jessica, one of the newest tellers at the bank. Jessica had been hired while Lou was in Hawaii, and Lou had only known her for a few days.

"You can call me Lou. Everyone does."

"Okay." Jessica stepped closer, her face lit with curiosity. "There's a very handsome man waiting for you in the lobby."

Lou's stomach clenched. Paul was here. She clutched her purse with the photographs tight to her side. "Can you tell him I'm coming? I need to go to the bathroom."

"Sure, but I wouldn't keep him waiting too long. The girls are circling him like sharks."

Lou gave Jessica a tight smile. "I'm sure he'll survive." Paul never even noticed when women looked at him. He was one of those beautiful people who was totally unaware of the effect he had on normal humans.

She went in to the bathroom and locked the stall door. There was just enough time to glance through the photographs before she had to get back to her desk. Let Paul wait.

In the bathroom stall, Lou leaned against the door and pulled the envelope out of her purse. She flipped through the photographs, each one spurring a memory as fresh as the Hawaiian breeze.

The first few pictures were from the airport. There was a shot of Keoni in black and white with a lei in his hand. Lou's heart slammed in her chest when she saw the glint of awareness in his eyes. The confident tilt of his head said he'd known her camera was trained on him and he didn't give a shit.

Lou suppressed the surge of emotion the picture elicited and flipped through the photos. There was the crooked tombstones of the graveyard and the Honolulu skyline from on top of the hill.

She flipped to the next photograph, and her heart threatened to pound out of her chest. It was a shot of Keoni standing on the hilltop. Dark sunglasses covered his eyes, and his hand was raised in the shaka sign. His hair was damp, and the white shark's tooth necklace winked against his throat.

That was right before their first kiss.

Tears blurred her vision, and the photograph slipped from her fingers to land on the bathroom floor. A sob caught in her throat as she stared down at the photograph.

At that moment, she realized she could never be happy with Paul. She didn't love him. Not like she loved Keoni. She might never see Keoni again except in photographs, but she would love him forever.

There was no way she could marry Paul. No way she could settle for a mediocre love knowing that spectacular love existed.

Lou picked up the photograph of Keoni and replaced it in the stack with the others. She checked the time and saw she was already late. Her boss was going to let her have it again. But, first, she had to deal with Paul.

She repaired her makeup in the mirror and walked out of the bathroom. It was time to tell Paul they needed to talk.

Knowing that Paul was out there waiting for her made her drag her feet. She didn't want to break his heart, but she couldn't pretend with him anymore. Not after seeing the photos of Keoni.

She walked through the central part of the bank, bypassed the tellers, and into the lobby. A strange sense of calm settled over Lou, and she knew she was doing the right thing. Hawaii had opened her eyes, and now she couldn't shut them.

Her gaze swept over the faces of the customers, and she didn't see Paul. Maybe he had decided not to wait any longer. Lou's shoulders sagged with a strange mix of relief and disappointment. She'd hoped to get this over with, but she didn't mind a few more hours to rehearse her lines.

When she turned to go to her desk, her gaze landed on a man sitting with his back to her. The guitar case and duffel bag at his feet made her take another look. There was no mistaking the broad shoulders or the unruly dark hair.

It was Keoni. He was here.

He saw her and got quickly to his feet. Lou stared at him, her mouth hanging open. He smiled. She smiled back. And then they were moving toward each other as if a magnet was compelling them.

One moment, she was gaping at him from across the room. The next, she was in his arms. She could smell the ocean in his hair. His arms cinched around her, holding her so tightly she couldn't breathe.

"What are you doing here?" Her words were muffled against his chest as she buried her face in his shirt.

Keoni pulled back and smiled down at her. "I never got to finish my story about Diamond Head."

Lou laughed. "You came out here to tell me a story?"

"You wanna hear it?"

The sound of his voice was just as enchanting as she remembered. She could listen to him talk all day. "Yes."

He pulled her closer, rubbing his chin in her hair. "Can we get out of here?"

Lou glanced around and saw that everyone in the lobby was staring at them. They were necking in the middle of the bank. She cleared her throat and tried to think. She'd already taken her lunch break, so she really couldn't leave again.

She took a step back. "I'll be right back," she said.

Lou went to the employee closet in the back and retrieved her coat. She told her boss she was feeling sick and needed the rest of the day off. When he tried to question her, Lou eluded to female problems and ducked out of his office before he could respond.

She walked back into the lobby and grabbed Keoni by the hand. "I'm leaving early."

Keoni picked up his guitar, slung the duffel bag over his shoulder, and followed Lou outside.

SCARS AND EVERYTHING

LOU REMEMBERED HOW SHY KEONI HAD BEEN WHEN HE'D welcomed her into his house, and now she understood exactly how he must have felt. Her apartment was such a personal space. She and Penny had carefully chosen every piece of furniture. The rug was a garage sale find, the sofa was a hand-me-down from one of Penny's friends at the dance studio, and the lamp was left by the last renter. But the quirk was all theirs. Colorful afghans made by Lou's grandmother draped across the back of the sofa, whimsical curtains softened the view of the brick building next door, and Lou's art lined the walls.

Her space might not have been as charming as Keoni's beach bungalow, but it was home. Lou's touches were everywhere. Driftwood she'd picked up on the shore of the lake served as a candle holder. A map of the United States with a red pin in all the cities they'd visited hung on one wall, and her photographs adorned the others. Framed pictures of Penny's numerous cousins lined the bookshelves alongside favorite novels and books of poetry.

Lou closed the door behind Keoni and turned the lock. Penny had lost her key in Hawaii, and Lou had been leaving the door unlocked for her until they replaced it. Penny wasn't due home from teaching class for another hour, but Lou wasn't taking any chances. She wanted to be alone with Keoni, and she didn't think they would make it to the bedroom.

She gave him a moment to set his guitar and bag down before touching him. Slipping her arm around his waist, Lou pressed against Keoni's back. His jacket was cold and damp, and his body was as hard as stone, but underneath the layers, she could feel his warmth. His soul. There was no one else like Keoni. He had a certain energy that drew people to him. Everyone wanted to know Keoni, to be near him, or catch his eye.

When his hand slid over hers and pulled her tighter against him, butterflies took flight in her stomach. She spread her hand under his jacket and felt his breath hitch. The little noise lit a flame inside her. She felt brave and free when she was with Keoni. Not afraid to take what she needed, she pushed the jacket off his shoulders.

He let the jacket drop to the floor and turned to face her. His brown eyes blazed with the same fire Lou felt scorching through her veins. She shed her coat, letting it fall next to Keoni's.

Keoni's gaze dropped over her, and Lou didn't have to wonder if he liked what he saw. His eyes darkened, and he reached for her. The distance between them disappeared as he lowered his mouth to hers. His kiss was soft at first, barely a whisper of his mouth across hers.

"I want you." His lips teased a path from her mouth to her jaw. He pulled her closer, anchoring her against his hard body. Lou felt exactly how much he wanted her. His hands kneaded the soft flesh of her bottom, molding their bodies together.

He trailed a hot path of kisses to her ear. "I've been lost without you." His breath was ragged. "So lost."

Lou cupped his face in her hands and dragged his mouth back to hers. "I've missed you." She spoke the words right against his mouth, not willing to break any contact with him.

"I want to make you mine." The words hummed against her lips in between kisses.

"You already have." Her fingers flew down his shirt, undoing the buttons.

"All the way mine. I want to show you everything." He shrugged out of his shirt and reached for the buttons of her blouse.

"I want to see everything." She toed off her high heels. "Scars." She kissed the healed scab on his bottom lip. "And everything."

Keoni pressed his forehead against hers, and she melted into him. Their noses touched, and then their mouths. They breathed as one. A long inhale and exhale of filling and emptying. Lou let go of her doubts. She breathed in Keoni's strength.

She lifted her gaze to his, and time stalled as their eyes locked. Lou felt a shift inside her so deep, it cut to the bone.

They kissed again, this time with an urgency that lit a fire in Lou's soul. The velvet warmth of his tongue filled her mouth to tease and stroke. His taste flooded her mouth as he kissed her in that expert way of kissing only Keoni knew. It was the kind of kissing that felt more like making love. The kind of kissing Lou couldn't live without.

Any trace of shyness she'd once felt vanished as his guttural groan vibrated against her chest. Encouraged by the expression of his pleasure, Lou grew even bolder. She knew what she wanted.

Keoni. Naked. Inside her. Now.

Without breaking the kiss, she walked Keoni backwards into the living room. When the backs of his legs hit the sofa, Lou placed a hand on the immovable wall of Keoni's chest and gave him a decent shove.

He sat with a muffled grunt of surprise. A grin took over his mouth as he looked up at her.

"What?" She raised an eyebrow as she hiked her skirt and wiggled out of her stockings and panties.

Keoni's eyes followed her movements as she tossed the under-garments to the floor. "You really did miss me, eh?"

Lou placed a hand on his chest and pushed him back against the cushions. "Let me show you how much." She bunched up her skirt and straddled his hips.

When she unzipped his fly, he lifted his hips so that she could ease his pants down and wrap her fist around his swollen flesh. He groaned as her fist tightened around him. When he threw back his head in pleasure, Lou feasted on the strong column of his throat.

"I can't imagine living without you," she said against his hot skin. The taste of him shot a bolt of lust straight to her core. He smelled so good and tasted even better.

She worked her hand between them, stroking him until he was like steel in her fist. Lou had never been so bold in her life as she was with Keoni. With him, she knew what she wanted and she took it. He gave willingly, lifting his hips off the cushions to give her better access.

He palmed her mound, then plunged a finger deep inside her. When he flicked her clit with his thumb, Lou gasped and ground against him.

"I need you now," she said, moving his hand away and fumbling to line his hard shaft up at her entrance.

"Wait." Keoni shifted and reached for his pants. He pulled his wallet out, flipped it open, grabbed a condom, and tossed the wallet aside. When he was covered up, he reached for her. "Come here."

The gravel in his voice turned her on even more than the sight of his hand fisted around his hard cock. She straddled him. Bracing her hands on his shoulders, she lowered herself onto him. As he filled her, Lou saw the edge of heaven. Lust zigzagged straight to her core as she sank onto him. She looked down at the sight of their bodies joined and shuddered.

Keoni thrust up to meet her, and her entire body throbbed with pleasure. He shoved the lacy cups of her bra down, and filled his hands with her soft flesh.

Her senses were so heightened that the brush of his calloused fingers against her heated skin made every muscle in her body clench.

Within moments, she felt herself losing control. She'd thought she was in charge, but maybe Keoni had been the one with control the whole time. One lick of his tongue against her nipple, and she was lost in a fog of desire so thick she had no idea what was happening.

She surrendered to the sensations as they rolled over her body. Wave after wave of pleasure consumed her as Keoni thrust into her with barely-restrained patience. His pace increased as Lou gave over to wild abandon.

"You're so sexy." He trailed wet kisses over her breasts and up her throat, finally capturing her mouth with his.

They kissed long and deep, their tongues tangling as their bodies slid together. She braced her hands on his shoulders, and felt his muscles bunch under her touch.

Keoni's fingers gripped her hard enough to leave bruises, and Lou was glad. She wanted him to leave his mark. She wanted to see the prints of his big hands spanning her hips tomorrow.

She could feel he was close. She was closer. She kissed him desperately, claiming his mouth as the first waves of the orgasm washed over her. A long moan escaped her mouth, and Keoni's tongue lapped it up. Her whole body seized, and then Keoni thrust into her, spilling his own release.

Lou's world turned upside down as she clung to Keoni. She held on tight, just like she'd done when he rescued her from the rogue wave at Makaha.

He gathered her against him, and their hearts beat as one. Lou wasn't sure how long they stayed like that. She felt like she had no bones left in her body, no blood in her veins. She was completely weightless, in love, and satisfied to stay connected to Keoni forever.

"I need the bathroom," Keoni said.

Lou groaned and buried her face in his neck. "I can't move."

Keoni chuckled and patted her bottom, shifting so that he eased out of her. He pushed to his feet and wandered down the hall.

"This the way?" he asked.

Lou cracked open her eye and watched his naked back. Smiling, she realized she hadn't even given him the nickel tour before pouncing on him.

"On your left." She flopped onto her back and contemplated the ceiling as if it had all the solutions to her problems. There were a lot of questions, and not a lot of answers. The only thing Lou knew for certain was that she loved Keoni.

"Lou?"

She stiffened. The sound of Keoni's voice told her something was wrong. She sat up and looked at him. He stood next to the front door where he'd dropped his belongings. He'd zipped his pants, but left them unbuttoned, and his chest was bare. The sight of his naked body made her ache for him all over again.

"What's wrong?"

"I brought you a gift." He bent to unlatch his guitar case. "I was hoping to make you fall in love with me."

"It's too late." Her heart raced as she boldly met his gaze. "I already love you."

A grin stretched his mouth and he dropped the case. He jogged over to the sofa and grabbed her hands, pulling her to her feet.

Lou laughed as he lifted her into his arms. "Does that mean I don't get my gift?"

Keoni's smile was like a beam of sunshine on a cloudy day. "It means I'm the happiest man in the world."

Lou's heart hammered, and her throat went dry. "Does that mean you love me too?"

Keoni crushed his mouth to hers. "I love you," he said between kisses. Eventually he set her down on her feet. "And you still get your gift."

Lou reached up and kissed the hollow of his throat. "You already gave it to me."

Keoni took Lou by the shoulders and looked down at her, his brown eyes soft. "That was my body," he said. "This is my soul."

The trembling in Lou's heart became a minor explosion as Keoni went to get his guitar.

PROMISES

ADJUSTING THE STRINGS ON HIS GUITAR, KEONI STRUMMED SOFTLY. His heart lodged in his throat as he looked up at Lou. The song he'd written for her somehow had come together so quickly, he didn't trust it was good. Although he could sing and play well, he wasn't much of a writer.

Lou was a beautiful distraction. She'd pulled on his shirt, and sat with her legs tucked under her on the other end of the sofa. Knowing that she was bare under the soft fabric of his favorite shirt made it hard to focus.

He strummed softly, still tingling all over from knowing she loved him. This song was no longer necessary, but he'd worked hard on it and wanted to give it to her anyway.

He smiled, feeling outrageously in love with the woman sitting so close by. He could hardly believe that he was here with her. His gaze swept across her living room, resting briefly on the items that made it her home.

Lou followed his gaze around the room. "My place isn't as nice as yours, but..." Her voice trailed off and she shrugged in a very Hawaiian gesture.

Keoni's smile grew. Bones had been right about Lou—she

would fit right in at home in Hawaii. He strummed the guitar, coaxing a sound out of the instrument that he hoped would touch Lou's heart. He sang the first few words and stopped when he saw Lou was crying.

"My voice isn't that bad, is it?"

She shook her head, and another tear leaked out. "I missed you so much." She sniffed, smiling even as she cried.

Keoni put the guitar down and reached for her. His heart was overflowing with everything he felt for her, including the guilt of what he'd done with Ryla.

He was dying to ask Lou to marry him, but he knew it was too soon. He would settle for her coming back with him to Hawaii. Hell, he would settle for anything she wanted to give.

Guilt stabbed his belly, and he knew he had to confess everything. Bones had told him not to say a word about Ryla, but Keoni didn't like secrets. He didn't like games.

His tongue tripped over all the words he wanted to say. The pounding of his heart made it impossible to hear his own thoughts. He took both Lou's hands in his and held them tightly, gazing down at their joined fingers.

He opened his mouth and started talking before he knew exactly what he wanted to say.

"I've been a wreck since you've been gone."

Lou nodded. Her pained expression told him she'd felt the same way.

"I was drunk for two weeks straight. And I did some stuff I'm not proud of."

Lou's eyebrows pinched together. "What kind of stuff?"

Keoni closed his eyes and drew in a deep breath. It was his last chance to keep him mouth shut, but he knew he wouldn't take it. Lou needed to know everything.

"The night Bones went missing, I…"

Lou interrupted him with a bruising kiss. She framed his face in her hands kissed him breathless. "I'm so sorry I left you that night." Smoothing his hair away from his forehead, she stared deeply into his eyes. "I should have been there for you."

Keoni's chest ached. "It's okay."

"It's not okay. It keeps me up at night, thinking of what you must have gone through waiting for news about Bones."

Keoni squeezed his eyes tightly shut. "Lou, try listen."

"Okay." She planted another kiss on his mouth. "Just tell me you forgive me. Tell me it's forgotten."

His eyes snapped open. "Of course," he said without pause. The thickness in his throat made it hard to talk. So did Lou's nearness. Her scent was driving him crazy. He wanted to bury his face in her neck and breathe her in. But, first, he had to come clean.

He dragged in a breath. "That night," he started again. "I was a little out of my mind." He hung his head. "It's no excuse, I know. I was crazy from saying goodbye to you, and a little nuts over Bones." He felt Lou stiffen, and he wished he didn't have to tell her. "I was drunk."

"What happened?" Her voice was a soft whisper.

Shame and anger warred in his chest. He hated himself, and he hated Ryla too. Hurting Lou was the last thing he wanted to do, but he knew if he didn't tell her the truth about what had happened, it would hang between them forever.

"I was with another woman."

The words fell between them with a thud. Lou dropped her hands and scooted to the edge of the sofa. Her eyes went wide, and all the color drained from her face.

"I'm so sorry." He longed to pull her into his arms, but he forced himself not to reach for her. "I can't take it back. I can only ask you to try to understand, and to forgive me."

Lou's expression underwent several changes. He watched as shock, sadness, and then outrage twisted her features.

Keoni shifted closer, and Lou flinched away from him. He sighed and clasped his hands in his lap.

"Say something. Please. Tell me to fuck off, or that you hate me. Say anything." The words tore from his mouth. He'd never felt more raw or desperate.

Lou blinked rapidly, swallowing her tears. When her eyes met his, a spark of hope ignited in his belly. She still looked mad as hell, but she also looked resigned. He prayed that meant she could forgive him.

"Lou?" He reached for her hand, and she let him take it.

A knock on the door sounded, and Lou's eyes shot to the clock on the wall.

"That's Penny." She stood and tugged his shirt over her thighs. "She lost her key."

Keoni stood and buttoned his pants. It was the best he could do since Lou was wearing his shirt.

Lou's eyes drifted over him. "Go wait in my bedroom," she said as the knock sounded again.

"Kay, then." He started down the hall. "But we have to finish this, yeah?"

Lou nodded and pointed him down the hall. "Second door on your right."

Keoni went to her room and sat down on her bed to wait, his heart lodged in his throat. If they hadn't been interrupted, what would Lou have said?

He swept his gaze around her room. The colors were vibrant—bright blue bedspread, purple paint on the walls, and dozens of photographs—but the view was awful. All he could see out the single window was the brick facade of the building next door. The view from his place was much nicer, but without Lou in his life, the ocean may as well have been a brick wall.

What the hell was taking so long?

Lou should have been back by now. Keoni's ears pricked up when he heard raised voices in the living room. He stood, walked to the door, and cracked it open.

"You're not making any sense," said a man's voice. "We've been planning this for two years."

"I know," Lou said. The rest of her words were too quiet to understand.

One thing was for sure, the person on the other side of the door hadn't been Penny. Keoni had a pretty good idea who it was. He opened the door and walked down the hall.

When he saw the tall man dressed in a suit and hat, he felt a crushing weight settle on his shoulders. He knew instinctively that the man was Paul.

"We're getting married." Paul put his hands on Lou's shoulders and bent down slightly to look into her eyes.

The sight of Paul touching Lou shattered Keoni's restraint. In two long strides, he crossed the room.

"Take your hands off her." Keoni's voice was a barely audible growl.

Paul's gaze snapped to Keoni. He looked him over with a smug smile and then turned back to Lou. "Is this him?" he asked. "The guy you told me about?"

Keoni stepped closer. His heart swelled with the knowledge that Paul knew about him. Keoni couldn't help thinking that was a good sign.

"You're gonna want to let her go, man."

The tension in the room increased another notch as Paul dropped his hands and turned to face Keoni.

"Lou told me about how she'd fallen under the spell of Hawaii and made a mistake," Paul said. "I guess you're that mistake."

"It wasn't a mistake," Lou said.

"Your little vacation fling." Paul sneered at Keoni.

"Vacation fling?" Keoni asked, raising his eyebrows at Lou.

"Lou told me everything. That's what people who love each other do. They forgive each other." Paul looked at Lou for confirmation. "Right, babe?"

Lou didn't answer. Her eyes were stuck on Keoni. His were stuck right back.

"I should be thanking you." Paul stepped closer and extended his hand to Keoni.

Keoni tore his eyes away from Lou and glared at Paul's hand. "Thanking me for what?" He cleared his throat, not at all sure what Paul was getting at, and not liking it one bit.

"You saved Lou's life," Paul said. "And because ever since Lou's been back from her vacation, our future has been even clearer." Paul took another step, inserting himself between Keoni and Lou. "She deserves security and a solid future. Can you give her that?"

"I can give her what she wants." Keoni locked eyes with Lou.

Paul laughed. "Lou doesn't want a surfer."

"I can speak for myself," Lou said.

"Kay then." Keoni crossed his arms over his chest, waiting to hear what she would say.

Paul buttoned his suit jacket. "Tell him, Lou. Tell him you don't want a high school drop-out as your husband and the father of your children."

Keoni's eyebrows shot up, and his eyes narrowed at Lou. Dropping out of high school wasn't something Keoni was proud of. "You told him that?" he asked.

"She told me everything, pal."

"Lou?" Keoni asked.

"You should go." Paul dismissed Keoni with a glance. "You don't belong here."

Keoni's eyes flashed at Lou. She still hadn't said anything. Her face was white as a sheet, and her jaw was tight. He wanted to pull her into his arms. "What do you want, Lou?"

Paul answered for her. "She wants a good life. A comfortable and secure life. She doesn't want to worry about her husband getting himself killed in the ocean. Can you give her that?"

Keoni's mind flashed to Sunset Beach on the day he'd pulled Eddie's body out of the ocean. He remembered every detail of what had happened, including calling Eddie's girlfriend to tell her Eddie was dead.

Would someone be calling Lou like that one day?

Keoni thought about standing up at Eddie's funeral and talking about what kind of man he was. A friend. A brother. A son. A role model.

What would they say about Keoni when he was dead?

"Keoni." Lou stepped forward and grabbed his shoulders. "Don't do this. Don't go away."

But it was too late. He was already gone. He'd been a fool to think he could give Lou or any woman a happy life. Whoever he married would always be watching the clock waiting for him to come home, wondering if he was okay.

Lou dropped Keoni's shoulders and rounded on Paul. "I'm tired of you talking for me all the time. You tell me how to wear my hair, what drink to order, what car to drive" Lou marched to the door and held it open wide. "Get out!"

Paul put up an argument but eventually left, saying he would call her later.

"I'm changing my number!" Lou yelled at him before slamming the door.

Keoni couldn't get the image of Eddie's girlfriend at the funeral out of his mind. Linda had been in so much shock that she hadn't even cried. She'd spent the entire ceremony staring off at nothing.

"Every time I go out in the water, I could get killed."

Lou flinched and wouldn't meet his eyes.

"I can live with that," he said. "Can you?"

Lou hesitated, and it was long enough for Keoni to have his answer.

"Yes," she said. She clutched his shoulders when he tried to pull away. "Yes. I can live with that."

But Keoni loved Lou too much to ask her to do that. The life she'd planned with Paul was worlds better than anything he could give her on his salary at the cannery, and a cloud of worry would surround them always.

Then there was Ryla. Lou still hadn't said whether she forgave him or not. It suddenly didn't matter. Keoni knew what he had to do. He took a step back.

Lou's face darkened. "I can't compete with a dead man, Keoni," she said. "You have to let Eddie go before you can let anyone else in."

"I'll never let Eddie go." Anger flashed at the very idea. "If you think that, then you don't know me at all."

"I don't mean you have to forget him," Lou said. "I only mean you have to forgive yourself." Lou clenched her fists at her sides. "We can't keep having this conversation, Keoni. You can't keep holding on to your guilt like it's a precious memento."

"I'm not."

"You're choosing pain over love."

"Nah." He shook his head. "I'm being smart." For once. "I can't let you give up your planned-out life for the unknown with me. I could die tomorrow."

"It isn't your choice to make." Lou crossed her arms and glared at him. "It's mine."

"You deserve better than worrying about me every day."

A blush crept up from Lou's neck to stain her cheeks. She stared hard at Keoni. "You know what I *deserve*?" she asked. She didn't give him a chance to answer before plowing ahead. "I deserve to make my own decisions."

Nausea filled his stomach. "What do you want, eh?"

Her shoulders hunched and she hung her head. Keoni's heart hammered in his chest while he waited for her answer. He was dying to fold her into his arms, to beg for her forgiveness and plead that she come home with him, but he held back. She needed to say the words out loud so that everything was clear, or else they didn't stand a chance.

After a long pause when she didn't say a word, Keoni had his answer. Whatever she felt for him wasn't enough. He went into the living room to grab his stuff, then realized he wasn't wearing a shirt.

He swallowed hard and held out his hand. "Can I have my shirt?"

Lou's eyes shot fire at him as she tore open the buttons, ripped the shirt off, and flung it at him. She glared harder at him as he stuffed his arms into the shirt.

Regret hung between them as thick as the mud at Manoa Falls, but there weren't any more words to say. He grabbed his bag and his guitar, and then, he was gone.

A FRESH START

Lou trudged up the four flights of stairs, cursing the fact that her building didn't have an elevator. She was tired. Every step felt like climbing a mountain. She had been feeling a little better that morning. She'd woken up earlier than usual, showered, and gotten dressed in normal clothes, and she hadn't even thought about Keoni until she was brushing her teeth. It was an improvement from dreaming of him and waking up with him already saturating her thoughts.

Lou had been feeling pretty proud of herself for getting outside and walking to the market. She'd bought fruit, and milk, and a loaf of fresh crusty bread. She hadn't been hungry in days, but the bread had smelled delicious and she was actually looking forward to eating it.

She finally made it to her door and heard the phone ringing as she fit the key in the lock. Her heart raced at the thought that maybe it was Keoni. Maybe he'd finally called.

She ran inside and grabbed the phone off the wall before it stopped ringing.

"Hello?" She was breathless from the stairs and sprinting into the kitchen.

"May I speak with Lou Hunter?" asked a woman's voice.

Lou's heart sank, and the hope that had been flapping its wings crash landed. "This is Lou."

There was a long pause on the other end, and then the woman spoke again. "This is Lou Hunter, the photographer?"

Lou froze, and the grocery bag she'd been holding slipped to the floor. She nodded and then realized that the woman on the other end of the line couldn't see her. She cleared her throat.

"Yes. This is Lou Hunter, the photographer."

It was the first time the words had come out of her mouth, and the smile that accompanied them warmed her broken heart.

"You're not a man?" the woman asked.

"No." Some of the pleasure faded. "Are you?"

"Of course not," said the woman. "Hold one moment, please."

The line went silent. Lou cradled the receiver between her ear and her shoulder and bent down to retrieve her dropped groceries, hoping nothing had been ruined.

A moment later, a man's voice came over the line. "Hello? Is this is Lou Hunter, the photographer?"

Lou pushed down her annoyance. "I thought we established that already."

"Just making sure."

"How can I help you?"

"This is Terry Orlandi calling from Los Angeles. I'm an editor at *Surfing Magazine*. I'm calling about your submission."

"My what?"

"This is Lou Hunter, the photographer, right?"

"Is this some kind of prank?" Lou asked, bewildered. "I didn't submit anything to you."

"Oh?" Mr. Orlandi said, clearly caught off guard. "Well, it must be a mistake. My apologies."

"Wait. Don't hang up." She hadn't submitted one of her pictures, but perhaps someone else had. "What do you want with the picture?"

"To buy it."

Lou's knees went weak, and she leaned against the counter for support. She tried to speak, but words didn't come out. She must have made some sort of noise because Mr. Orlandi spoke up again.

"Listen, lady," he said. "I've got a lot of stuff to do today, so tell me, is this your picture, or not?"

Lou cleared her throat. "Yes."

"Okay. Good. I want to buy your picture and print it in my magazine," he said, enunciating slowly and carefully as if Lou was a small child. "Do you want to sell it?"

Lou wet her lips. Her throat was dry, but her hands were damp with sweat. She gripped the phone tightly. "Yes."

"Good," he sighed. "What's your address?"

Lou recited her address automatically.

"You should get something from me in the next week. Sign the consent form, and I will get a check to you as soon as possible."

"Okay." Lou had a million questions, but she was too excited to ask any of them.

"We want to do an interview with the man in the picture. Can you give me his name?"

"The man in the picture?" Lou asked.

"Yes. The man in the picture." The man sighed so loudly, Lou could practically see his eyes rolling.

"Can you describe the man?" Lou had taken a lot of pictures in Hawaii, she didn't want to assume the man was Keoni, even though she had a pretty good idea it was him.

"He's tall and dark-haired. Looks like something out a Hawaiian history book." He paused. "The surfboard is a Dick

Brewer model, *The Himalaya.* He only made about a dozen of those in '63."

"That's Keoni." She felt a stab of pain in her heart as she said his name. "Keoni Makai."

"Do you know how I can get in touch him?"

"He lives in Hale'iwa, Hawaii."

"Wait, let me write that down. Holly-what?"

"Hale'iwa," Lou said, slowly and clearly, pronouncing it the way Keoni did, with the glottal stop and the *w* like a *v*. *Hah-lay-ee-vah.*

"Thanks," he said.

"You're welcome."

Lou held the phone to her ear for a long moment after Mr. Orlandi hung up in California. Finally, the dial tone sounded, snapping her out of her daze. Lou pressed the button to disconnect, then found the Seattle phone book and dialed up Pacific Camera. Her finger shook as she spun the oscillating dial on the face of the phone. She felt like she might faint.

Until she spoke with Mr. Tollison, she wouldn't believe this was really happening.

When Mr. Tollison answered the phone and confirmed that he had been the one to send in the photo of Keoni, Lou sighed and slumped against the counter.

"I hope you aren't angry," Mr. Tollison said, sounding embarrassed.

Lou was far from angry. She was ecstatic. She hung up the phone with tears of joy streaming down her face and sank down to the kitchen floor. She was still sitting there staring into space, not quite believing her luck when Penny came in the front door.

Lou hadn't cleaned up the mess she'd made when she'd dropped the groceries. Oranges had spilled out of their container and rolled across the kitchen floor, and the carton of milk was lying on its side getting warmer by the minute.

"Lou?" Penny came into the kitchen with an orange in her

hand. When she saw Lou crumpled on the floor, her mouth dropped open. "Lou! What happened?"

Lou transferred her glazed stare from the linoleum up to Penny. Emotion clogged her throat. "I'm going to be in a magazine."

Penny squatted down next to Lou and picked up the milk carton. "What are you talking about, honey?"

"Mr. Tollison sent in one of my photos, and they want it. They want to publish it." Lou pushed herself to her feet and paced across the room. Her blood started flowing again as she moved, and she was struck with the urge to break into a run. She settled for climbing on top of the sofa and yelling, "They want my picture!"

Penny stared at Lou for a moment and then she dropped the milk and ran to join her on the sofa. They jumped up and down, hugging each other.

"Congratulations," Penny said. "I knew you could do it."

Lou's smile spread across her face. "I have to tell Keoni!"

After the words came out of her mouth, Lou's smile crumpled. Her first thought had been to share her joy with Keoni. He would be so proud of her. But then she remembered how he'd felt about the photo of him in the tourist pamphlet. He'd been embarrassed by it, not even wanting her to see it. How would he feel about being featured in an international magazine? He might not be pleased at all. He might be angry.

"I don't know what to do." Lou sank onto the sofa.

"Call him," Penny said.

"I've tried." Tears welled in her eyes. "He never answers."

"That's because you hang up before he gets the chance."

Lou squeezed her eyes shut. "If I talk to him, I'm never going to get on with my life."

"You call this living?" Penny asked. "You've been moping around here for almost a month. You haven't looked for a real job. You haven't even taken any pictures." Penny took Lou by the shoulders when she tried to look away and pinned her with a glare. "Have you even brushed your hair today?"

Lou winced. Penny's words cut deeply. She'd just been feeling so proud that she'd bought oranges and milk and hadn't thought about Keoni until five whole minutes after she'd woken up.

"The world isn't over just because your plans didn't work out the way you wanted," Penny said.

Lou stared at Penny, who had seemed to shake off her misery over losing Bones with admirable resilience. She'd sworn off men and had been focusing all her energy on her career.

"The way I see it," Penny said. "We got a gift when we went to Hawaii. Our eyes were opened."

Penny's voice sounded strange, and Lou took a closer look at her friend. "What are you saying?"

"I'm saying that there is a whole world out there for us to explore."

Lou shook her head. "I don't understand."

"I didn't want to tell you this yet, but I guess now is just as good a time as any." Penny hesitated and then said, "I'm leaving Seattle."

Lou's mouth dropped open. "When?"

"Next month."

"Why?"

"Why not? I need a change. A fresh start."

A sudden burst of anger blinded Lou. "I can't believe this. We were supposed to be a team, Penny. And now everything is ruined."

"It isn't ruined." Penny bent to retrieve another orange that had rolled under the coffee table. "It's just different."

Lou stood and walked down the hall to her room. She closed the door and then went straight to the record player on the dresser. She picked up the needle and started the record that was already on the turntable. The first strains of Otis Redding's "(Sittin' on) The Dock of the Bay" filled the room as Penny opened the door.

"Not this song again," she said, shaking her head. "I can't bear to hear it one more time."

"So leave," Lou said. "What's stopping you? You're leaving me anyway."

"I'm not leaving you." Penny sat on Lou's bed. "I'm leaving Seattle."

"How's that different?"

"You should think about leaving, too. There's nothing here for you."

"Where would I go?"

Penny gave Lou a pointed stare. "You know where."

"I can't."

"Of course you can."

"What am I supposed to do, show up at Keoni's door and tell him I forgive him, beg him to change his mind?"

"Sure, why not?" Penny asked. "He came here for you, Lou. He wants you. He knew about Paul the whole time, and he didn't hold it over your head. So what if he fooled around? You'd already left him."

Lou dragged the needle off the record. "But he left me."

"And you let him."

"Maybe you should take your own advice and go after Bones."

Penny shook her head. "No. It's not the same. He didn't even call me after he went missing and we thought he was dead. He doesn't love me. But Keoni loves you. He loved you from the moment he saw you get off that plane. You'd be crazy to give that up."

"I have to think about all this." Lou paced to her window and gazed out at the brick building next door. She sniffed back tears, thinking of the view from Keoni's bedroom of the soft sands of Hale'iwa Beach.

"Don't take too long," Penny said, letting herself out. "Men like Keoni don't sit around waiting."

The thought had already struck Lou. Maybe Keoni had already gone back to the woman he'd tried to replace her with once before.

Lou had nightmares about Keoni in the arms of another woman, but she'd gotten used to it.

After Penny left, Lou went to her closet and opened the door. Keoni's jacket, which he'd left her behind at her apartment, hung next to her favorite dress. Lou touched the sleeve of the jacket, running her fingers along the coarse duck cloth as if she was touching the man and not just the fabric. Although the scent was fading, the jacket still smelled like Keoni. Lou slipped her hand into the pocket and pulled out the photograph she kept there. It showed Keoni on the top of the Pali Lookout.

He was facing the camera, leaning against the railing in a relaxed pose. The beauty was behind him in the green cliffs that overlooked Kaneohe Bay and the distant peak of Chinaman's Hat, but Keoni's eyes were soft as if he was looking at something even prettier. The wind blew his hair away from his face, revealing the cut on his forehead.

Keoni had said he didn't want Lou worrying about him, that's why he was ending things. He didn't want her ever to experience the pain he carried over Eddie's death.

But Keoni's argument made no sense.

Thoughts of Keoni filled Lou's every waking moment. She dreamed of him at night and woke up missing him. Being apart didn't make her worry less about him. At any given moment, he could be launching himself off a huge wave, or risking his life to save a stranger.

Lou would never stop worrying about Keoni, wondering if he was safe, or missing him. And no matter what, she'd never stop loving him.

She pulled the jacket over her shoulders, threaded her arms through the sleeves, and zipped it up tightly. Then she lay down on the bed and cried herself to sleep.

The next morning when she woke up, Lou had a plan. She had always been excellent at planning, now she just had to hope Keoni was still available.

THE PLAN

HALE'IWA, HAWAII
A Saturday in March

LOU STOOD IN THE DRIVEWAY OF KEONI'S HOUSE. IT WAS JUST AS charming as she'd remembered. The sloping shingled roof was framed by the blue sky. The white paint on the porch looked fresh, and flowers spilled from their beds onto the lawn.

Lou took a deep breath of the fragrant air and marched up the steps of the front porch with her suitcase. She knocked on the door, but there was no answer.

Keoni's beige VW Bug was in the driveway, so she knew he was home.

He could be asleep. He worked nights at the cannery, so it was possible.

Lou knocked again, louder this time in case Keoni was in bed. The doubts she'd managed to push aside grew stronger.

What if he turned her away?

What if he didn't love her?

What if he wasn't alone and another woman was sharing his bed?

She shook off her worry and raised her hand to knock again. Before her knuckles could touch the wood, the door flew open.

Keoni stood in the doorway, wearing only a towel around his hips.

Lou sucked in a surprised breath, shocked at how his appearance affected her. Keoni was just as stunning as she had remembered. His wet hair dripped onto his shoulders, and water clung to the perfection of his muscled chest.

Keoni's presence was a dynamic force. He exuded quiet power and strength. Lou remembered seeing Keoni for the first time at the airport and thinking he was majestic. He was no less so right now, even dressed in a towel.

Lou dragged her eyes up to Keoni's face. His mouth was pinched, and his eyes were guarded.

"What are you doing here?"

She had rehearsed this. She was going to lead with the picture in the magazine and the interview. She was going to apologize for not asking his permission to submit it, even though she hadn't submitted it. Anyway, she was going to hope that he still loved her and tell him she didn't care about the past. The past was gone, and all she wanted was him.

She realized she still hadn't said a word. Then, it didn't matter, because Keoni took her hand and drew her inside. As soon as they touched she knew they still had whatever it was that glued them together. Their connection hadn't faded. If anything it was stronger than ever.

Keoni closed the door behind her, but didn't let go of her hand. With his free hand, he reached up and tucked a lock of hair behind her ear. His calloused fingers trailed down her neck, then dropped away. "Why are you here?"

"The magazine article. The picture."

His eyebrows pinched together. "I'm sorry, what?"

"The picture in the magazine," she said. "Didn't they call you?"

Keoni shook his head.

"*Surfing Magazine* is publishing one of my pictures," she said. "They were supposed to call you for an interview."

Keoni stopped staring at her mouth and seemed to register her words. A smile spread across his mouth. "Your picture is going to be in a magazine?"

Lou nodded. "Your picture." She chewed her lip. "I hope you're not mad."

"Mad?" His eyebrows rose. "Why would I be mad?"

"You were embarrassed about that picture in the tourist pamphlet."

"That's different, but…" He shrugged. "This is you. You should know me better than to think I'd be mad."

He sounded disappointed, and Lou realized this was going all wrong. She steered things back to her plan.

"I was hoping you would take one look at me and fall in love with me."

Keoni stiffened. "It's too late for that."

"Oh." Lou's heart dropped to her stomach. She turned and reached for the door.

Keoni's hands shot out to stop her. "I fell in love with you the moment you stepped off the plane."

A tingle of awareness shot down her spine. She'd noticed him the moment she'd stepped foot on Hawaiian soil.

"Are you alone?" She peeked around his shoulder, steeling herself for his answer.

A muscle in his jaw tensed, and he nodded. "I can't be with anyone, Lou. I told you that."

Lou blew out a frustrated breath and hung her head. She was glad that Keoni wasn't with anyone else, but this wasn't exactly good news.

The tension mounted between them.

Lou couldn't take being so close to him and not touching him. She could smell the coconut shampoo in his hair and it was driving her crazy.

She abandoned her plan. It wasn't working anyway. She took a big step and threw herself into his arms. After taking a step back to steady himself, Keoni slid his arms around Lou's waist. He pulled her against his chest so hard that all the air rushed out of her lungs.

His mouth was on hers, and the plan was right on track again. Lou raised up onto her toes and threaded her fingers through Keoni's hair.

He groaned and backed her against the wall, kissing her as if his life depended on it. The stubble on his chin chafed her skin, his fingers bruised her hips, and his hard body pinned her to the wall.

Lou clutched Keoni's shoulders for balance as her knees went weak.

"Are you sure?" His voice was hoarse, and his body was heavy against hers. "You forgive me?"

Lou pressed her palms against his chest. "There's nothing to forgive."

His eyes softened and he rested his head against hers. She liked the solid feel of him pressing into her and the intensity of his hot gaze trapping hers in such tight quarters. When she breathed, he breathed.

"Keoni?"

"Yeah?"

"You're crushing me."

"Oh." His eyes crinkled in the corners and he laughed. "Sorry."

Keoni lifted his head off Lou's and scooped her higher into his arms. He carried her into the kitchen and set her down on the counter so that they were eye to eye. Standing between her legs, he planted his hands next to her hips and resumed looking her in the eye with the same intensity as a moment ago. The towel had fallen off his hips sometime in the last few minutes. Lou saw that he was blissfully naked and completely unconcerned with it.

"You deserve the best," Keoni said. "I don't know what I can give you."

"You gave me everything already." Scars and all. "Are you taking it back?"

Keoni flinched, and Lou knew her plan had worked. She had counted on his pride not letting him take back something he had given her.

While he was vulnerable, she pressed her advantage, peppering his face with kisses. She kissed his chin, his jaw, and finally his mouth. She took her time on his mouth. She kissed him just like he kissed her. Exactly how she wanted to be kissed. Her mouth made love to his until slowly, and then hungrily, Keoni kissed her back.

"So, can I stay?" Lou asked when they parted.

Keoni gathered her closer, until they were lined up with their chests touching. "Do you want to?"

She shrugged, clutching Keoni's shoulders as he scooted her even closer. "I don't have anything better to do," she said.

EPILOGUE

Sunset Beach, Hawaii
Late March 1968

The breeze blew across the sand, kicking up skirts and ruffling hair. The sun was bright, and the sky was cloudless. It was a perfect day at Sunset Beach, not unlike the one when Eddie had died.

It was the second anniversary of his death, and Eddie's closest friends and family had gathered on the beach to have a party in his honor.

It seemed like the entire island of Oahu was crowded onto Sunset Beach to celebrate Eddie. The group was eclectic in age, ethnicity, and social status. Old people stood in small groups, while young children dashed away from their parents to build castles in the sand. Surfers popped up on glassy waves, and snorkelers explored the marine life swimming in the coral reef. They were all there to honor one man who'd been ripped away from them too soon.

A small stage had been set up on the beach, and Ryla Aikau's band was performing. Couples swayed on the sand, holding each other tightly while Ryla crooned a traditional love song from the stage.

The scene was just as Eddie would have wanted. Everyone he loved was in attendance. His family. His friends. The girl he had loved. They were all there for him.

Eddie's best friend was in love with a beautiful *haole* girl from the mainland.

Eddie's other best friend had just won the most prestigious championship in the world of surfing.

Eddie's girlfriend was living her life without him.

The waves were bigger than usual at Sunset Beach, and the conditions were perfect. Everyone's lives had gone on without Eddie, and that was exactly how he would have wanted it.

The End

WANT MORE FROM KEONI MAKAI?

Grab this Bonus Scene from Keoni when you sign up for Jill's newsletter.

TRY ME

KEEP SWIPING, SCROLLING, OR TURNING TO READ THE FIRST chapter of *Try Me*, Declan Bishop's story. Available now HERE

THE TRUTH WILL SET YOU FREE... OR IT WILL RUIN EVERYTHING.
Hawaiian surfer Declan Bishop is living a lie. Haunted by his role in his best friend's death, he can hardly face himself in the mirror. When he gets the opportunity to compete in the most prestigious contest in the world, he must decide if the title he covets is worth the pain of facing his past.

She knows what she wants, and love isn't on the list.
Pearl Sunn has sacrificed everything to fulfill her mother's surfing legacy. But it's easier to catch a dangerous wave than it is to catch a break in the male-dominated industry of surfing. She's desperate to get noticed. Desperate enough to fake-date surfing's bad-boy Declan Bishop for a chance to compete.

Nothing this fake has ever felt so real.
It only takes one kiss to realize breaking up will hurt worse than an epic wipeout. Declan's reputation is on the line. Pearl's

career hangs by a thread. And if they don't bail out of their affair on schedule, their dreams will be swept away like yesterday's tide.

TRY ME : A FAKE RELATIONSHIP ROMANCE

Sunset Beach, Oahu
Summer 1966

The fire was hot enough to burn Declan's skin, but he didn't move.

He took another swig from the bottle of whiskey and savored the sting of the alcohol going down his throat. The pain felt good. Declan wanted to hurt. It made him remember he was alive, even though he didn't deserve to be.

Life was good for him. He was rich, talented, handsome, and he was one of the best surfers in Hawaii, which was pretty much the world, because everyone knew Hawaii produced the best surfers. Six months ago, Declan had signed with the best-known agent known to sports. Soon, he would be flying all over the world competing in contests, and probably winning.

Six months ago, things had been good. Better than good. Declan had been flying high. Drinking a little too much maybe, but it was all under control. He'd had his best friends, Eddie and Keoni, who were better than brothers. He'd had a shot at Linda Cooke for the first time, and he'd been on his way to stardom.

Then the accident had happened. Eddie had died. Everything had changed.

Noises from the party floated down the beach, but Declan barely heard them. He was reliving that terrible day when Eddie had disappeared beneath the waves. Declan had been right there, on the very same wave, and he'd been so self-absorbed, so stuck his own head thinking about his upcoming trip to South Africa, and what he was going to do about Linda that he hadn't seen Eddie go under the waves. He'd only seen him come up — blue and lifeless.

"'Ey? You okay?"

Declan looked up from the bottle of whiskey he'd been drowning in and saw Keoni towering over him. Keoni had been there the day of Eddie's death, but he hadn't saved Eddie either. Declan had no words for Keoni. Ignoring the best friend he'd ever had; Declan tipped the bottle to his mouth and drank deeply. He wished he hadn't come tonight. It was supposed to be a celebration in honor of Eddie, so Declan had dragged himself off the barstool he'd been permanently glued to and driven to Sunset Beach.

If he'd known everyone would insist on having such a good time, he would have stayed put.

"Why's everybody so damn happy?' he growled.

Keoni laughed. The sound was just as hollow as a wave at Pipeline Beach, and it took him back to a time when laughter was a possibility. Now, it seemed like he would never laugh again.

"Shut up!" Declan yelled toward the crowd of people partying down the beach.

His protest was caught in the wind and carried out to sea. The outburst taxed him, and he slumped over. Declan lifted his head to pour whiskey down his throat, but before the sweet liquid could touch his lips, Keoni slapped away the bottle.

"Cool out, brother," Keoni said. "You're wasted."

Declan scrambled across the beach to where the bottle lay on its side. The precious contents leaked onto the sand before he could grab the bottle.

"Whaddyah do that for?" Declan asked, looking up at his best friend.

Shadows danced over Keoni's face, highlighting the lines etched by grief. "I'm not lookin' to lose another friend," he said.

Declan threw the empty bottle into the fire. He was tired of Keoni. Tired of everything. He pushed to his feet, wobbling a little as he stood. "I'm gonna split," he said.

Keoni stood in his path, his big shoulders blocking where Declan wanted to go. "Nah," Keoni said. "You're not goin' anywhere."

"Since when was you my dad?" The words sounded fine in Declan's head, but they came out garbled as if he had a mouthful of pebbles.

"Sit down." Keoni pointed.

Declan tried to shove Keoni out of his way, but the big oaf didn't move. Keoni was six-three and all muscle. Keoni didn't move unless he wanted to. Declan glared up at him.

"Get outta my way." Declan cocked his fist, but they both knew he wouldn't raise it.

"You can't drive like this. Lemme' drive you."

"You want to play the hero?" Declan asked. "You shoulda saved somebody who mattered."

Keoni winced as though Declan had socked him in the belly. The look on his face was worse than if Declan had punched him. Declan recognized that look. Guilt. Shame. Anger. All rolled into one big fist that knocked your lights out. Keoni had watched Eddie die, but he hadn't been the one kissing his girl the night before. No, that would be him, Declan Bishop, king of assholes.

"You shoulda saved him!" Declan yelled, spit flying from his lips. "Where were you? You let Eddie die! It's all your fault!"

Keoni's eyes narrowed, and he clenched his jaw hard enough to shatter his perfect smile. Declan watched Keoni's throat work as he swallowed his own accusations instead of hurling them at Declan. Keoni wouldn't fling blame. He was a strong, proud, noble Hawaiian. Keoni would bear the shame, lugging it on his broad shoulders like a canoe full of sorrows.

Keoni's jaw tightened, but his voice remained steady. "I'm not gonna fight you, but you gotta pull yourself together. You gotta quit this shit."

A movement behind Keoni's shoulder caught Declan's attention. The silver moonlight caught on Linda's pale hair as she strode toward them. Every step revealed a flash of her long tanned legs from the split in her wrap skirt.

Great, just what Declan wanted now. Linda Cooke, with her pretty, forgiving smile and her sad, sympathetic eyes. She'd been Eddie's girl, and Declan had tried to take her. His behavior was unforgivable.

"Are you guys fighting?" she asked, her baby blue eyes wide with concern. "I can hear you yelling."

Keoni slung an arm around Declan's shoulders. "Nah, nah, nah," he said. "We was just discussing how Declan was getting home. He doesn't want to drive."

"Oh, yeah?" Linda said, scrutinizing them both.

"Yeah," Keoni said.

Declan tried to maneuver away from Keoni's hold and he stumbled toward Linda.

"I'll take him," Linda said, grabbing Declan's arm. "I'm dying to drive the Stingray."

Declan let Linda lead him away. He couldn't take another moment of Keoni, and besides, he wanted a drink. He needed a drink like he needed another wave at the end of a surf session. His bottle was empty, thanks to Keoni, but he had a flask of whiskey in his car.

His Corvette Stingray, painted Rally Red, stood out from the other cars and trucks in the dirt parking lot. The long, sleek hood shined in the darkness, reflecting the full moon. It seemed like a long time ago when he'd bought the Corvette brand-new in celebration of winning his first major surfing contest. Declan loved the Stingray more than anything, but he would trade it for one of the dented-up beaters in the parking lot if it would bring Eddie back.

"Keys," Linda said, holding out her hand. She was practically drooling over the prospect of driving the Stingray. Declan never let anyone drive his precious baby.

"You're not driving," Declan growled. "I'm fine."

Linda stamped her foot in the dirt. Her fists balled at her slim hips. "You're not fine," she said.

Declan reached for the handle. "I don't need your help."

Linda inserted her body between Declan and the driver's door. "What's going on, Declan?" she demanded. "I've tried calling you a dozen times."

"I've been busy."

"Too busy to call me back after the night we had together?"

To Declan's horror, Linda's eyes filled with tears. The night she was referring to had been years in the making. Declan had always had a thing for Linda. But she was Eddie's girl. He'd never made a move on her until they had officially broken up. And then, right when Declan got the up the courage to ask Eddie's permission to go for Linda, they'd decided to go to Sunset Beach instead of Patterson's to surf and Eddie had died.

Declan reached around Linda for the door. He didn't want to talk about that night a few weeks ago when he'd gone back to Linda's apartment, mostly because he was mortified, but partly because he didn't remember what had happened. For the better part of his teenage years and into his second decade, Declan had coveted Linda and couldn't have her. Now, all he wanted was to get away from her.

"Declan, stop," Linda said, putting a hand on his chest. "We need to talk."

"Not now," he said, pushing her out of the way.

"You're too drunk to drive," she said, attempting to close the door. "You don't even know what you're doing."

"I know what I'm doing," he said, suddenly sober. "I know exactly what I'm doing—getting away from you," he said. "That was a mistake. Whatever happened," which, unfortunately he couldn't even remember, "it was a big mistake. You're Eddie's girl!"

"Eddie's dead!" Linda shouted, her voice cracking on a sob.

Declan yanked the door open and slid into the seat.

Comforted by the familiar feel of soft leather on his skin, he pulled the door shut and put his hands on the wheel. The dashboard slipped in and out of focus as he leaned forward to fit the key in the ignition.

Linda pounded on the window. "Declan, you can't drive right now."

He turned the key, and the hum of the V-8 engine rumbled to life, muffling her words.

"You're going to get yourself killed," she yelled as Declan shifted into reverse and peeled out of the parking lot.

As soon as Declan hit the highway, his head cleared. Everything made sense. Linda was in the past. Eddie was in the past. He was leaving in a few days for a world tour on the surfing circuit, and he might never come back. His agent was already on the island, come to escort him on the trip. Nate McKenna had promised him fame and fortune and a life he'd only dreamed of having. They didn't appreciate him in Hawaii, but soon the world would know Declan Bishop's name.

The road unfolded in front of him, weaving like a black snake in between the blue Pacific and the green mountains. Declan punched the gas and watched the speedometer crawl past fifty, then sixty miles per hour.

Switching on the radio, Declan sang along with Marvin Gaye for a few bars before remembering his flask of whiskey. He opened the glove compartment and fumbled around until he grasped the cool metal. Using both hands to unscrew the cap, he steered with his knee around a sharp bend in the road. He took a long swig, and the memory of Linda's tears receded.

The whiskey burned, just like he liked it. Declan pressed harder on the gas, craving speed. If he drove fast enough, he could leave Hawaii behind.

An image of Eddie's lifeless body came to mind, and Declan lost his grip on the flask. It clinked and rolled across the floor. Declan bent forward to get it. Groping around on the floorboard, he hoped it hadn't spilled. His fingers closed around the cold metal, and he sighed in relief.

He grabbed the flask and straightened just in time to see a light pole a few feet in front of him. What was a pole doing in the middle of the road?

A moment later, he crashed into it.

WANT MORE OF DECLAN BISHOP?
Keep reading the second book in the Aloha Series. Try Me

ACKNOWLEDGMENTS

Writing *Try Easy* allowed me to wallow in my obsession with the Hawaiian Islands. When we visited Oahu in 2014, I walked up the Diamond Head Crater Monument two times. Once because it was the touristy thing to do, and the second time because I was so enchanted with the magical views.

I was inspired by the rugged landscape, the colorful sunsets, and the resilience of the native people. I hope that the setting of *Try Easy* is three-dimensional enough to be one of the characters and that my readers fall in love with Hawaii as well as Keoni and Lou.

I couldn't have written this book without the support of my husband. When I told him I wanted to write a book, I was terrified that he might think I was insane. I mean, it's crazy, right? I had another career at the time and two young children. How the hell was I going to write a book? But he just said, "You can do it!" And he kept saying that every time I wanted to give up. Thanks for believing in me, Drew.

Thanks to my children, who had to put up with me dragging my laptop to every sporting event or function they participated in so that I could sneak in a little writing time. Grace and Michael, you two are the reason I hung in there when I wanted to quit. I hope you have learned a few valuable life lessons from all my ramblings—and now you can tell all your friends that I finally finished!

Thank you to Lew Rauton for sharing Hawaii with your family and for inspiring the name of the main character. *Aloha and Mahola.*

Thank you to my wonderful Beta Readers—Jana Spencer, Michele Hochstrasser, Jane Marcus, and Cynthia Matz.

Thank you to my developmental advisor, Shari Box.

Thank you to Rian Harris for inspiring the title of *Try Easy* one day in hot yoga class. We were all trying way too hard to fling ourselves into arm balances, and you advised us in your loving voice to *try easy* instead. For one brief moment, as Drake played over the speakers and sweat dripped into my eyes, I owned crow pose, and life made perfect sense.

Thank you to my readers for picking up a new author. I know there are many other choices you could have made, and I am grateful to you for giving me a chance.

ABOUT THE AUTHOR

Jill Brashear is an author who believes in love at first sight and the existence of soulmates. In her books, you'll find compelling characters, sexy settings, and plenty of happily-ever-afters. She can't imagine a world without dirty martinis (straight-up with blue-cheese olives), yoga, and romance.

She loves connecting with her fans! Reach out on any of the social media platforms, and she promises to write you back.

Don't miss a thing! Sign up for Jill's newsletter at www.jillbrashear.com

ALSO BY JILL BRASHEAR

Aloha Series

Try Me

Try Right

Blue Ridge Book Club Series

Love, Lacey Donovan

Sign up for my newsletter and get

Free Vacation Romance Series

Made in the USA
Middletown, DE
24 July 2021